1/95

Out of
the Shadows

Out of the Shadows

—— / ◆ / ——

EDWARD MATHIS

WST C 1

CHARLES SCRIBNER'S SONS
New York

COLLIER MACMILLAN CANADA
Toronto

MAXWELL MACMILLAN INTERNATIONAL
New York Oxford Singapore Sydney

F
MAT

Charles Scribner's Sons
Macmillan Publishing Company
866 Third Avenue, New York, NY 10022

Collier Macmillan Canada, Inc.
1200 Eglinton Avenue East, Suite 200
Don Mills, Ontario M3C 3N1

Library of Congress Cataloging-in-Publication Data
Mathis, Edward.
    Out of the shadows / Edward Mathis.
        p.   cm.
    ISBN 0-684-19038-9
    I. Title.
PS3563.A836409   1990
813'.54—dc20   90-8090   CIP

        10   9   8   7   6   5   4   3   2   1

Printed in the United States of America

In Memory of
Hazel McCoy

Out of
the Shadows

/ 1 /

The highway shimmered and danced in the rising air warped by the bristling September sun. Wide, smooth, relatively straight, a monument to man's ingenuity, high taxes, and revenue sharing, it stretched from Laredo on the Rio Grande to the northern border of Texas. It had no understanding of its innate seductiveness, no appreciation for the lulling hum of singing tires, the muted murmur of a sweetly tuned motor, the inexplicable allure of its own lean sinuous shape cleaving the rugged heartland of Texas, projecting a subtle image of limitless time and space, the promise of a mind free for esoteric formulations, a spirit that could soar like the keening wind.

Ordinarily it captivated me, stirred dormant feelings, like old sad songs well sung, like sweet memories not often remembered.

But now, encapsulated in my cool cocoon of glass and steel, the highway's pervasive tune went unheard. My mind was a long way from flying free, my attention distracted from the undemanding highway by my passenger, Letty Medlock.

She wore jeans, black, with crisp white stitching. A wrinkled, short-sleeved pink blouse. Adidas without socks. Her hair was long and brown, parted in the center of her small round head. Glossy with the sheen that only nature can bestow, it fell in shallow waves to her shoulders, bunched there in a dark mass of tangled curls around the faint outline of a square dimpled chin and full curving lips. Seventeen years old going on thirty.

With her legs tucked on the seat between us, she leaned

into the nook formed by the backrest and the car door, her arms folded across her breast, head canted against the blazing sun, eyes open and staring straight ahead. They were big and brown, impossible to read.

She had slept all the way from Port Aransas to Austin, only rousing long enough to visit a gas station rest room and drink a canned Coke, giving me one fleeting glance and a smile before settling into her corner of the seat. I couldn't tell if she was angry or sad, embarrassed or glad, or, more likely, plotting heinous retribution.

Then, after a stop near Hillsboro for a hamburger and fries, as if the greasy food had unleashed some font of energy inside her, she began to liven up, stretching and yawning, facing forward in her seat.

We even began to talk, keeping it light and trivial, discussing everything from the courses in communications she'd been taking in college to the storm clouds hanging over west Fort Worth. We talked about her high school and the woes and tribulations of being in the high school marching band.

I told her about some of my recent cases, the few that had ended happily.

Make-talk, as inconsequential as lint.

Thinking about it later, it seemed we talked a lot, and it wasn't until I finished helping her unload her belongings, chatted a few minutes with her tearful mother, and drove the short distance to my eighteen hundred square feet of emptiness and stale air surrounded by Old English brick, it wasn't until then that I realized she hadn't said a word about why she had run away, or, more important, how she felt about my arbitrary behavior in bringing her home.

I found seven calls on my phone recorder. Three were obvious come-ons for sales promotions, one from Captain Homer Sellers of the Midway City police, and three from a man named Phillip Arganian.

Homer probably wanted to talk about the upcoming deer-hunting season, I thought, or maybe the return of Letty Medlock. He could wait.

Phillip Arganian sounded like a job. I didn't want a job, but three calls in two days indicated persistence, quite possibly a degree of urgency. The name seemed familiar, but I couldn't put a face to it.

I sighed and lit a cigarette. Only one way to find out; I dialed the number. He must have been waiting by the phone; it rang only once.

"Phillip Arganian speaking." It was an odd way to answer a phone in your home, but I had to admit it saved time.

"Mr. Arganian, this is Dan Roman. I'm returning your call."

"Yes, Mr. Roman. We seem to be having some trouble getting together." His voice was soft and precise, excellent diction, a hint of humor, a faint trace of annoyance.

"I'm sorry, but I was out of town until a few minutes ago."

"Yes, of course, I understand. However, I am rather anxious to discuss the possibility of your employment on a matter of . . . shall we say, delicacy?"

"Mr. Arganian, I feel it's only fair to tell you now that I don't handle cases involving marital infidelity or divorce, or—"

"Oh, no, Mr. Roman. It isn't anything like that. I hesitate to discuss it over the phone. However, if you would be so kind as to call at my home tomorrow?"

"Your home?"

"Yes, if you don't mind. I am on vacation, you see."

I hesitated, lit a cigarette. "Mr. Arganian, are you certain this isn't something the police couldn't handle—"

"Mr. Roman, you are a private detective, are you not?"

"Yes. I have a license, but I don't take very many cases. The ones I do take are concerned with finding people."

"Yes. I am aware of that. It is precisely that type of case. You were recommended by a mutual friend . . . a policeman, incidentally. Chief of Police Cliff Hollister."

I was stunned—Cliff Hollister—not exactly a friend, not anymore.

3

"Oh. Well, Mr. Arganian, if you would give me your address?"

The line hummed for a moment, then his voice came, lightly amused: "It's the house on the hill, Mr. Roman, at the intersecton of Claymore Road and Arganian Drive."

"Oh! Oh, yes, of course. I'm sorry, the name didn't register. Yes, I've been to your home—a disturbance call, prowler on the premises. I was riding a patrol car at the time—that was a few years back."

"I'm afraid I don't remember."

"No reason why you should. We didn't find anything except a neighbor's horse."

He laughed dryly. "We still get those occasionally."

"What time would you prefer, Mr. Arganian?"

"Would nine o'clock be suitable to you?"

"Nine o'clock's fine."

"Very well. I'll expect you at nine, then."

"Good-bye, Mr. Arganian."

"Good day, Mr. Roman."

I replaced the receiver and whistled softly. I lit a cigarette and shoved on the arms of the recliner, bringing the footrest up to first position.

Phillip Arganian. Scion of one of Texas's oldest and wealthiest families. If you could believe the stories, most of Midway City, as well as portions of Haltom City, Colleyville, and Grapevine, had at one time been part of the Arganian ranch. Old money. Cattle and oil money.

Then came the Texas population explosion, and the land, much of which was clay and sand sparsely covered with scrub oak and sagebrush, was worth millions due to its strategic location between Dallas and Fort Worth. And the Arganians were suddenly skyrocketed from among the modestly rich to the very rich, one of the wealthiest families in Texas. So went the local scuttlebutt, and such tales generally carried at least a germ of truth.

I came forward in the chair, and the footrest disappeared with a clunk. I picked up the receiver and dialed again.

"Police Department, Captain Sellers's office."

"Hi, Mitzi, let me speak to the bear, will you?"

"Oh, hi, Dan." She lowered her voice. "That's what he's been today all right, like an old bear with a bee-stung nut." I lifted the receiver away from my ear as her laugh rang shrilly.

I heard a sharp click, and Homer Sellers rasped brusquely: "Don't go taking a lot of my time, boy. I'm busy as a one-armed cotton picker, and I'm just getting ready to go home."

"Hell, Homer. This is your call I'm returning. A little civility wouldn't hurt, especially from a civil servant."

"Civil servant, my butt. Civil slave is more like it. I swear I don't know what's getting into people. If we stop for five minutes, the thieves and bandits will take over the whole damn town."

"Jesus, Homer, you sound pretty low."

"Yeah. Did you find Letty?"

"Sure. I took her home to her mother."

"She okay?"

"I think so. I found her down on the coast singing with some half-assed rock band. They were all stoned out of their minds."

"Letty, too?" His voice was tight; Letty Medlock was his favorite niece.

"No, but she was drunk. She said she won't touch dope, but she seems to think drinking's okay."

He coughed, then cleared his throat. "Want you to know I appreciate this, Dan. I mean bringing her back and all."

"I don't usually mind. Not when they consent to come. She didn't seem to care one way or the other."

I heard his cigar lighter snick and the faint sound of smacking lips. "Arganian give you a call yet?"

"How did you know about him?"

His laugh was a mumbling grunt. "You know damn well I know everything that goes on in my town, Dan'l. . . ."

"Cliff Hollister told you."

"Naw, I was sitting right there in Cliff's office when old man Arganian called to ask about you. Cliff gave you a great buildup. I didn't agree with him, but I didn't want to butt in."

5

"Yeah, thanks, buddy. Did he say what it was all about?"

"Nope. But I'll bet you fifty it'll be about finding his sister."

"Sister?"

"Yeah, younger sister. Run off about twelve years ago. Wanted to be a movie star."

"How come you know so much about it?"

"Well, back then we got a query from the Las Vegas police about a private investigator named Murdock. Seems he'd gone out there on a case for Arganian, looking for his little sister. He won a bundle of money on the roulette wheel and got knocked in the head in his hotel room. Killed him. You'd think a private detective would have more sense than to carry a wad of dough—I think it was around eight thousand—to a hotel room with him. Vegas cops thought someone had followed him from the casino. Never heard no more about it, so I guess that was what it was about."

"Why do you remember it so well, Homer? It doesn't sound like the kind of case you'd remember for twelve years."

He barked another short gusty laugh. "You kidding? I got a memory like a steel trap."

"Cut out the bullshit, Homer. You pull the missing person file on the girl?"

"Yeah. Figured I'd have to anyway. Figured you'd come sniffing around wanting me to do your work for you as usual."

"What you mean is you heard Cliff and Arganian talking and got nosy. Okay, since you've got it there handy, give me what you've got. Just in case."

He grunted. I heard a desk drawer slam shut and paper rattling. "Didn't your mama ever teach you to say please?"

"Please."

"That's better. Okay, only thing here is some field investigation reports we did on the girl's friends, classmates, relatives, like that. Nothing that amounted to a damn . . . well, there was one thing. Friend of hers named Virginia Adams— best friend, she said—got a card from her from Las Vegas a short time after she run off. Said she throwed it away, though, so nothing came of it."

"Did the department query Las Vegas?"

"Don't look like it. I don't see anything here. Sloppy work."

"How about boyfriends?"

"Her boyfriend at the time was a guy named Sackett, John Sackett. Said he didn't know anything about her running away. Notation here, though, says the investigating officer thought he looked nervous, like he might've been lying."

"Do you have addresses on Adams and Sackett?"

"Yep. Don't know how good they are. The Adams girl had just got married, so I don't know if this is her current address or not. The Sackett boy's father owns Sackett and Son Construction Company, so he shouldn't be hard to find."

He read off the addresses, and I copied them down.

"How old was the Arganian girl?"

"About sixteen, I think. I remember thinking she must have been a menopause baby. I guess it happens. That would make the girl about twenty-eight now." He made a sniffing sound then lustily blew his nose.

"You didn't do any good at all, huh?"

"Nope. Not even a smell. There's thousands of kids who run away every year and more leaving every day. Boy, I tell you, I'm sure glad I never had any. That's one worry I don't have."

For a moment, I thought of the child I had had, my son. Tommy. He'd disappeared, too, many years ago, around the same time as the Arganian girl. Disappeared in a burst of flame against a bridge abutment, chasing PCP dreams in a stolen car. He was fourteen.

I willed myself not to look back, but to concentrate on the present, on what Homer was telling me.

"Well, there was one other thing I remember," he said. "Not about this exactly. Four, five years before that. I was in uniform back then, and I didn't have anything to do with the case, but if I'm remembering it right, the Arganian girl's daddy killed himself. Shot himself, I think. Seems like there was some kind of flap about it for a while, like maybe he had some help or something. But I'm almost sure it was finally

7

ruled a suicide by the coroner, although as I remember, Sid Croft didn't agree. Sid handled the case."

"What would that have to do with the girl running away five years later?"

"Hell, Dan, I don't know. You asked me and I told you. Probably no connection at all, but you asked—"

"Yeah, I appreciate it, Homer. Think you could dig back in the files and see what it was all about? Turn old Mitzi loose down there. She's a whiz at this kind of thing."

"Old Mitzi's up to her stays in work the way it is. Anyhow, all that stuff is on film now. They hired some half-assed college kids to do the cataloging, and it's a damn nightmare finding anything over ten years old. But, we'll see. I can't really spare the time, but I'll see what I can do. Damn cheap-assed city. Understaffed and underpaid—"

/ 2 /

Due to some complicated and arcane interaction of flywheels and cogs, camshafts and springs, my J. C. Penney clock radio made a grinding popping noise approximately five seconds before erupting into soothing wake-up music.

Generally speaking, five seconds gave me ample time to snake out a vengeful arm and beat the beast into submission, turn it off completely, or stab the snooze-alarm button allowing ten more minutes of uneasy slumber, at which time, if I was so disposed, the ritual could be repeated.

It was a frivolous waste of time, a self-indulgent luxury I could afford only because I was my own boss.

In a manner of speaking.

I worked for other people but not very often and sometimes

not very well. But whether I worked diligently or hardly at all, I made it a point never to be late for appointments, which goes a long way toward explaining why my alarm was set for eight o'clock on that particular Tuesday morning in late September.

I had a nine o'clock appointment with Phillip Arganian, a foolish commitment I was already regretting. I was tired, solvent, and in no mood for a rich man's problems. Even more disturbing was the realization that I had let the startling fact of Police Chief Cliff Hollister's recommendation stampede me into agreeing to see Arganian.

Cliff Hollister was not a friend. I had once, a long time ago, pounded him into insensibility after he had made a move on my first wife, Barbara. We had not spoken since that time, and his promotion to chief had been one of the many reasons I left the police department. Whether he was an enemy had yet to be determined, but accolades and endorsements came totally unexpected and made me a little wary.

Thinking those thoughts slowed my reaction time, and the radio hummed gently, triumphantly to life. I swung my legs off the bed to the accompaniment of Willie Nelson's muted nasal twang, the thrum of guitars, and a rousing advertisement for life on the road again.

I found a cigarette with one hand and rubbed my eyes with the other, and then sat slumped, staring at the carpet and waiting for the song to end.

I punched the radio silent; the droning sound grew in intensity, coming from somewhere behind me in the empty house.

I was halfway down the hall before recognition struck me like a shout of derision.

Vacuum cleaner!

I stopped, disoriented, mentally scratching my head.

Tuesday. My cleaning lady came on Friday—when she came at all, and then only in the afternoons, when our tacit agreement ensured that I would be gone.

Not my cleaning lady—then who?

I went back into the bedroom and slipped into my clothes.

Curious and bewildered, I clumped down the hallway again, into the ever-increasing drone of the vacuum cleaner, into the peripheral vision field of Susan Roman busily zipping around and about the furniture in the den.

Domestically fetching in old jeans and a short-sleeved blouse, raven hair yanked back and lashed into a rippling ponytail, she glanced up quickly, smiled, and held up one finger.

I nodded and walked around through the living room into the kitchen. I poured a glass of milk and sipped the cool liquid reflectively, wondering how she had managed to get into the house, since she had dramatically thrown her house key on the kitchen table when she left—wondering why she had decided to mark her return by cleaning the den carpet.

The vacuum cleaner whined to a halt; I heard a low nervous cough, the slap of cord on shaft as she rewound the extension. A moment later she appeared in the doorway, face flushed, the smile back, crooked and hesitant, warm brown eyes meeting mine squarely, almost defiantly.

"Hi. I was beginning to think I'd have to wake you up. If you don't hurry a little, you'll miss your nine o'clock appointment with Mr. Arganian."

I stared at her, back to a bewildered state again. "How did you know about that?"

She laughed. "No big mystery. He just called a little while ago. I caught the phone on the first ring, I guess that's why it didn't wake you."

"I had it turned off in the bedroom. What did he want?"

"Nothing really. He just wanted to be sure you were going to make it. I assured him you were." She looked at me and blinked slowly. "That's right, isn't it?"

I nodded and finished the milk. I rinsed out the glass and started to put it back in the cabinet.

She made a clucking sound and took it out of my hand. "Honestly, Danny. You know better than that." She slipped the glass onto a hook in the dishwasher.

"What's this bit with the vacuum cleaner?" I said, trying to look properly chastened. "I have a cleaning lady come in every Friday . . . well, almost."

"She may come in, but I have a big news flash for you, partner. She's not doing any vacuuming, at least not for a long time."

"Really? How can you tell? It always looks great when she's finished."

She crimped her mouth in amused disbelief, then glanced at the clock and shook her head. "You'd better be moving, Danny. You don't want to be late. You know you're never late." Her voice was light and dry and gently chiding, in remembrance of past lectures on the moral imperatives of punctuality.

"I'm usually not careless, either. Which means I probably locked the door last night. And that brings us to how you got in."

A long fat second ticked by while she reshaped her features to wide-eyed innocence, a disarming smile.

"Why, I had two sets of keys, Danny. I thought you knew that." Her face fell in counterpoint to her rising voice, reformed smoothly to rueful chagrin. "I've had the second one all the time." She hesitated. "Do you want it back?"

I killed a moment lighting a cigarette, and before I could answer, she rushed on.

"I really came over to get the rest of my winter things. I have some dresses and a couple of coats in the front bedroom closet. I thought you were gone. Uncle Homer said you were down in south Texas looking for Letty Medlock. When I saw you were home, I almost didn't stop . . . but then I thought what the hell, we have to meet sometime." She leaned against the counter next to the sink and folded her arms, her features composed, noncommittal.

"So, you decided to vacuum my house?"

"You know it makes me nervous to wait. Anyway, I only did the den and living room." She paused and smiled wryly. "I think you need a new housekeeper."

"Or an old wife," I said, then winced inwardly and went on to bury the line in a gush of meaningless verbiage before she could interpret it as a sign of weakness. "Like you said, I'll have to be moving along if I'm to make my meeting with Arganian, so feel free to look around and take what you want." I moved across to the door to the utility room. "As for the key, Susie, keep it. You may forget something and want to come back." I hesitated. "Homer said you were sharing a place with Janey Petroski."

She nodded, her eyes suddenly cool and remote. "Yes. We found a larger apartment, though. Her old one was a little too small for two people."

"Sounds good," I said briskly, and opened the door. "Sorry I can't stay and talk but, well, you know how it is, busy, busy."

"Yes, I know," she said, forming a tight little smile with her lips only, the rest of her face immobile, unchanging. She disappeared through the living room door.

I went through the utility room into the garage, a dry, hollow spot in my chest expanding, a part of me crying out in disbelief at the opportunity that was slipping away. I stood for a moment with my hand on the door of my Ramcharger pickup, then wheeled and went back into the house. I trailed through the rooms until I found her rummaging in the front bedroom closet. She turned and looked at me when she heard my voice.

"Look, I'll call you. We'll have dinner. Maybe it's time to talk. I don't know. Maybe it's not, but we won't know until we try."

She nodded wordlessly, one tanned hand drifting up to touch her throat.

"All right," she said finally, voice muted, unrevealing.

I nodded and left.

/ 3 /

As houses go in Texas, rich men's houses, Phillip Arganian's wasn't overly pretentious: a two-story colonial-style brick, complete with towering white columns, dormers, and a steeply pitched red tile roof. Plain, but also proportionate and aesthetically pleasing. Possibly nine thousand square feet of air-conditioned living space, nestled among towering native elm and a scattering of scrub oaks. Constructed in a time when the dollar was still worth fifty cents, the house must have cost in the neighborhood of a million dollars to build, and would now sell for at least three times that amount.

A slender man of medium height opened the door; I had almost decided he was the butler when he acknowledged my name with a quick easy smile and extended his hand.

"Mr. Roman. I'm Phillip Arganian. So very nice to meet you." He had thin blond hair, a narrow handsome face, and irises so dark blue they were almost violet. Deep vertical lines etched the corners of his mouth, and there were plum-colored pouches under eyes set deep into their sockets. He appeared to be a man at ease with himself and his environment, self-assured and content with his niche in the overall scheme of things, confident of his right to be there.

"Could I get you something to drink, Mr. Roman?" He led the way into a large airy room with a dominant male theme: billiard table, poker table, and an ancient player piano that had been restored to its original cherry-wood finish. Stuffed animal heads festooned the walls, and on a long table near a window a full-grown mountain lion hung suspended at the apogee of its hunting strike against a wild-eyed deer.

"No, thank you. It's a little early for me."

"Perhaps some coffee, or orange juice . . . ?"

"No, thanks, I'm fine."

He nodded and smiled, and I followed him across the room to a desk under a giant draped window that used up half of one wall. He gestured toward a leather chair with wide thick arms, and I sank into it—and kept sinking until I found myself looking up at him seated behind his desk. Surprisingly enough, the chair was comfortable.

He clasped his hands together in the middle of his desk and regarded me steadily.

"Mr. Roman, you come to me very highly recommended. I assume you are therefore a busy man, and I will not waste your time or mine with a lot of questions that would be necessary if, in fact, you had not been so highly recommended."

He opened the top drawer in his desk and withdrew a manila envelope.

"Mr. Roman, I would like you to undertake the task of finding my sister, my baby sister. I say task, because it may very well be just that. She has been missing twelve years." He tapped the envelope against his palm and waited for my reaction, his eyebrows lifted quizzically. "That's a very long time," he added.

"Yes, it is," I agreed. "Twelve years. Almost anything could have happened in that time. She could be married, have a family, be living in another country—be dead."

His lips tightened. "Yes, I'm aware of that. Actually it isn't quite that long. My mother received a letter from her four years after she left—it was at Christmas—so it is only eight years that we have had no word from her." He opened the envelope and extracted a photograph. "Here is the very latest picture we have. She sent it in the letter."

The picture was a black-and-white snapshot of a young girl in a waitress uniform, and despite the poor quality, it was easy to see that she was extraordinarily pretty in a plump baby-faced sort of way. Her hair was long and either dark brown or black.

I nodded and handed the photo back to him. "Very pretty girl, but that's not going to help much. She still had her baby fat then. She's not going to look much like that now. Even her hair could be a different color, blond, red, auburn, anything."

He nodded patiently. "Of course, I understand that. But this is what she looked like then, and I'm afraid that is where you'll have to start." He withdrew a slip of paper from the envelope. "My mother did remember the name of the girl Loretta said she was staying with in California. Lacy Wynters. Spelled with a *y*. She remembers also that the letter was postmarked Chatsworth, California. And I'm afraid that's all there is, Mr. Roman."

"Would it be possible for me to see your mother?"

"I'm sorry, no. She isn't allowed visitors beyond the immediate family. It wouldn't matter. She's told me all she remembers."

"Mr. Arganian, after twelve years . . . may I ask why you are suddenly interested in finding your sister?"

He nodded again. "My mother. She is seventy-eight years old and, as I just explained, in very poor health. She wants to see her baby before . . . well, let's just say it's for her. I gave up on Loretta before she ran away, Mr. Roman. She was not just wild, she was incorrigible, sexually promiscuous, and into drugs. Heaven only knows what she has become." A self-righteous tone had crept into his voice, and somehow it surprised me.

"Sometimes they fool you."

"I pray that is so for my mother's sake . . . and Loretta's too, of course. She was such a lovely child, so sweet and even-tempered. She just couldn't seem to control herself. She wanted to experience everything and to do it all at once. Impatience, I'm afraid, was her downfall as much as any one thing." He smiled faintly. "I sometimes considered her more of a daughter than a sister. There were almost thirty years between us." He ran a slender hand through thinning hair and down the back of his neck, a pained look on the narrow handsome face. "There is, of course, another consideration. With our mother's death, Loretta will inherit half the Arganian estate. If she can't be found, her half will go to charity."

My surprise must have shown in my face.

He smiled faintly. "We are half brother and sister, you see. We shared the same father, but Loretta's mother is my step-mother. She is, I believe, trying to make up for the years she emotionally neglected Loretta as a child. Either way it goes, it will be a gesture of atonement."

"I understand."

"So you see, Mr. Roman, Loretta must be found in any event. The disposition of a great deal of money depends on your efforts."

"How do you think Loretta would react to her inheritance going to charity?"

"I wouldn't know. Loretta was never very much concerned with money. Of course she may well feel differently as an adult."

"Apparently not, if she hasn't bothered to ask."

"That's true," he said, a slightly incredulous edge to his voice, as if the idea of someone not caring about money was an enigma.

"Could I see the letter?"

He smiled ruefully. "I'm afraid not. My mother has mis-placed it. There was very little in it. No return address, al-though she did say she was rooming with the woman in California. The trail ended in Las Vegas the first time."

"You tried before?"

"Yes, when she first disappeared. It ended almost before it began, however. A Mr. Murdock, a private detective. He some-how tracked her to Las Vegas and had the misfortune to win at the roulette tables. A respectable sum, I believe. Someone robbed and killed him in a Las Vegas hotel room."

"Did he send you any kind of report?"

"No. He called me from Las Vegas the second day after he left Midway City. He said he had followed her trail to Las Vegas, but I didn't ask for details. I suppose I should have."

He caressed the faint hook in his thin aristocratic nose, idly scraping the edge of one nostril with a manicured nail.

"It probably wouldn't matter by now. Las Vegas is a transient town. People come and go all the time."

He drummed his fingers on the desk, then picked up a pencil and rubbed it between his palms. He tapped the eraser against his teeth. "Well, Mr. Roman, what do you think?"

"To be honest with you, I don't think I have a chance of finding her. Maybe anywhere in the country except Los Angeles and Las Vegas I might have a fighting chance. But there's a constantly shifting mass of humanity on that end of the continent. Nobody seems to stay anywhere for very long. Besides, they're all half-crazy."

He smiled politely. "But will you try?"

I lit a cigarette and mulled it over. I thought of Los Angeles, all that teeming restless humanity rushing to nowhere, the madness of the freeways, the strangling smog—and I almost said no. Then I thought of Susie; it would give me a few more days . . . time to think.

"If you like. I'll give it my best swing."

He slapped his hands on the desk and pushed to his feet. "Done. I understand that your fee is three hundred a day plus expenses. That will be satisfactory, and perhaps a small bonus will be in order if you succeed. One thing, Mr. Roman, I insist on knowing everything you find out about Loretta. That means *everything*. I truly hope there will be nothing that will distress me. I would like nothing better than to have my former opinion of her invalidated . . . but, nevertheless, I must know everything in detail that you learn. Agreed?"

"Agreed. I just hope I can find out something for you."

"Oh, I'm certain you will. I have every confidence in you."

He replaced everything in the envelope and handed it to me. "Oh, incidentally, Loretta changed her name after she left home. She told us in the letter. She was using the name Nancy Taylor." He smiled wryly. "She said Arganian sounded foreign."

He walked outside with me, into the sunny morning.

17

"She never wrote for money, then?" I asked.

"No. I'll have to give her that. She was evidently determined to make it on her own. She knew she could always get it, but she never called for help."

"Maybe she wasn't as spoiled, as willful, as you thought."

He nodded solemnly. "Perhaps not. We tend to judge young people too harshly sometimes. We tend to forget." He smiled his quick friendly smile again and extended his hand. "I'll be looking forward to seeing you again, Mr. Roman. I hope you can understand the reason for all possible haste. My mother—" He broke off as a small yellow sports car, its mufflers throbbing gutturally, whirred into the lane from the street.

We stood silently and watched the car approach, then slide to a stop next to my pickup, watched the woman in the kelly green suit alight, smile toward us, and wave her hand gaily.

Arganian walked forward a few steps to meet her. "What are you doing here?" he demanded in a voice that had picked up a touch of roughness.

She laughed, lifted on tiptoe, and kissed him. "Darling! I live here, remember?"

He returned her laugh, but when he turned to me, his face seemed strained, taut.

"Mr. Roman, I'd like you to meet my wife. Honey, this is Dan Roman, a business acquaintance of mine." He smiled down at her. "What I meant was, I thought you were going to be late. You said the game wouldn't be over until noon or later."

She shook her head in mock dismay. "Men! They never listen to you." She strode forward and extended a small tanned hand. "I'm very pleased to meet you, Mr. Roman. I don't think I've heard my husband speak of you before."

She was small and stunning. I received a swift impression of meticulously planned beauty, of elegance, before she turned back to her husband. Her hair was golden blond streaked with dark gray. Arranged in graceful swirls and curls, it formed a pleasing backdrop for her pale smooth skin.

He's at least twice her age, I thought irrelevantly.

She linked her arm with her husband's and shook him gently. "The games, darling. Games. You know I always get knocked out in the first round. The games won't be over before noon, but I told you that I'd come home as soon as I lost." She wrinkled her nose and smiled at me. "He never listens." Her eyes were an intense dark blue.

I smiled back at her, then looked up to find him watching me closely; I had an uncomfortable feeling he was gauging my response to her, an uneasy realization that I was in the presence of an extremely jealous man. His smile was amiable, however, and after I mumbled a polite good-bye to her, he followed me out to my truck.

"I don't expect you to call me every day or anything like that, Mr. Roman. As a matter of fact, I would prefer that you wait until you have something concrete to report. It would be a waste of your time and mine otherwise."

"Good. That suits me fine. I'll be in touch, Mr. Arganian." I paused, then brought up the subject I had been evading. "What can you tell me about Loretta's reasons for leaving home?"

He looked away, his face clouding. "I can't tell you anything specific. I hadn't seen her for . . . for some time before she left. She lived with our sister Alice for a long time, you see, and Alice would never tell us much about Loretta. I'm sorry to say there was a great deal of dissension in our family, Mr. Roman."

"Maybe I should talk to your sister."

"I'm sorry, she's dead."

"Your father, perhaps?"

He turned to face me. "Our father's been dead a long time."

"I see. I'm sorry." He obviously wasn't going to talk about his father's death, and short of a few blunt questions, I couldn't see any reasonably sensitive way of pursuing the subject further.

He looked toward the house. "I—I wouldn't like my wife to find out . . . you know, about Loretta's past."

"Of course. Everything will be put directly into your hands."

"Fine. Fine." He stepped back and gave me his friendly

smile again and went up the walk toward the house, his shoulders bent slightly, head bowed.

All that money, I thought. All that money and a beautiful young wife half his age; some men were just born winners.

Virginia Adams lived on the north side of Highway 183, the contemporary equivalent of the wrong side of the tracks in Irving, Texas. A small frame house with an untidy yard and peeling paint that squatted humbly beneath threadbare native cottonwood and transplanted mulberry. Here and there, small patches of yellow-green grass fought for survival, and I could see the blocked hulk of a fifty-seven Dodge Polara quietly gathering rust in the backyard. Moldy, pus-yellow leaves stippled the graveled driveway and gathered in thick dank tangles beneath a row of bedraggled hedge that was the only overt attempt at landscaping. A rusty air-conditioning unit whirred busily in one of the two front windows.

Virginia Adams had gleaming auburn hair and warm green eyes that belied the toughness of a pinched pixie face. She was short and petite, as neat as a Barbie doll in a pleated skirt and ruffled blouse. Her voice, a pleasantly husky contralto, unaccountably stirred memories of adolescent passion.

"Loretta Arganian?" She shook her head in amazed disbelief as she ushered me into a small living room only a notch above the sad decrepitude of the house's exterior. "After all this time? Good Lord, how long has it been? Ten years, twelve?"

"Twelve," I said, accepting the narrow-armed Naugahyde chair she offered, successfully controlling a wince as something sharp attacked my right buttock. "Her brother said you were her best friend." I gingerly shifted my weight.

She snorted, an unfeminine, derisive sound. "How would he know? Loretta wouldn't go around him. She hated him. And I guess the feeling was mutual. She hadn't seen him since her father's funeral."

"When was that?"

She shrugged thin shoulders. "I don't know exactly, but it was when she was eleven or twelve, around in there." She paused, chewing on her lower lip. "Eleven, I guess. She came to my school in the fifth grade. I heard that her father had just died. I didn't find out until later that she had come to live in Irving with her older half sister after that happened." She hesitated again, head tilted to one side. "Did you know he killed himself?"

"No, I didn't."

She nodded. "I didn't find that out until later, either. After Loretta and I became best friends." She stopped and smiled, a sardonic smile with curiously poignant overtones. "That must have been something to see. The beautiful fairy princess and the little pixie ragamuffin. It was a strange friendship, at least in the early stages. On my side it was mostly a kind of slavish devotion, and on Loretta's—well, I've never been sure what she got out of our relationship. Counterpoint, possibly. I couldn't help but make her look terrific—not that she needed it particularly." She stopped again and grimaced gently. "I shouldn't say that. Lorry was a sweet gentle person. One of the few truly kind people I've ever met. She was beautiful, but I honestly don't think she knew it. It always seemed to embarrass and confuse her when people told her that. Particularly when the boys began to notice her, started hanging around stepping on their tongues." She began a laugh that dwindled quickly, as if the memories had touched some swollen tender spot.

"Did she have a lot of boyfriends?"

She gave me a pitying look. "She could have had them all.

21

They flocked around her like crows on new corn. The fallout was terrific. Even I made out like a bandit." The laugh this time was quietly mocking, filled with self-derision.

"One boyfriend in particular," I said. "Her last one, I believe, before she ran away. John Sackett. What can you tell—"

"That bastard!" She spat, her face tightening, drawing in on itself until it looked almost wizened, the green eyes alight with coruscating splinters of fire, the thin lips losing all definition. "That woman-beating bastard! I think he was mostly the reason Loretta left, maybe the only reason that mattered. She was in love with him, deeply, totally committed, the way she was about everything she believed in—and . . . and that no-good creep . . . he beat and raped her like she was some . . . some . . ."

Her voice failed, ending in a heaving sob. Her eyes were bright and shiny with unshed tears.

I wasted a moment lighting a cigarette, giving her time to stabilize her emotions, feeling a sympathetic response of my own. I smoked silently for a few moments, then cleared my throat.

"Why didn't she break it off?"

She shook her head without looking up. "She tried. He wouldn't leave her alone. And she loved him. She stood up for him, said he couldn't help it. Something about Vietnam—he was an ex-marine or something. She made excuses—my God, she'd be walking around with bruises the size of my hand, and she made excuses."

"She could have told someone, her brother, her sister—the police."

"She never would. She didn't want to hurt him, to have him hurt any more, she said. By that time her sister was an alcoholic, divorced, and half crazy. Lorry didn't want to worry her, I guess."

"If he bruised her up that bad, couldn't her sister see it?"

"He never marked her face—except once when he gave her a black eye. That's why I never believed what he told her, that it was some kind of reaction to what he saw and did over there. He told her he lost control, couldn't help himself." She paused, blinking slowly. "It only seemed to happen when they were . . . making it. She was willing. That's why it was so stupid, the way he acted." She shook her head, lips crimped tightly again. "I just think he liked to do it. Maybe that was the only way he could get it . . . get it on." She threw me a quick sliding glance.

"You didn't know she was running away?"

"No. But I wasn't too surprised. She was upset all the time about her family, her sister's drinking. Her father's death had hurt her terribly. I don't think she cared much for her mother. She said her mother was fifty when she was born and that she didn't want her. She said she always knew that right from the first. It was her father, I guess, who loved her and spent a lot of time with her. I know she loved him. You couldn't be around her very long and not find that out. She talked about him all the time."

I stubbed out the cigarette and asked her the question I had come to ask. "You have heard from her, though, since she left?"

She nodded without hesitation, eyes downcast. "A card from Las Vegas not more than a week after she left. She had lied about her age and got a job as a waitress in a café next door to one of the big casinos, the Sands or the Sahara—one of those."

"Do you still have it by any chance?"

"No. I gave it to a man named Murdock, a private detective like you. That was right after I got it. I—I really didn't want to, but he convinced me that Loretta could get into a lot of trouble out there . . . and he gave me a hundred dollars." The self-deprecating tone had crept back into her voice. "I guess I found out something about myself that day."

I nodded and smiled. "I find out things about myself all the time."

She looked up and moved her lips in a faint parody of a smile, looking me squarely in the eye for the first time.

"When did you hear from her the second time?" I asked

casually, catching an almost imperceptible flicker in her eyes, a faint tightening about her mouth that told me my stab in the dark had found a tender mark.

She spread her hands in an unnecessary gesture of negation. "I never heard but that once," she said, a faint tremor in her voice, the slender hands falling to her lap to tug and smooth the pleats in her skirt.

I chuckled, a hearty sound meant to reassure. "That's one way you and I are alike, Virginia. I can't lie worth a damn, either."

She made a face, then smiled her little small-toothed smile. "I know," she sighed. "I never could lie. But that doesn't mean I have to tell you about it." Her chin tilted defiantly. "And I'm not going to. If Lorry wanted to be found, she'd be found, and that's all there is to it."

I nodded and lit another cigarette. I leaned forward. "Okay. That's fair enough. Now let me tell you why I'm trying to find her. Her mother's dying. She wants to see her—if that's possible. If not, then she'll be satisfied to know that she's alive and well. That's all there is to that. Now, let me tell you about me, what I do. I find people, mostly. I find them if and when I can, but I don't take them anywhere. That's up to them. I try to persuade them to come home with me. If they say no, then that's that. I don't push them. I don't hound them. Once in a while, when in my godly wisdom I believe they're better off where they are than where they've come from, I don't even find them at all—if that makes any sense."

She was smiling, the tough face softer, the green eyes warmer, a glimmer of gold in the auburn hair as she bobbed her head.

"Yes, that makes sense," she said. "All right, Mr. Dan Roman. I'll tell you what little I know if you'll promise me that if you find her, you'll ask her first before you tell anyone." She paused. "And you won't tell anyone if she doesn't want you to."

"You've got it," I said solemnly.

She smiled crookedly. "And if you offer me money, I'll be angry."

"Don't worry. Nothing scares me more than an angry woman."

"I'll bet," she said, then blushed and quickly stood up. "All I have is an address in Los Angeles, California. She wrote me a letter a year after she left. She was living with a man named Wade Chance. He belonged to a bunch of bikers called the Desert Devils. I remember that much. I have the address written down. I answered her letter, but I never received a reply, so I don't know how much help it will be." She turned and marched out of the room before I could reply.

I stood up and rubbed my buttock where the spring had been drilling for blood. Another name, another link in a chain. I hoped there would be another name after that, another link. That was the way it was done, one link at a time. Sometimes the chain was broken, and that was the end of it. At other times it seemed endless, stretching to nowhere. I had a sinking feeling this was one of those times.

Virginia Adams came back, holding a slip of paper in her extended hand like a sacred offering. She looked worried, her pixie face clouded. "I hope I'm doing the right thing."

"You are," I assured her. I tucked the paper in my wallet without looking at it. I thanked her and moved toward the door.

"John Sackett," she said, the name tumbling off her tongue like a curse. "Sometimes I think of what he did to her and I— I . . ." Her voice clotted, choked off.

"There must have been more to it than that," I said, opening the door and stepping out onto the small concrete porch. "A woman doesn't have to put up with beatings any—"

She made a sound like a cat spitting, eyes blazing. "Don't tell me about wife beaters!" Her voice was shrill, thready. "I just got rid of one of the bastards. Twelve years I put up with that—that—" Her voice failed her again, and she threw up her hands and fought to bring herself under control. She swept one arm outward in a fierce half circle. "This is what it got me, this mansion in a slum. As soon as I can unload this cracker box, I'm leaving this damn town for good." She fairly hissed with anger.

There was nothing I could say to that, so I smiled my most sympathetic smile, shook her hand, and took my leave.

I hadn't been lying when I said that nothing frightens me like an angry woman. Well, almost nothing.

/ 5 /

John Emerson Sackett, Loretta Arganian's long-ago boyfriend, turned out to be the son in Sackett and Son Construction Company.

A telephone call to the company office sent me to south Midway City to a strip of gently sloping land a half mile from the south fork of the Trinity River. There were rows of tract homes that seemed only slightly larger than my two-car garage, brick veneer on slab foundations, single-car garages suitable only for the new generations of minicars, and not a single tree left standing. The once-wooded tract of land had been swept by clanking bulldozers, stripped to bare earth, eliminating the expense of contour planning, allowing the small houses to be lined up and evenly spaced like row houses in a New York slum.

I found John Sackett in a tiny mobile office at the end of one of the arrow-straight streets. A tall lanky man in white jeans and hand-tooled cowboy boots, he greeted me amiably, coming around his desk to shake hands, then sitting down again and resuming his late lunch of take-out chicken, French bread, and beer.

"Have a seat, Mr. Roman. I'm running a couple of hours behind today. I hope you won't mind if I eat while we talk. I hate cold chicken." He bit into a drumstick with obvious relish, grease glistening on wide full lips, steady blue eyes appraising me with a salesman's ruthless scrutiny.

"Go right ahead," I said. I moved a folding metal chair near the corner of his desk and sat down. I busied myself selecting a cigarette and lighting it, giving him time to masticate the huge mouthful and wash it down with canned beer.

"Well, Mr. Roman," he said, "what can I do for you? For some reason I don't think you're here to buy one of my small mansions." His tone was genial, his smile wide and friendly— maybe just in case he was wrong.

"As a matter of fact, I'm not. I'm here to ask you about someone you used to know, Mr. Sackett, someone you knew a long time ago." I hesitated a beat. "Loretta Arganian."

For the better part of a second he seemed to freeze, drumstick suspended before his open mouth, cerulean eyes flickering to life, focusing on mine, growing cold.

He put the drumstick down and methodically wiped his fingers on a paper napkin, the flicker in his eyes turning to shiny pinpoints of flame.

"What do you want from me?" His voice had turned shrill, harsh, and abrasive.

I had his full attention; that much was certain. I puffed smoke across the desk at him and let the small silence grow, smiling what I hoped was a gentle sardonic smile.

"What do you think I want?" I asked finally, breaking the ominous silence.

He shoved abruptly to his feet, the wooden swivel chair crashing against the wall.

"Not a goddamn penny, you son of a bitch!" He stormed around the desk to the outside corner and stood there glaring at me. "I want your ass out of this office! And I mean right now!"

I took one last pull at the cigarette and dropped the butt in the ashtray. I stood up, keeping my smile intact despite the familiar stillness inside, the vigilant part of me that watched, assessed, made judgment, and waited.

2 7

"Ask me nice."

"Out! Out, you son of a bitch! I mean right—" He broke off and took a step forward, an involuntary step in all likelihood, prompted by his unaccountable, irrational anger. But it was a hostile action, and I was feeling my own drumbeat of anger.

I took a half step to meet him, hooked him with a right in the solar plexus from a foot and a half away.

Done right, the shock can paralyze you for seconds, sometimes minutes, leaving you with presentiments of mortality through an illusion of imminent suffocation.

It can also, and often does, empty your stomach, and Sackett, hunched and tottering, eyes blearing, mouth gaping, made liquid warning sounds deep in his chest.

I scooped up the wastebasket just in time, and held it in front of his stricken face. I turned my head and listened with a sort of detached pity as he brought up his take-out chicken, bread, and beer, and probably a good part of his breakfast and last night's supper.

When he finished I walked him around his desk and sat him down in the swivel chair. I handed him the paper napkin.

"Wipe your mouth and chin. You look like hell."

He hunched forward, breathing heavily through his mouth. He swiped the napkin across his lips and gave me a reproachful look.

"What—what did you do that for?"

I shrugged and took out a cigarette. "You didn't smile," I said. "Either time."

Face clouded with bewilderment, he scrubbed carefully at his chin. Finally he grimaced, looked up, and scowled. "That ain't funny."

"Being called a son of a bitch isn't funny, either. Not where I come from."

He sat up straight and fingered his stomach gingerly. "Aw hell, that's just a figger of speech, sort of. I think you kinda overreacted."

"The way you overreacted to Loretta Arganian?"

His face clotted again, rapidly, then just as quickly paled. "Who the hell are you anyway?"

"I told you my name," I said. "I'm a private investigator—" I broke off as his shaggy head bobbed up and down, fleshy lips curling in a sneer.

"Just like that goddamn Murdock! All you sons of bitches—" He bit it off quickly, flashing a weak smile. "I didn't mean anything by—"

"What about Murdock?"

His lip curled again. "Money-grubbing scumbag! I paid him a thousand—" Once again he bit it off, looking like a man who had just swallowed a worm.

"A thousand dollars. For what?"

"None of your damn business."

"How old are you, Mr. Sackett?"

He glared at me, mouth crimped tightly.

"It's easy enough to find out. And I'll do that. But I'm going to guess right now that you're at least thirty-six or seven. That would mean that you were a legal adult when you were screwing Loretta Arganian. Did you get her pregnant? Was that why she ran away? Was that why you paid Murdock a thousand dollars? Or did he find out something else, something far worse about you?"

"Get out of my office." His voice hovered barely above a whisper.

"Or maybe," I said, "he found out that you were a sadist. That you beat and raped a sixteen-year-old girl who loved you—not once, but repeatedly."

"No! No! I loved her—goddammit, I loved her!" His head wagged wildly from side to side. "It—it wasn't like that—not at all like that."

"Then what was it like, John? Did she like it? Did she get off on being brutalized? Is that what you're telling me?"

"No, no, not . . . that, either." He crashed forward in the chair, elbows on the desk, his face buried in his hands. "I—I kept flashing—flashing back to Nam. . . . Man, I'm no goddamn shrink, but I know what . . . this gook bitch . . . mama-san, she got a knife into me, my guts, my back. I lost a kidney, a lot of gut . . . and I damn near died."

"How did she manage that? She invite you over for tea, or what?"

He washed his face roughly with both hands, dropped them to the desk, and looked at me dully.

"You know, man. I was humping her in a hootch. She had this damn knife. . . ." His voice trailed off. He broke eye contact.

"You mean you were raping her, and she defended herself. So, what's new? What happened to her?"

His chin lifted, and a fleeting look of belligerence crossed his face. "I blowed her damn head off."

"So, what did that have to do with Loretta?" I knew what he was going to say, but I wanted to hear him say it, to listen for the crystal ring of truth or the hollow whine of falsehood.

He sighed and looked past me out the dirty window. "Some-times, man, sometimes I'd flash back—back to Nam. Usually when I'd been drinking. I kept seeing these dark eyes staring up at me, big and shiny . . . just like the gook's when she cut me. . . ." His voice faded again, came back stronger, surer. "I loved her. I—I guess I still do. I can't tell you how much I hated it when I hurt her. I hated me. I still do."

"Why did she run away, John?"

He shook his head wearily. "Man, I don't know. I was half-crazy for a long time thinking it was me, yet knowing in some deep-down kind of way that it wasn't. I don't know which was worse, thinking I run her off or knowing that I didn't mean that much to her." His head sank forward on his chest like an old man nodding off in church.

"You never heard from her?"

"Not once, man. Not once in twelve years." His voice thrummed with sadness, a familiar aching litany, as if he had said the words a thousand times before.

I got up and turned to the door. I lit a cigarette and looked at his lowered head. "I'll take your word for that, John. If I find out you lied, I'll come back." I opened the door, then turned back once more.

"Sorry about your lunch."

He gave no indication that he heard me. I looked at his bowed head for a moment, shrugged, and went out the door.

A black three-quarter-ton pickup with an eight-foot stake bed had pulled into the parking slot next to mine. Oversize tires and high-sprung body combined to give it a top-heavy, ungainly look, raising its roofline six to eight inches above my Dodge. Pretentious and impractical, I thought, descending the steps and watching a tall massive man alight, a pseudo-cowboy in whipcord pants, hand-tooled boots, and a flat-brimmed Stetson hat. He wore a cream-colored cowboy shirt with brown piping, embroidered pocket flaps, and mother-of-pearl snap buttons down the front and on the cuffs. A real dandy. He had probably never been closer to a cow than the meat counter at Tom Thumb. A neatly trimmed beard and mustache, dark shades, and a string tie rounded out whatever image it was he was trying to project. He moved up the walk at a long-legged lope, passing me without so much as a glance.

I shut down my friendly smile and turned to watch his broad back disappear inside the small building.

"I'm fine, thanks, and how are you?"

But of course he didn't hear me, and I climbed into my Ramcharger pickup and started the engine, wondering just where in hell I had been when the whole damned world had shifted gears, when rudeness and indifference had become the uniform of the day. A symptom of some deep psychological change, no doubt, an ominous harbinger of things to come. The thought added a dirty smear to an already muddy day.

I lit a cigarette and let the pickup ease backward, then tromped the brake frantically as the imperious blast of a car horn came from behind me. I ducked my head into my shoulders and watched in the rearview mirror as a mint-green Cadillac crept around me, nosed into the parking space on my right.

I eased the pickup forward again, a silly apologetic grin on my face. I leaned across and looked into a pair of warm dark eyes peeking from behind a luxuriant mass of chestnut hair. I lifted my hands, winced, and tapped a finger against my temple to indicate lunacy.

Her head bobbed almost imperceptibly, full pink lips edging upward briefly in a smile. She turned away immediately, busying herself with keys and purse and alighting from the car.

I straightened up behind the wheel and went into reverse again, moving the truck slowly, watching her go up the walk, a shapely compact body in a sleeveless blouse and ubiquitous designer jeans, the dark hair glinting with golden highlights, breaking in deep waves across her shoulders.

Sackett's wife? I wondered. Girlfriend? Secretary? Customer? Whoever she was, someone had almost certainly been using her as a punching bag. My one fleeting glimpse of her face had told me that much—yellow-green bruises high on both cheekbones, a purple welt along the curve of her jaw. That would account for the peek-a-boo hairdo, the reluctance to maintain eye contact. Like too many victims, she felt shame and guilt at being a victim, probably convinced she had brought it on herself.

I felt a sharp shiver of disgust, a throbbing drumroll of helpless anger.

I drove out of the housing tract, wondering if it could be Sackett, if his hairy knobby fists had bruised the pale tender skin, marred the lovely face, wondering if he still used Vietnam as justification.

It was a melancholy notion.

/ *6* /

"California, huh?" Susie said, a bit of sirloin poised on the tip of her fork while her eyes drifted around the rough-hewn dining room of Texas' Best Steak House. She chewed the bit of beef along with a chunk of baked potato and brought her gaze back to mine. "Must be nice romping around all over the country, chasing girls, going to exotic places."

"Los Angeles isn't exactly an exotic place, and I'd rather be horsewhipped than ride a plane."

"Why don't you drive? You could take your new station wagon. It would be a nice trip."

"Too far." I took a sip of tea and watched a red-faced brat in a high chair across the room bombard his mother with a fistful of green peas. She ignored him; he turned over his glass of milk. The father reached a long arm across the table and swatted one of the fat cheeks. The kid howled. I brought my attention back to Susie.

"I've been thinking," I said. "You need a car. That little foreign crate of yours was on its last legs when ... when you left. That's one reason I ordered the station wagon. Why don't you use it while I'm gone, and you and Janey look around, find something you like, and I'll get it for you when I get back."

Her fork stopped en route to her side order of green beans. She looked up, a startled expression on her face, quickly replaced by something I wasn't sure about.

"Why?"

"Why what? What do you mean, why?"

"Why should you buy me a car, Danny? Why would you want to?"

"Well—hell, Susie, that's a hell of a question to ask. Why not, for Pete's sake?"

Her face tightened. She looked toward the red-faced kid still crying across the room. "Once and for all, Dan Roman, I want you to understand that you don't owe me a single solitary damned thing." Her face swung back to me, olive skin dark with heated blood, eyes sparking fire, a transformation so rapid and so complete, it caught me totally off guard.

"Look, all I wanted to do was to help out a little. It's no big thing—"

Her head bobbed. "Oh yes, it is a big thing. A new car is a big thing. It's a little too much to pay me back for doing a little housecleaning. I assumed that was what this date was for, paying me back for what I did. Don't worry, I never for a moment imagined you were asking me out simply because you enjoyed my company."

I stared at her, bewildered by the sudden turn the conversation had taken, sifting through her convoluted speech for some clue to her anger. I bought a little time by sipping my tea and, after a while, decided I had it.

"The one thing doesn't have anything to do with the other," I said. "I invited you out because I do happen to enjoy your company. And for no other reason. I'm not trying to pay you back for anything. After all, we are still man and wife."

"And the car?"

"What about the car?"

"Why do you want to buy me a car?"

I threw up my hands. "Because you need it, dammit!"

"That's no answer, Danny."

"It's the only one you're going to get." I pushed back my empty plate and lit a cigarette, feeling a tiny rill of righteous anger of my own.

She brought back the meager smile. "Thanks anyway, Danny. I'll buy my own car. I'm going to look next weekend."

"Good," I said, and glanced at my watch. "You about finished? The movie starts in twenty minutes. We'd better hustle."

She took a sip of tea and blotted her lips, then gave me a cool searching look. "I'm not really in the mood for a movie tonight. I've got so much homework, I'd just sit there worrying about it. Maybe I could have a rain check?"

"I'm devastated," I said lightly, dredging up my own smile despite a jabbing pang of disappointment. "But I'll get over it."

"I'm sure you will," she murmured, picking up her purse. "I'm ready if you are."

She waited near the door while I paid the cashier. I watched the old lady's arthritic fingers count out my change and wondered what the hell had happened, wondered how I had managed to blow the heart right out of the beautiful September evening.

*　*　*

They were waiting at the rear of the restaurant near the edge of the parking lot, standing quietly in the shadows of a Dempster Dumpster set at right angles to the building. Wide-brimmed western hats shielded their faces from the pole lights, casting darkness.

Susie saw them first; I heard a small smothered gasp and felt her hand clutch my arm.

"Mr. Roman? Mr. Dan Roman?" The voice was deep and rumbling and slow, Texas dripping from every syllable.

I stopped and turned, instinctively gripping Susie's hand, bringing her around to the side away from them.

"Yes, that's right, I'm Dan Roman. What do you want?"

"We startled you," the slow voice said. "I'm sorry, young lady, please don't be alarmed." I zeroed in on the voice this time: the taller of the two, a good four inches above my six feet even.

"I'm not," Susie said tartly, her suddenly ice-cold hand tightening on mine.

"Why don't you send your daughter on to the car?" another voice suggested—the short bulky one. "We'd like a few words with you—if, of course, you don't mind."

I nodded and took the keys out of my pocket. I pressed them into her hand. "Wait in the car. I'll only be a minute."

"Danny, I don't—"

"Go on, Susie. It's all right. Business."

She gave me an uncertain look, then backed a few feet away. "Okay," she said, her voice an octave higher than usual. "I'll watch from the car." She emphasized the word *watch*, and off to my right one of the men laughed.

"No trouble, little lady. I promise. We want to be your daddy's friends."

"He's my husband," she snapped. She whirled and stalked toward the car, not an easy thing to do in high heels.

"Pretty little lady," the tall one said.

"Spirited, too," his companion added.

"Okay," I said, slipping my hand inside my jacket for a cigarette. "Talk."

35

"Don't try to scare us, okay?" the big one said. "You're not wearing a gun."

I brought out the cigarettes and lighter. "What do I call you? Big shadow and fat shadow, or what?"

The short one laughed. "He's got a busy mouth."

"You can call me Harpo," the tall man said. "This here's Chico."

"Groucho couldn't come; he's looking for the secret word." Chico guffawed and slapped his thigh, head tilting. I caught a fleeting glimpse of a round face and a thick drooping mustache. I lit the cigarette, feeling a little better. There was something eerily disquieting about talking to shifting shapes, faces I couldn't see.

"You're looking for a certain person," Harpo said, speaking noticeably faster. "We've been asked to tell you not to look for that person anymore."

"By whom?" I asked politely.

"Groucho," Chico said. "Groucho don't want you to look for the young lady anymore." He bent forward as if ready to convulse with laughter.

"Could you give me a reason?"

The two hats turned broadside as they looked at each other. In silhouette I could see that Harpo wore a beard, a thick mustache under a long humped nose.

"We can give you two," Chico said, voice bubbling with merriment.

"Muscle," Harpo said succinctly, and banged his fist against the Dumpster; it sounded a lot like a rock.

"And steel," Chico added, taking a half step forward, shoving his hand into the light. The hand was closed; I heard a snick, and five inches of knife blade shot through a crack in his pudgy fingers.

"Slick," I said. "But I've seen junkies who could do it better stoned."

"I'm just learning," Chico said, his thin voice aggrieved. "What I need is practice." His hand disappeared, blended with his barrel-shaped body's silhouette.

36

"What may I tell our principal?" Harpo said politely.

"He means Groucho," Chico said. "Whatta we tell Groucho?"

"Tell him I'll take it under advisement."

"He'd like a yes or no answer." Harpo's feet grated on the asphalt as he changed position. I changed my own, tensed, ready to bolt. Muscle and steel—I knew my own limitation.

"What would happen if I said no?"

"Groucho would get mad, for one thing," Chico said.

"Nothing," Harpo said, spreading his hands. "This time. We promised the little lady."

"It's comforting to see you're men of your word." A babble of voices drifted around the corner of the restaurant, a patter of feet, laughter.

"We are," Harpo said. "What does a man have if his word's no good?"

"The next time, though," Chico said, "we'd have to put you in the hospital a couple of months."

"Six months," Harpo corrected.

"Six months, yeah, that's right." Chico practiced, extending his hand, the blade snapping out into the light again, disappearing just as the group of people came around the corner, laughing and talking, passing us by without a second glance.

"Hey," Harpo said, after they were out of earshot. "You're cool. I thought sure you'd take off with them."

"Why?" I asked. "I've got your word. Besides, you know my name; you must know where I live."

"That's right," Chico said. "We do. Well, good buddy, what's the good word?"

"I already told you. I'll take it under advisement."

Harpo sighed. "I reckon that means no. Well, this time we're only messenger boys. . . ." He let it drift away.

"Well," I said, turning, skin crawling between my shoulder blades. "I guess I'll see you."

"No doubt about it," Harpo said.

"Soonest," Chico added.

"Until then," I said, already fifteen feet away, feeling tension sloughing off in almost painful waves, the valves in my heart relaxing, adrenaline tapering off.

I was grinning cheerfully by the time I climbed into the pickup.

"Couple of old drinking buddies," I said. "Wanted me to go off on a toot."

"How could you tell?" she asked sweetly. "They never came out into the light."

I wheeled out of the parking space, feeling her eyes singeing the side of my face.

"Oh, I recognized their voices right off. They were just having their little joke."

She leaned forward and looked at my face as we passed a lighted intersection. "Then why are you so pale?"

I grinned, shrugged, and lit a cigarette.

She sat back in her seat and folded her arms across her breasts. We rode in silence. All the way to her apartment.

She snapped out a tight-lipped good-night, flipped out the door, slammed it, then before I could blink my eyes, snatched it open again.

"I'd like to know," she said furiously, "just how big a damn fool do you think I am?"

She slammed the door again before I could answer and dashed up the walk. I waited until she was inside the apartment before driving off, sucking the cigarette like a pacifier, forcing my tangled nerves to unwind.

I discovered I had a headache, a hollow spot just under my breastbone, a faint tremor in my fingers, a dry mouth. By-products of fear. I knew the symptoms well. The exchange by the Dempster Dumpster had unnerved me to an unusual degree, out of proportion to the overt menace offered by the two shadowy buffoons. I wondered why.

I discovered the answer a few minutes later. Seated at the kitchen table, staring at an unopened bottle of Wild Turkey, I realized that it had been Susie's presence, the possibility of harm to her that had triggered my inordinate reaction of fear. I had always kept my job and my private life in two different compartments, a sharp dividing line between the two. It had been a hard, fast rule when I was a cop, one of the few I brought with me when I quit.

One thing was clear: whoever sent Harpo and Chico to brace me when I was with Susie was either too damn dumb to rot, or he simply didn't understand the risk inherent in breaking the unwritten rule.

Sooner or later I'd get a chance to enlighten him.

"I simply don't understand it, Mr. Roman." Phillip Arganian's voice corroborated his self-proclaimed confusion. He had repeated the same words three times since I began telling him about the incident behind Texas' Best Steak House. I could hear music in the background, muted voices, snatches of laughter, a tinkle that suggested ice cubes rattling against glass.

"You mentioned money the other day, the Arganian estate inheritance? Could there be some connection?"

"I can't possibly think of one. Loretta and I are the only ones left ... and that's assuming she's still alive, of course. After our mother's death, failing an appearance by Loretta, I would inherit half the estate and the balance would go to charity. There is no one else involved."

I cleared my throat. "No one?"

A moment of silence was broken only by a soft rasp of breathing. "If you are referring to my wife, Mr. Roman, please forget it." His voice was stiff, his tone formal. "We have prenuptial agreements. She is wealthy in her own right. She has no need for Arganian money nor any desire for it."

He was silent again, and I wondered if he was expecting an apology.

"The men I saw earlier this evening were not fantasy. Neither were the threats they made."

"What did they look like? If you could describe them, perhaps I—"

"One was tall, the other was short and round. The short one had a mustache. The tall one had both a mustache and a beard."

"That's it?"

"That's it. I would recognize their voices, I think, but I don't know how to go about describing them."

"I'm sorry, Mr. Roman. I simply don't understand it. I can't believe anyone other than my mother and I would be interested in Loretta's whereabouts."

"Someone obviously is, and at the risk of sounding cynical, I have to believe the money's involved somehow."

"I don't see how." He coughed; I heard the tinkle of ice cubes. "Does this mean—I mean, are you going to allow this incident to . . . to dissuade you from—" He broke off, letting it hang there like an accusation.

"If you mean did they scare me, yes. If you mean do I intend to quit, no. They caught me completely unaware. With a lady in the line of fire and no way to defend myself. That won't happen again. If they're serious, they made a bad mistake."

"I don't know . . . violence. I wouldn't want you to endanger yourself on my account."

I was getting a little tired of this; I decided to call his bluff. "It's your decision, Mr. Arganian. You say call it off, I call it off."

There was no response.

"Go back to your party, Mr. Arganian. I'll call you when I get back from California."

"Very well," he said stiffly.

I hung up thinking maybe I was being too hard on him.

*   *   *

I hate to fly.

The flight to Los Angeles was no exception. I heard the solid chunk and felt the quiver as the landing gear on the big jet locked into place and, as usual, wondered fleetingly if perhaps a section of wing could be ripping away.

Logic and airline advertisements will tell you that, for miles traveled, flying is by far the safest way to get from point A to point B. And the fastest. And that is reassuring—right up to the time I step aboard one of the thin-skinned monsters and begin wondering if it is absolutely necessary that I get to point B the fastest way possible—or to get there at all, for that matter.

Finally we dove under the dirty clouds, rocketing over rows and rows of houses, as far as the eye could see. The ground moved under us at an incredible speed, and when the tires bumped, skipped, bumped again, and the faint sound of brakes blasting reached our ears, there was a concerted movement of tensed bodies, a relaxing of taut faces, quick smiles, and nonchalance returning.

It was fast approaching darkness by the time I retrieved my bag and settled on a stool in the bar for a damn-I-made-it-again drink.

I unfolded Arganian's slip of paper and looked at the name: Lacy Wynters. Beneath it, in parentheses, he had written the word artist. What kind of artist, I wondered?

Lacy sounded like the kind of name someone might pick for a stage name—particularly if one had been originally dubbed Ethel or Tillie or Hortense. Not surprising, there had been only one listing for a Lacy Wynters in the directory according to the long-distance operator. The number hadn't answered, but it was still connected, so I had hoped that she still lived there.

The street name was an unpronounceable Spanish word, located in Chatsworth, a suburb of Los Angeles twenty-five miles or so to the north. I refolded the sheet and tucked it back into my billfold. Twelve years was a long time.

I stared at my sun-browned face in the mirror behind the

bar and thought about the changes that twelve years could bring.

The hair was good: still thick and black, with only a slight salting of gray, and over the years I had found that blue eyes were damn nigh irresistible to a good number of females. My nose was hooked in a manner I liked to think of as aristocratic, and I had been blessed with a friendly mouth. But the years were there, too, especially around the eyes and just above the mouth. Well, I was stuck with it, the same way I was stuck with this undoubtedly fruitless quest for a woman who, for reasons of her own, had disappeared twelve years ago.

Computer data banks, fingerprints, and Social Security numbers notwithstanding, it was still comparatively easy to lose yourself in this, the greatest hodgepodge of human beings in the world. Particularly if you weren't wanted for a crime somewhere along your back trail.

Fortunately for those in my profession, finding people could still sometimes be ridiculously easy; at other times it was absurdly difficult, even impossible. It was almost always frustrating, tedious, and dull. Long nights in strange places, with lots of time for reflexive introspection. Too many bars and too much booze, too many hours spent with people living on the razor's edge of survival—nobody runs away to hide at the top.

Sometimes, counting sheep in some tawdry, penumbral motel room, I'd find myself thinking about my quarry, wondering if maybe we weren't chasing the same rainbow, following the same ill-fated star, searching for our own particular epiphany, a better dream.

And in some strange way, that would ease the restlessness, the guilt, and bring about the realization that whatever the outcome, it would only be one small ripple in a vast sea of indifference.

I rented a car and drove halfway to Chatsworth before I pulled in at a motel, a redwood-and-stucco creation with a subdued western motif, real palm trees, and a giant swimming pool. I ate at a fast food restaurant down the highway and sat for a while in my doorway watching the tourists frolic in the pool. They were abrasively noisy and seemed grimly determined to wrest every second of enjoyment out of their precious vacation.

They wound down around midnight. I turned off the television during the most interesting scene of an X-rated movie that would have had a goodly portion of the residents of Midway City, Texas, marching on city hall with fire axes and hangman's nooses.

/ 8 /

I drove straight to the house. I stopped the car, lit a cigarette, and sat congratulating myself and studying the mailbox with the name L. Wynters painted in black by an artistic hand on its rusty side.

The paint looks fresh, I thought. I climbed out of the car and contemplated the thirty or so wooden stair steps that led to the top of a high bank where the upper portion of a dirty yellow stucco house was visible. The steep bank was covered with ivy, droplets of water still glistening from either an early-morning watering or a late-drying, persistent dew, the leaves so waxy they looked artificial.

I threw away my cigarette and climbed the stairs, and whomever I was expecting, it certainly wasn't the incredibly old wrinkled man who eventually answered my knock.

He stared out at me silently, the grooves in his face like scars in the west side of a Texas clay hill, the ridges worn smooth and parchment-thin by the winds of time, the furrows dark and black-speckled and unclean.

"Lacy Wynters?"

He stared some more, and I was about to repeat my question when the gray cracked lips parted, revealing startlingly white false teeth with peach-colored gums.

"What'che want with her? You a bill collector?"

"No, sir. My name's Dan Roman. I'd like to talk to her if it's possible?"

He blinked at me slowly.

"You here about the rent? I got one more day 'fore it's due. I got all her stuff ready here now. I'll have it out of here by tomorrow. I ain't payin' you a dime, neither. You got more'n enough out of her the last ten years."

"I'm sorry. I'm afraid there's been some misunderstanding. I just wanted to talk to her for a few minutes."

He studied me again carefully. "Who are you?" he asked finally.

"My name's Dan Roman. I came here to talk to Lacy Wynters about a girl she used to room with."

He shook his head slowly. "I'm Greta's pa. Her name ain't Lacy, it's Greta. She just took that 'cause she thought it was prettier. Don't matter no more, nohow. Greta's dead."

"I'm sorry," I said. "I didn't know."

He opened the door wider and looked past me. "Happened right there on them stairs. I allus told her she'd kill herself on them stairs someday. Girl wouldn't listen to me. Never would listen to anything I said. It finally got her killed. I told her about them stairs."

I turned and looked at the stairs, then back at him. "They seem all right to me."

He nodded and wiped his thinning hair with a gnarled hand. "Nothing wrong with them, I reckon, but she was a clumsy girl. Allus was, even as a kid. Allus fallin', hurtin' herself." He shook his head wearily. "I warned her, but she never would listen to nothin' I told her since she was thirteen."

"Mr. Wynters—" I broke off at the sudden fierce intensity of his expression.

"Name's not Wynters, it's Wynkowski. Perfectly good name, but she didn't like it, said it didn't sound American enough,

said nobody could spell it right. She had these fancy ideas—
wanted to be better than what she was. Left home at fifteen.
We didn't hear from her for ten years about. My old lady had
died by then. Never thought I'd bury my own daughter,
though." The old eyes watched me steadily. "I reckon you
might be talkin' about that Taylor girl. Greta wrote us about
her. How much you want to pay to find out about her?"

My sagging spirits revived; I felt a spurt of adrenaline.
"Well, that would depend on what you could tell me, sir.
Maybe as much as fifty, hundred dollars."

"I can't tell you nothin', but everythin' Greta ever done or
seen in her whole life she wrote down. She had these books
she wrote in every day of her life, I reckon."

"You mean she kept a diary?"

He nodded at me, his eyes glinting shrewdly. "She's got half
a dozen of them things in her stuff. I know, I just finished
packin' 'em." He looked away from me. "I reckon they ought
to be worth twenty dollars apiece."

"That sounds fair, Mr. Wynkowski. But I may not need
them all . . ."

He waved his hand. "Nope. I couldn't go for that. They're a
set, like. They'd all have to go together. Greta'd want them to
stay together."

I smiled and nodded. "I'd like to see them if you don't mind."

"You have to take them as is, I reckon. I ain't got time for
you to set around readin'."

"All right, I'll take them. You say there are six? I believe
that would come to one hundred and twenty dollars."

He looked at me for a moment, as if regretting his easy
bargain, but he was evidently figuring the sum in his head. He
nodded briskly and showed me his chalky teeth again.

"I reckon that would be about right." He stepped back and
held the door open. "Come on in while I get 'em for you."

He limped across the room to a metal trash can in the
corner. He picked it up and casually dumped the contents on
the floor. He dropped awkwardly to one knee and rummaged
in the debris.

"You were going to throw them away, huh?"

He gave me another shot of his beautiful teeth. "Yep, I was. Now I'm gonna sell them."

"Not interested in what they say?"

"Nope." He climbed to his feet, his arms filled with small red books, each with a strap still firmly attached to its lock.

I handed him the money and accepted the books. "If you'd like, I can take your address and mail them to you. I won't need them for very long."

He was thumbing through the twenty-dollar bills, counting slowly, carefully. "Nope. Don't know what I'd do with them." He folded the bills and pushed them deep into his pants pocket.

I looked at the two suitcases and three small cartons by the door. "She didn't have any other papers of any kind? Old letters, things like that?"

"Nope. Them diaries was all she had 'cept for a little insurance policy to bury her."

"How old was your daughter, Mr. Wynkowski?"

He scratched above his ear. "I reckon she was about thirty-five, or thereabouts. Don't rightly remember how old I am, come to think about it."

I stopped at the open door. "Well, I'm sorry about her death," I said.

"Don't need to be," he said curtly. "You didn't know her."

I smiled and nodded and turned to the stairs. I heard his shuffle behind me.

"Watch them damn steps," he said.

It was an eerie feeling, reading the words of a dead woman, a dead woman I hadn't known.

I began with the oldest diary and waded methodically through the small neat printing, each letter formed meticulously, as if she were being graded on her penmanship ability. It was the last entry on the first day in December when I came to a reference to a Nancy Taylor: two short sentences squeezed in at the bottom of the page:

46

A new girl came to work at the restaurant today. Her name is Nancy Taylor and she is the sweetest person I've ever met.

An ambiguous statement, one young woman's evaluation of the personality of another. Innocent. It gave no indication of what was to come.

Each day thereafter the journal contained references to Nancy Taylor, until, by the middle of the next month it contained little else. I gradually became aware that what I was reading was not merely frothy extravagant praise of one girl by another, but instead a declaration of love. I read the January eighteenth entry with a slight tingling sensation of shock:

She's moving in with me! Oh, God, I don't think I can stand it if she rejects me. I love her! I love her!

And then the entry on February first:

Last night! She let me sleep in her bed for the very first time! If only she loved me—but that will come in time. To love her is enough for now. So help me God, I'll drive all thoughts of men right out of her head!

Grimly, doggedly, feeling like a ghoulish Peeping Tom, I followed the progress of their love affair. It soon became clear that it was very much one-sided, that Nancy Taylor was permitting herself to be loved. For reasons known only to her, she was allowing Lacy Wynters access to her body, submitting to, but not reciprocating her love and her passion.

In March, the two of them flew to Las Vegas for the weekend. They spent Saturday sightseeing, shopping, doing a little gambling at the slot machines. Sunday morning Nancy rented a car and drove them to a small town not far from Las Vegas. Talon, Nevada. They visited an old friend of Nancy's, an Indian named Joe Lightfoot. Lacy watched them laughing and talking and realized they were once lovers. She took that as further evidence that Nancy was growing restless, slowly slipping away.

Lacy's frustration grew, permeated her writing, vicious at times, humble and adoring at others. The entry for May third:

> Oh, God! I should have left! I can't bear listening to them! The way he grunts, the terrible sounds she's making! If I go now, I'll see them. . . . I couldn't bear that. Hearing them is terrible enough!

The last Nancy Taylor entry came on the twenty-fifth of May:

> She's gone. Gone to him . . . Spencer Osgood. Oh, God, how I hate him! I know what he's done. He's promised her a part in a movie. And she bought it . . . poor stupid, stupid Nancy. God, can't she see? Doesn't she knew what they'll do to her? Oh, God, I could kill him!

I quickly leafed through the rest of the book, but there were no further references to Nancy. There were two more journals, but I didn't expect to find anything more, and I got up and washed my burning eyes. I stretched out on the bed and opened my fourth pack of cigarettes of the day.

Spencer Osgood—never heard of him. Maybe someone in the movie industry: producer, director, actor. He could be anything, anyone. Agents, stuntmen, even prop men had been known to use the promise of an introduction, a chance of a part, as leverage to pry open the reluctant legs of a gullible young would-be actress.

Tomorrow, I thought groggily, tomorrow I'll find out who Spencer Osgood is.

/ 9 /

Sheriff's Investigator Paul Thurgood closed the manila folder and shook his head. "Everything's pretty straightforward, Mr. Roman. There was no reason to suspect anything other than an accident. Miss Wynters's next-door neighbor thinks she heard her cry out when she fell. She went to her window and looked out, but she couldn't really see anything because of the brush and trees between their houses. No signs of violence. One of her shoes was found near the top of the stairs. It appears that she just tripped and fell." He picked up a pencil and worried it with his fingers, his hazel eyes regarding me quietly. "You have reason to think otherwise?"

"No, not at all. I talked to her father, and he seemed pretty vague about the details." I lit a cigarette and smiled. "At any rate, I like to check in with the local law when I'm working in their territory."

He nodded. "It's a good idea. You're working on something connected with Miss Wynters?"

"Yes, more or less. I'm trying to locate a girl who used to room with her years ago. I don't imagine it would have panned out anyway. I believe they parted company several years ago."

Thurgood leaned back in his swivel chair and laced his fingers behind his head. "They come and go. I understand from her neighbor that she's had a number of female visitors over the years." He smiled faintly, his slight hesitation and the smile an indication that he was aware of Lacy Wynters's sexual proclivities.

"I won't take any more of your time, Sergeant, but just one

more thing—I was wondering if you might know of a Spencer Osgood. I understand that he was connected with—"

He came forward in his chair abruptly, laced fingers dropping onto his desk with a thump, his eyes no longer uninterested. "Spencer Osgood? May I ask what your interest in him would be?"

I met his eyes, startled at the sudden change. "He—his name came up in connection with the woman I'm looking for...."

He lifted his hand. "Just a moment, please." He pressed a button on his phone. "Mabel, would you bring in the Spencer Osgood file, please? Yes, that's right."

He leaned back in his chair again. "Go ahead."

"That's it. His name came up as someone who may have known the lady I'm looking for. All the information I have is that he was somehow connected with the movie industry."

He nodded. "And who is the lady you're looking for?"

"Her name is Nancy Taylor."

He pursed his lips and inclined his head slowly, as if confirming a known fact.

"Why?" he asked bluntly.

There was a light tap on the door; then it opened, and a young woman came in with another manila folder. She handed it to him, glanced at me, and left. He placed the file in the middle of his desk and folded his hands over it.

"Why?" he repeated.

I shrugged. "I have a client."

"Who? Mrs. Osgood?"

I shook my head. "I'm sorry, Sergeant, I can't reveal my client's name. You know that."

His eyes gleamed. "I don't know any such thing. You're in California, Mr. Roman, not Texas. Your license is no damn good here . . . and you know that."

I smiled. "Yes, I know that. But I still won't reveal my client's name, Sergeant."

"A few days in our jail may very well change your mind about that."

50

"I doubt it. But before you do anything rash, I wish you would contact Captain Homer Sellers of the Midway City Police Department in Texas. He'll vouch for me."

He made a deprecating gesture. "The fact that you're from the Dallas area in Texas tells me that it must be Mrs. Osgood. She's a persistent lady. You're the third private detective she's sent looking for Nancy Taylor. She thinks Texas is the place to start. She just won't give up until she is face-to-face with her husband's murderer."

I stopped in the middle of lighting another cigarette. "Murder?"

He smiled. "I take it that she didn't bother to tell you that the reason she's so eager to find Nancy Taylor is that Nancy's the number one suspect in her husband's murder. It happened a couple of years ago. She hasn't given up, just keeps sending out fresh private detectives."

"The murder wasn't solved, then?"

He looked nettled. "It was, to my satisfaction. She killed him. Nancy Taylor killed Spencer Osgood, as sure as I'm sitting here."

"But you couldn't convict her?"

He waved his hand angrily. "We couldn't find her. She disappeared the day of the killing—" He broke off and stood up. He went to the water cooler in the corner and filled a small paper cup, then threw back his head and downed it like a shot of whiskey. He turned to face me.

"I handled that investigation. I'm certain that she killed him. It's been a burr under my saddle ever since. Not so much that we didn't find her, but that we couldn't find her—if you know what I mean. She disappeared like a puff of smoke. We were able to trace her back as far as the restaurant where she met Lacy Wynters, where she worked as a waitress, but she may as well have been born that day. No fingerprint record anywhere, not even a Social Security number. She gave one at the restaurant, of course, but by the time they found out it was false, she was gone. As far as we could determine, that was the only place she ever worked." He held a match to a cigar, sucked industriously until his head was shrouded with blue-white smoke.

"What about after she left the restaurant? Was she with Osgood all that time?"

He nodded and opened the file folder. He leafed through it slowly, not really looking at any one thing, obviously thoroughly familiar with its contents. He extracted a five-by-seven photograph and sat looking at it, his face softer, enigmatic.

"She was beautiful. I guess I can't blame him." He looked up, smiled faintly, and flipped the photo across the desk to me. "I guess you know though, huh?" His face had darkened and there was an embarrassed note in his voice.

It was an excellent job of photography, but then the photographer had had a lot to work with. Her face was still round, still youthful, but infinitely more lovely than in the picture Arganian had given me. This was the face of a woman, somewhat overweight to judge by the fully fleshed arms, the barely discernible pouch under her chin, but the extra flesh seemed only to add to her allure, to enhance the startling beauty of her smile and her serene eyes.

I felt a faint flutter somewhere in my chest, a dryness in my mouth. I looked up to find Thurgood watching me, his lips forming a crooked smile.

"She gets to you, don't she?" he said quietly.

"You never met her, then?"

"No. Sometimes I think maybe I'm not too sorry. I'm sure she killed him, but I imagine she had a good reason, considering his reputation."

"How so?"

He shrugged. "He was a womanizer. His only two interests were making movies and women, and from all reports, he spent more time on the latter."

"He was a producer?"

He nodded. "And director. Never very big. He made a lot of movies, but mostly B-grade, some for television, like that. His one big success was his first: *Death's Last Bow*. You probably

52

remember that one. Hell of a box-office success. Made him a lot of money." His crooked smile returned. "Made him a lot of women, too."

"You must have checked him out pretty thoroughly."

He shrugged. "He spent about half his time in my county. Had a small ranch up close to the north line. Rugged country. He shot some of his outdoor footage there. He made several westerns, did most of the shooting on his and his neighbor's ranches. Yeah, I knew a lot about him. Besides, my wife is in the business—costume design."

"How about Mrs. Osgood? She give him any problems?"

"Not that I know of. Oh, they had a few fights, I suppose. Rumors about separations, divorce, the usual kind of stuff. But nothing ever came of it. She stayed in Beverly Hills most of the time. He used the ranch for his heavy stud work." His cigar had gone out, and he paused to relight it. "The way he went through women, I think it says something for the Taylor woman that she was with him for two years."

"Maybe he loved her," I suggested.

He shook his head. "I got a theory about men like that. I think they're woman haters and don't know it, or maybe they do know it."

I grinned at him. "Man in your line of work needs to know a little psychology. It never hurts."

"You used to be a cop." It was more a statement than a question.

"Ten years. I got tired of holding the revolving door for the punks. Half the time they'd be out of the station before I was."

He nodded. "I know what you mean. I know there were a lot of abuses, but I think we were a hell of a lot more effective in the old days. Hell, the crime stats will tell you that." He brushed his hand through his graying crew cut.

I looked down at the picture of Nancy Taylor still in my hand. "How was Osgood killed?"

"Shot. His own gun. A .22 caliber. Twice in the chest at close range. The damn gun would fit in your pocket, but they don't have to be big if they're close and in the right place."

"I don't suppose you would let me see that file?"

"No. I don't think so. There isn't really anything here that would help you find her. That's your only interest, isn't it?"

"Yes. That's my only interest."

"I'd like to help, but you understand."

I nodded. "Do you have other copies of this print? It's much clearer and later than the one I have."

He looked inside the folder. "Yeah. You can have that one."

"Thanks." I got to my feet and slipped the picture into my inside jacket pocket. He pushed back from his desk and rose also. He followed me to the door and extended his hand.

"Sorry about getting horsey with you there for a while, but this damn case upsets me."

"The unsolved ones always do." I turned to go out the door, then stopped as he touched my arm.

"You'll let me know if you find her?"

I studied his broad face for a moment. I shook my head. "I don't know," I said honestly.

/ **10** /

I drove back to my motel through a hot dry wind blowing in from the desert. A liquor store on the highway provided me with a bottle of bourbon, and I stopped at the ice machine on the way to my room and wrapped a few ice cubes in my handkerchief. Inside, I dropped two of the melting cubes into one of the wrapped plastic glasses on the bureau and poured a drink.

I propped the photograph of Nancy Taylor against the ceramic lamp and sat on the edge of the bed sipping my whiskey and staring glassily at the picture, my mood as barren as the desert outside my window.

I was homesick for the untainted air of Texas, the relatively simple life I lived there. Somewhere in the deep recesses of my illogical self I had decided that if something bad had happened to this sweetly smiling woman, I didn't want to know about it.

And whatever had happened would almost have to be bad. Her kind of simple uncomplicated beauty would draw the spoilers like insects to a flame; the ones who couldn't stand to see beauty go intarnished, the ones who would have to possess it at any cost.

I was afraid of what I might find.

I paced the floor. Her eyes seemed to follow me around the room, pulling at me relentlessly, drawing me finally back to stare at her again. I finally had to turn the picture face down on the end table.

I picked up Lacy Wynters's fourth diary and turned to the dog-eared page where I had found the name of Nancy's Nevada boyfriend. The Indian. Joe Lightfoot, Talon, Nevada. A saloon-keeper.

I called information at the airport and discovered that Talon, Nevada, was a short distance outside Las Vegas. I booked a flight for early morning and spent a restless two hours tossing on the hard lumpy bed watching late-night movies on a black-and-white TV. Finally, I got up and turned it off. I fell back into bed, firmly convinced I'd never sleep again, and when I did, my dreams were wild and unlikely and filled with fantasy, an impossibly pastel world where all the boys grew straight and strong and all the girls were beautiful.

The well-used battered building was set back from the highway. It was stucco, with a redwood front, and the side nearest the gravel parking lot still bore the faded ghost of someone's long-ago dream: yard-high letters boldly proclaiming to the world that this was El Hacienda, a place of fine foods and fine wine in an elegant setting. But now the sign under the sagging portico simply promised beer, whiskey, and food at reasonable prices.

Joe's Joint. Simple and direct.

I parked my rental among the other vehicles in the parking lot: four or five rusty old pickup trucks and a ten-year-old Cadillac with a broken spring. I stepped out into blazing sunlight and stretched, trying to shake the effects of a fitful night and too much booze. I had to squint against the brightness until I crossed the lot and stepped into air-conditioned twilight, into silence broken only by the boom of my footsteps on a hollow wooden floor.

It was my kind of bar, dim and homey, with a frontier motif, deer heads at each end of the bar, ancient wagon wheels mounted on the walls, and heavy cane-bottomed chairs and wooden tables. The kind of place you could lodge in on a broiling afternoon, contemplate the sorry situation of the dying planet, and bemoan your own deplorable niche in the muddled scheme of things.

A man and a woman sat quietly at a table near the door; country people by the look of them, with simple rustic clothing, sunburned faces, and narrowed eyes that looked me over carefully before cautiously returning my nod. I spotted a juke-box and angled to take a stool at the end of the bar farthest away from it. Sooner or later someone would wander in with a gut full of misery that could only be assuaged by a lot of booze and loud music.

The man behind the bar was tall and lanky, with skin the color of old copper. He nodded amiably and took one last swipe at the grill he was cleaning before tossing his rag under the bar and coming toward me in the forward-leaning, rolling stride you usually find in the cowboy bars in Fort Worth.

"Afternoon," he said. He stopped in front of me, produced another rag from under the bar, and gave my section a courtesy wipe. "What'll you have?"

"Beer," I said. "Something out of the tap. Any kind will do as long as it's cold."

He grinned. "You got it." He was wearing Levi's and a western shirt turned up two cuff lengths on his forearms. Straight black hair framed a narrow handsome face and hung almost to his shoulders. His eyes in the dim light were as black and shiny as the carapace of a beetle.

He placed the mug of foaming beer in front of me. "Going in or coming out of Vegas?"

I put some money on the bar. "Coming out. But I didn't light. I came straight through from the airport, so I still got my shirt."

He laughed. "That's the only way to beat them, believe me." He picked up his rag and wiped his way a few feet from me, close enough to talk if I wanted to, far enough away if I didn't.

"You'd be Joe," I said, and when he nodded, I extended my hand. "I'm Dan Roman from Midway City, Texas."

He came the few feet to reach my hand. "Joe Lightfoot," he said, "from the reservation." We both laughed. He leaned his folded arms on the bar. "I was kinda wondering. You didn't look like a local, but in another way you did. You don't talk much like a Texan."

"It's a matter of survival. My instructor in basic training in the army was an Oklahoma U. grad. He didn't like Texans. I didn't like the garbage detail too much, so I lost my accent real fast."

He looked at me appraisingly. "You look about right for Nam."

I nodded. "Sixty-nine."

He had a slow wide smile that revealed large even teeth. He reached down and rapped his knuckles against his right leg just below the knee. It made a dull hollow sound.

"Some of us were lucky. They only got a piece of us."

I wagged my head. "It doesn't show. I thought you were a cowpuncher wearing boots. You have the same rolling gait."

He nodded. "You get used to it after a while. Sometimes you almost forget it—until you take off your pants."

I upended the mug, then set it down and slid it toward him. "Just fill it again. No point in washing another one. Join me?"

"No, thanks. You know how it is with us redskins and liquor. We go crazy, scalp the white folks, and rape their women."

"Speaking of women," I said lightly, "you ever see Nancy anymore?"

He stopped wiping the bar in midstroke. We faced each other in silence for a moment, his dark eyes appearing to recede in their sockets, his wide mouth a thin line.

"Nancy? Nancy who?" he said quietly.

"Nancy Taylor. You know, short, darkhaired, little on the plump side, pretty face. You remember Nancy."

"No," he said, his eyes never leaving mine, "can't say I do."

"That's funny. She remembers you real well. Said you two were pretty tight at one time."

His hand began the slow wiping stroke again. He shrugged. "Must be some other Joe."

"Joe Lightfoot, Talon, Nevada. Left part of his leg in Vietnam. Damn, that's some coincidence."

Without appearing to move, he came closer to me. "Who are you?"

"Just a guy from Texas who knows Nancy Taylor."

"You a cop?"

I shook my head. "I used to be. Haven't been for several years now. I gave it up."

A man came in and sat down at the other end of the bar. Lightfoot moved away to wait on him, and I concentrated on my beer and the drifting smoke from my cigarette. In a few minutes he was back.

"If you're not a cop, what, then?"

"I'm looking for her."

"Why?"

"I'm a private detective. Her brother hired me to locate her. Their mother is dying. She wants to know if Nancy is still alive, see her if possible."

I tugged out my billfold and showed him my Texas ID. He looked at it for a long time. I knew he was stalling for time.

58

He handed it back. "I don't remember her mentioning that she had a brother."

"Might not have. He was thirty years older; they didn't get along. Maybe she wanted to forget him. I don't know. I do know her mother hasn't much longer to live." We made eye contact again in silence. I sipped my beer and waited. Finally I said: "I know about Chatsworth. About Osgood. It doesn't enter into this." I could tell from the flicker in his eyes that I had struck a chord.

"You know about it," I said flatly. "You've seen her since then?"

He went away to serve another customer; I finished my second beer and lit another cigarette and patiently waited. This is not really a hell of a lot better than being a regular cop, I thought. You still spend most of your time asking questions and waiting. But at least I could drink on duty.

He came back with a folded slip of paper between extended fingers. "This is my address. It's only a couple of blocks from here. If you want to talk about Nancy, come by around seven tonight."

I took the paper and slid off the stool. "I'll be there, Joe. I'm on an expense account, so . . ."

He made a short violent gesture. "I'm not talking for money. First you're going to have to make me believe in you." He wheeled and abruptly walked away. His limp was hardly noticeable.

I drove around and located his house, a dreary one-story stucco with a dead brown lawn, then drove back toward Las Vegas until I found a motel.

I left a call for six o'clock, sprawled across the bed in my shorts, and went immediately to sleep.

/ 11 /

The inside of Joe Lightfoot's small house bore no resemblance to its antiquated exterior. The walls were covered with grained ash paneling, and a large airy living area complete with picture window encompassed the entire front of the home. In one corner, a big air-conditioning unit hummed busily.

"Have you eaten, Mr. Roman?" Joe was in an alcove off one end of the living room that served as a kitchen. I could see him stowing the contents of two large paper sacks onto shelves and into the refrigerator. I heard the clink of bottles.

"Yes. You go right ahead, though."

"I ate at the bar. How about a drink, then? I have vodka and gin and bourbon, mix for Bloody Marys, gimlets. . . ."

"Bloody Mary would be fine."

The living room was crowded with furniture, old and heavy and well used. It was a room of various shades of browns, the only color provided by a half-section of wall that had been converted to shelves and filled with books, both hardcover and paperbacks.

"You read a lot, Mr. Lightfoot?"

He came in with the drinks, his limp much more noticeable. "All the time. If you don't like to gamble or can't afford the shows, there's not much else to do around here." He handed me the Bloody Mary and eased himself into an imitation-leather chair with arms a foot wide. "But I'm not used to being called mister. I answer better to Joe."

I tasted the Bloody Mary. "You make a good drink, Joe."

He smiled. "I should, I've had enough practice." The drink

in his hand appeared to be clear liquid with two ice cubes; I wondered if it might be soda. He saw my look.

"Vodka," he said. "It's all I drink. I never get a hangover."

We sat in silence for a moment.

"You wanted to know about Nancy," he said at last.

"Yes. I'd like that very much."

He emptied his glass in one long draft, shuddered, and climbed slowly to his feet. He nodded toward my glass on the table. "You?"

"No thanks. Not just yet."

I heard the clink of bottle against glass; he came back and sank into his high-backed chair, bad leg extended in front of him. He laid his hand on his thigh and massaged gently.

"She never minded this. Not at all. Not many women could handle it like she did."

"I don't know," I said. "There were a lot of casualties in Nam. A lot of them are married."

He lifted his hand listlessly. "A hell of a lot of them aren't, too. Not anymore. And a lot more wish they weren't. A woman has to be pretty special not to show something sometime—maybe just a look when they're not on guard, a cringing, a pulling away, or, just as bad, being too eager to show that it doesn't matter, touching the stump, rubbing it, even . . . even kissing it." He turned to look at me, his face darkly sardonic, his eyes mocking.

"Then there are those who get off on cripples. I guess maybe they're the worst of all."

There wasn't a hell of a lot I could say to that, so I sampled my drink, and we sat again in silence. I lit a cigarette. After a few moments, he cleared his throat.

"It was in the spring, I remember that. I hadn't had Joe's Joint very long. She came in early one morning, riding behind a bum on a motorcycle, her hair stringy, dress filthy and torn. She was obviously pregnant. They had some sandwiches, and the guy she was with drank three or four beers. He was noisy and mean, and she was like a little mouse, smiling and taking

61

his shit like it was her due, like that was the way it was supposed to be and she was willing to accept it because she was nothing at all compared to him. By the time they finished, I was ready to throw his ass out in the street. She went into the rest room, and he came to the register and paid. He went outside then, and I heard him start his bike, and so did she, because she came flying out of the toilet with a small scared smile on her face and got to the door in time to see him blast off down the highway. . . ." His voice caught, and he shook his head angrily and took a drink of vodka.

"She sat on the bench outside my place for hours, looking down the highway like an abandoned puppy waiting for her master to come back. Jesus! I'll never forget that. I finally went outside and asked her if he was coming back. She just shook her head. I asked her if she had any money, and she didn't bother to answer that one—she didn't even have a purse." He stopped and drew in a long shaky breath.

"Well, to shorten it some, we, my waitress Josie and me, took her into the back room I had used as living quarters before I bought this house. Josie helped her get a bath, then ran over to her place and got her some decent clothes, a little too big, but clean. It was easy to see she was half-dead for sleep, so we fed her and Josie put her to bed in the back room. She was still sleeping when I went home at two in the morning." He shook his head, his face working with something like awe. "Jesus, she was a mess. Skinny, scratches, bruises on her arms and legs. That big son of a bitch must have been an animal. By then I was wishing . . . hell, I was praying that he would come back. I don't guess I ever hated any human as much as I hated that bastard right then—not even the gooks in Nam. It's good that he didn't come back. I don't think anything short of killing him would have satisfied me." He turned to face me, his lips twisting in a weak convoluted smile. "Us savages have a great sense of vengeance, a need for retribution, you see."

I nodded and smiled.

"When I came into the Joint the next morning, she was

62

sick. She was all huddled up on the bed, and it was bloody. There was . . . something in the bathroom wrapped in a towel. She had aborted. I took her to the hospital, but I never did find out if she had done something to herself or if it just happened. I asked the doctor, but he gave me a hard look and walked off. I guess it was easy for him to believe I'd done something to her, me being a bloody savage and all. We've always been notorious for treating our squaws like workhorses and dogs." He flashed me that crooked smile again, but there was no bitterness in his voice, only mocking self-denigration.

"We all have our little idiosyncrasies," I said.

He laughed loosely, his eyes slightly out of focus, the vodka making its presence in his bloodstream known. It showed also in his shambling gait as he went to make two more drinks.

"She came back fast, man. Inside a month she had gained twenty pounds, her hair looked like it was gonna live and 'long about then I discovered she was the best damned thing that had ever happened in my life. It wasn't only her looks, man, and she was beautiful, but it was *her*. I couldn't believe anybody could be that sweet, that kind, that generous. But there was a kind of dignity about her, too, long-suffering dignity. Oh, I didn't consciously think about all that stuff then; all I knew was that I was in love with her, crazy about her. I wanted her in the worst way. And the hell of it was, I knew I could have her any time I wanted. I could tell she expected it from the first, seemed puzzled because I didn't. I'd catch her looking at me, and I figured she was wondering if I was queer or something. But I didn't want her that way. . . . It was too easy that way. I—I guess I wanted to earn her . . . if that makes any sense. I wanted her to come to me because she wanted *me* . . . not because she owed me. . . ." His voice drifted off, dark eyes shadowy with pain, features clouded with recollections of other times, bad endings, the bankruptcy of hope.

"That's easy to understand."

"Is it? I don't know. I wasted a lot of my time with her. Sometimes I regret that now."

His head fell forward, his chin on his chest, and I wondered after a while if he had passed out on me. But then he spoke again.

"It was sometime in May before I decided that I'd have to make the first move. I'd convinced myself that she loved me back, the way she looked at me, the smile in her eyes. And we had necked some, nothing really heavy, but enough for me to know that she could respond to me. One night I waited around until Josie and my other bartender had gone. . . . She knew . . . I could tell by the way she looked . . . pleased and at the same time almost shy. She was still living there at the Joint, and I hung around talking, talking . . . all of a sudden scared to death because of my leg. But she knew, man, and she finally smiled and came and took my hand and led me to her room. She began undressing me . . . making a soft crooning sound, like I was a baby, her baby . . . and I was shaking, man, shaking . . . like I had never had a piece in my life before. And it was almost like that. She'd never seen my leg before, and she examined it . . . kinda curious like. Then she looked up at me and smiled and pulled herself against me and asked me if it would be better with it off or on, Jesus, I almost cried. It was so . . . so *right*."

"I can imagine," I said, my voice tight.

"I was off the end, man! I was crazy in love with her, and I wanted to marry her. But she wouldn't. She told me she loved me—right then. But she said it might not last, that some other man might come along and she would leave with him— and that would hurt me too much. We spent hours and hours talking about it, but I could never change her mind. There was something she wanted; she didn't know what it was, but she had to keep looking until she found it. It was crazy, man! I was crazy! She moved in with me here. That helped some. She worked at the Joint, wouldn't have it any other way. I didn't want her to. I wanted to keep her here, in this house—I didn't want her to see any other men, I guess. . . ." He lifted his head and turned away from me, but not before I saw the glistening slicks on his high cheekbones, the smears under his eyes.

I sat in silence and waited for him to work it out.

"It happened," he went on dully. "Just the way she said. August, somewhere around the middle. A man in a Caddy convertible. She waited on him. I noticed him talking to her, but I was busy and didn't pay much attention. Then, later, I saw them talking again, and I saw her look in my direction. God, Dan, I felt a freezing numbness. I knew . . . I knew even before she came over to the bar and waited for me to finish with a customer. Her face was sad. I managed to smile . . . God . . . and I wished her the best of luck. But I didn't fool her. She knew what it was doing to me . . . but she had to go. I don't think she could help herself. . . . I want to believe that anyhow." He lurched to his feet and, without asking, plucked my empty glass out of my fingers and sidestepped cautiously into the kitchenette.

"Hey, partner," I said. "Maybe you ought to lighten up a little."

He whirled and glared at me, his eyes glittering crazily. "Goddammit! Don't try to tell me how to run my life!"

"Okay," I said. "Just thought I'd mention it."

It took him longer than usual to make the drinks; when he shambled back, he was grinning.

"Sorry. I get meaner'n a snake when I get drunk. And I ain't even all the way drunk yet."

"Just give me a little warning is all I ask."

"We always war-whoop first. Man, don't you ever go to the movies?"

"I haven't seen an Indian since *Gunsmoke* went off TV."

"Yeah," he said glumly. "We ain't even worth killing anymore. John Wayne used to keep half the tribe working, but ever since he died, they ain't making no more westerns."

"Was that the last time you saw her, Joe?"

He looked at me and his face tightened. "Give me one good goddamned reason why I should tell you anything else."

"Because you want to," I said. "No, because you have to. Because you want me to find her. You want to know as much as I do whether she's still alive, safe, not broke and cold and hungry somewhere, hiding, having to take men into her bed to—"

"Shut up!" he said savagely. "She ain't no whore!" He glared at me. "Anyhow, what do you care if she's cold or hungry? You haven't even met her."

"I don't know," I confessed. "But I do." And surprisingly enough, it was the truth. I wanted to see her in the flesh, find out what it was that others saw in her beyond the beauty, what there was behind those haunting, brooding eyes that pulled at me so relentlessly.

"Yes, dammit," he said harshly. "I saw her after that. Several times after about a year. She was with some producer, director, something like that. He came to Vegas a lot. She always rented a car and drove out to see me."

"Spencer Osgood."

"Yeah. She had changed some. She was heavier, more nervous. Jesus! I wanted to see her, and I hated it. I never gave up hoping, I guess. One time we were in the back room talking . . . well, I tried to . . . but she wouldn't. She had a crazy kind of sense of honor, I guess. Something. She said she couldn't, that she was with him now. Christ! I wanted to hit her, but in some kind of stupid damn way I was proud of her." His head wobbled as he turned to peer at me, and his eyes were suspiciously moist again. "Damn, she was one hell of a woman. But . . . but it was the damnedest thing, man. You could never reach her, you know, not really. Never get down there inside where she lived. Jesus, I don't know. Maybe there wasn't anything there—maybe what you saw was all there was. You'd get to thinking that; then all of a sudden she'd say something, do something that would throw you for a loop, make you realize that she had some thoughts of her own, that she wasn't just a pretty doll made out of clay that could be molded any way a man wanted. Jesus, I don't know, man, maybe I just wasn't smart enough to figure her out." He slumped awkwardly in the chair, his legs strung out at an uncomfortable angle. I had a feeling he was going to fold on me at any moment.

"When did you see her last, Joe?" My tongue wasn't working well, either, and I tried unsuccessfully to remember how many Bloody Marys he had fed me.

His head wobbled, eyes trying to bring me into focus. "See her?.... Never saw Nancy ... not once. ..." His head fell back, then slowly began to roll on the axis of his shoulders. He slid sidewise in the chair, tilted forward, and would have fallen if I hadn't caught him.

I tried to pick him up, but my head was whirling, and when I bent over, I almost fell. I settled for dragging him into the bedroom and wrestling him onto the bed. He immediately turned on his back, flung his arms wide, opened his mouth, and began snoring.

It was chilly in the air-conditioned room; I found a blanket in the closet and spread it over him before I left.

Outside, nightfall had brought a quick cooling of the air. I stood beside my car and lit a cigarette, waiting for the hollow sizzling sensation in my head to go away.

Three drinks, I thought, that's all I had. I shouldn't be feeling like this after only three drinks. A sharp pulse of pain pounded the back of my neck, and my joints burned and ached; I felt sapped, as if I had just come off a twenty-six mile hike with full pack and combat boots.

I leaned against a fender and breathed deeply, coughed, then gave it up and climbed into my car and drove out onto the highway. The desert slipped by around me, sparkling and bright in the moonlight; just ahead the horizon blazed with the orange glow of Las Vegas's greedy all-consuming fire.

/ 12 /

When I awoke the next morning, I was sick, my head a buzzing hornet's nest, my body slick and slimy with fever sweat. With my joints aching and nausea swirling in my stomach, I sat on the edge of the bed and tried not to think about breakfast. I felt too sick to live and decided that if I had to die, I was going to do it in Texas and not in some godforsaken motel in an even more godforsaken desert.

I called the airport and found that the next flight to DFW was leaving in something over an hour. I calculated times and distances fuzzily and decided that I could make it. I wasted ten minutes getting through to Homer, overwhelming his barrage of questions, convincing him that I was not drunk but sick, and that I would wreak a terrible vengeance if he was not waiting for me when the plane landed at DFW. I wasted another ten minutes checking out and paying my bill, and if there hadn't been a fifteen-minute delay, I would have missed the damned thing.

I remembered very little of the trip home. A stewardess looked at me queerly when I refused lunch, and a few minutes or maybe hours later, a portly man in custom Levi's and a loud sport shirt sat down next to me. He carried a small bag the size of a shaving kit. He poked and prodded at me for a while before pronouncing in an authoritative voice that I was sick. I could have told him that in the beginning. The stewardess stood nervously in the background; I dimly heard references to "liquids" and "aspirin."

They moved me to a section of the plane where I was all by

myself, arranged the seats so that I could lie down, and began stuffing me with water and juices and aspirin. The plane touched down somewhere. I was halfway down the aisle before my stewardess-nurse collared me and firmly led me back to my bed. She covered me up again, made motherly clucking sounds, and told me in a soft tender voice that if I got up again, she was going to kick my ass.

Finally, they took me off in a wheelchair to meet Homer, who hovered around skeptically, then lumbered off to bring his aged Plymouth to the front entrance. The man in the loud shirt was there, too, talking to Homer, who listened to him intently, head bobbing up and down, his broad face red and strained.

Big oaf's afraid he's gonna catch my flu, I thought fondly.

The night was long, intermittently filled with startled moments of clarity, a soft voice, and water and pills, roaring noises and throbbing quiet, my body alternating between burning and freezing.

Once during the night I saw a lovely silhouette in the dim glow of the night-light, and I felt safe and loved, but I was so cold.

"Susie. I—I'm freezing, honey." I clenched my jaw to keep my teeth from chattering.

"All right, darling." I felt the movement of the bed, a chill blast of arctic air, then her body tight against me, incredibly hot, waves of blessed heat slowly working through my flesh, dissipating the chill. I tried to shrink, to curl, to creep deep within that life-giving warmth.

I slept deeply, without dreams.

I awoke to find Susie watching me quietly, raptly, mouth parted slightly, as if she found breathing an effort and her nose needed help. Her dark eyes were fixed somewhere on my face, her own features relaxed, open in the way of someone watching something of interest, blithely confident she is not being observed.

69

In itself, that was not in the least disconcerting; it was a lovely face, a pleasure to watch, a work of art by some master genie's hand. It was not the face itself that set bells crashing like cymbals, adrenaline racing like fire; it was the fact that it was only inches from my own; so close I could feel the soft puff of her breath, see the faint line of freckles that bridged her nose and swirled and faded at her cheekbones, so close that I became acutely aware that the body welded to mine was sans clothing.

Her eyes shifted, met mine, the parted lips curving instantly into a smile, brown eyes widening in a mixture of humor and concern.

"Are you warm enough now?" she said primly.

"Any warmer and I'd burst into flame." My mouth was dry, coated. I sounded like Johnny Cash on a bad day.

"You were pretty sick," she said, moving minutely away, a slow blush building under my scrutiny.

"Maybe I should get sick more often. Kinda like old times."

"You were freezing, Danny. I had to warm you somehow." Her smile slipped, became small and lopsided. "You begged me to help you. You were shaking to pieces. I had to do something."

"You did exactly the right thing." I moved to regain the lost distance between us. "I ever tell you your body is like a furnace?"

She chuckled uneasily. "That's an exit cue if I ever heard one." She slid out of bed and into her robe with one fluid graceful movement. She cinched the belt and leaned forward to pull the covers around my shoulders. Then she felt my forehead, her expression businesslike and reserved. "Your fever is down, but it'll be back in the evening. That's what the doctor said."

"Susie," I said. "I—Jesus, I don't know what to say . . . except thanks for taking care of me. I'm sorry about . . . uh, about all this. Homer had no business . . . he should have gotten me a nurse."

Her eyes gleamed. She straightened, hands propped on her hips.

"Never mind that now," she said. "It's time for your medicine. There was a doctor on the plane with you. He wrote you a prescription and everything. You've got the flu. He said it would take two or three days for it to run its course. So, you'll have to settle for me, mister." She was talking rapidly, her voice crisp. I opened my eyes in time to see her small round bottom flip around the doorjamb.

"Susie!" But she was gone—and it was just as well, I thought morosely, trying to remember the dreamlike delirious hours of the long night.

She came back, pills in one hand, a glass of water in the other. She was dressed in a puff-sleeved yellow cotton blouse and black designer jeans, her face severely composed, her eyes avoiding mine.

"Four times a day, with lots of water," she said curtly, all business. "And sleep. That's important. You mustn't be disturbed." She was already at the door before I could speak.

"Susie! I have to know. . . . Did . . . anything . . . you know, happen?"

"We'll discuss it later, Daniel," she said with the cool smile and frosty voice that all women seem able to muster at will. She closed the door with a gentle click of the latch.

As she had predicted, with the advent of evening came the chills and fever: times of flushing, swelling, sweating, followed by periods of relative calm that gradually gave way to bone-shattering chill.

She gave me alcohol rubs and pills and water, washed my face, and sat quietly reading the rest of the time. In moments of calm, of lucidity, I watched her face and wondered.

In the early hours of the morning the chill reached its zenith again, the piled-on blankets providing little relief; and this time it was with complete awareness that I watched her remove her clothing. I steeled myself for the rush of icy air as she lifted the covers and came inside, moving in one swift sinuous movement to bring that body with its life-giving warmth to mine.

"There now," she whispered. "I'll take care of you."

/ 13 /

In the afternoon of the third day I sat leaning against the headboard, Susie cross-legged in front of me, balancing the tray across her legs while I slurped soup ravenously.

"Not too fast," she advised. "You'll throw it up."

I put the spoon back on the tray and leaned my head back, exhausted.

"Is that all I get?"

She laughed and slid the tray to a corner of the bed. "That's it, buster. You can have some more tonight. Maybe even a piece of toast and some milk." She folded her arms across her knees and sat for a moment in silence, waiting for me to look at her. When I didn't, she sighed and said: "You don't need to act so humble, Dan. I'm still your wife, after all. I don't mind taking care of you."

"Who's acting?" I said dryly.

She made an exasperated sound. "You're being silly. You know what I'm doing is the right thing to do. You'd do the same for me." She cocked her head and tilted an eyebrow. "Wouldn't you?"

"Sure I would, but I know it's bound to be an imposition— all the time you've been spending over here."

"Not as much as you think, Danny. I haven't missed but two classes and no tapings at all—"

"Whoa. Class? Tapings? You lost me somewhere back there."

She sighed and tilted her head, a mocking glint in her eyes. "I guess you don't know, do you? Well, I'm going back to school to finish out my degree."

"So that's what you meant the other night about homework. But what about your job with TNS? Won't there be a conflict?" I felt a sudden rush of confused emotions, not the least of which was a small blip of exhilaration. Throughout our four-year marriage her job as co-anchor and special assignment reporter for the Texas News Service TV broadcasting network had presented a spate of problems not conducive to a smooth-running love life and had eventually led to a marital blowup that sent us stalking off in different directions to "reconsider our commitment."

Susie's words, not mine. Four long lonely months, and I was convinced more than ever that the real culprit was the sixteen years' difference in our ages. Middle-aged stodginess versus the vicissitudes of youth, paranoia versus boundless optimism.

She caught a loose strand of hair and wound it around her fingers, her eyes bright but unreadable. "No. I'm not reading the news anymore. I'm still working for TNS, but I have a different job, more of a part-time job. I'll be taping interviews with celebrities, politicians, covering civic functions and things like that. With a little luck I'll be able to fit the interviews into my class schedule. If it doesn't work out, I'll have to quit."

"Pretty sudden decision, wasn't it?" I said, keeping my voice flat and neutral. "Last I heard, your career was the most important thing in your life."

Her head lifted slightly. "I never said that, Danny. Not once did I ever say that. It isn't true."

I wanted to ask her what *was* the most important thing in her life, but I couldn't make myself say it. Stubbornness or fear, I wasn't sure which. Instead I deftly turned the conversation to more mundane matters. "Will you be making the same money?"

After a momentary hesitation, she shook her head. "No. I had to take a cut in salary, but—"

"Then you'll be needing some help—"

She smiled faintly and shook her head again. "I don't think so. Mother said she would pay my school expenses, and I'll be making enough to live on, so ..." She let it fade away and broke eye contact, tracing the seam along one leg with a slender finger.

"I see. Mother dear to the rescue. I keep forgetting you don't have money problems like us poor folks—"

She lifted her head, eyes flashing. "That's not fair, Danny! And I'm certainly not going to apologize for my mother. She deserves everything she has. She wasn't born rich, you know. She and my dad put in their time being poor. More time than they deserved, and just because you don't like her—"

"Hey, now wait a minute. I like Lucille, dammit! I respect the hell out of her. She's a fine woman, but I think she's a little too free with her money when it comes to my wife—"

"Your estranged wife," she put in grimly. "Let's tell it like it is. And another thing, I think you're a little hypocritical coming down on my mother for being wealthy, when you have all that money for the coal from your land."

"That's right, I do. More than enough to see my wife through a dozen years of college—"

"That's not the point, Danny."

"Well, suppose we pause for one breathless moment while you tell me what the point is."

"I told you. We're ... estranged ... we're separated, we're not living as man and wife, and I don't know—" She broke off, tossing her head to flip her hair back across her right shoulder, the movement bringing a goodly portion cascading forward, effectively hiding her face in shadow.

"You don't know what?" I reached for a cigarette on the nightstand by the bed, creating my own diversion to mitigate the growing tension, a sudden swooping chill of premonition adding definition to my sore and aching joints.

"I don't know, Danny. Four months ... you never once tried to see me ... call me. I—I don't know what to make ... of that."

74

I lit the cigarette and gained a few seconds; then I coughed and cleared my throat. Eventually, I had to answer.

"Okay, I won't make the obvious comment that streets and telephones work both ways. What I will say is that you were the one who left. I didn't kick you out or even ask you to go. As I recall, you marched out under your own steam, your jaws tight and your teeth clenched—"

"I don't see how you could recall anything. You were smashed."

"You're right, I was, but I won't hide behind alcohol. I remember everything I said and did that night—"

"Then you must remember calling me a tramp!"

"No. I said you were acting like one. There's a difference." I stubbed out the cigarette. "I didn't follow you and Sy Deacon away from the Golden Crown Restaurant, so I don't know what went on later. I didn't want to know, I guess."

"Nothing! I tried to tell you that, but you wouldn't listen, and when you did finally listen, I could see you didn't believe me. You already had your mind made up. That hurt, Danny, it really hurt. I knew you were jealous of Sy, but I had no idea you didn't trust me!"

"I know what I saw."

"And what did you see? You saw me sitting in a restaurant having dinner with my co-anchor—and incidentally, my boss. Did you happen to notice that the next booth had four people from TNS? Did it occur to you that those booths hold only four people, and that was why Sy and I had to take one by ourselves? Big secret. Sitting right in the damn window having an after-show sandwich with my co-anchor, who also happens to be a friend—"

"Friend, huh? I guess that accounts for the friendly kiss I saw him give you after you came out."

"No," she said evenly, "it doesn't. He surprised me. And it wasn't a friendly kiss, but if you were watching like you say, then you must have seen that I didn't respond."

"It was hard to tell there in the shadows that way, but I do know I didn't see you slap the hell out of him or knee him in the crotch the way a—" I broke off, not sure how to end it.

"The way what?" she said crisply. "The way a decent woman would have done?"

"I didn't mean that, Susie. Don't put words in my mouth— Look we've been over this before. If you say nothing went on between you and Sy Deacon, then I'll take your word for it. If you told me that before, and I acted like I didn't believe you . . . well, it must have been the liquor bringing out the cynic in me."

"Did it bring out the spy in you, too? Was that why you were skulking around watching me?"

"No. I was cold sober. I came to the restaurant because the girl at TNS said a bunch of you had gone down to the Golden Crown to eat. I got home a day early, and I thought I'd surprise you. Some surprise. I saw you eating with a man who's been after you for years; I saw him kiss you and finally saw you both get into his car. I didn't need to be a detective to follow that chain of events to its logical conclusion. I left."

"If you hadn't been so quick to leave, you would have seen him drop me at my car in the TNS parking lot. I came straight home from there. *I* didn't go out and get roaring drunk, then come home and accuse *you* of being unfaithful . . . and a tramp."

I sighed and reached for another cigarette. "I think we've been at this water hole before. We're going around in circles. What do you want from me, Susie? An apology? Okay, I apologize for coming home a day early. I apologize for caring that another man kissed my wife. I apologize for my unreasonable, narrow-minded attitude and my dirty thoughts. I apologize for any name-calling or swearing I might have done— does that about cover it?" It didn't, and I understood that, but the pain of doubt was still prickling under my skin, like the sting of a cactus needle, and I couldn't make myself humble and penitent no matter how much I wanted her to come home.

She nodded slowly. "It's a start," she said crisply, and rolled sideways, coming to her feet at the end of the bed. "I think you're about well, Danny. I don't think you really need me anymore. At any rate, I have to run, or I'll miss another class." She moved the few steps to the door. "I'll call later this afternoon, and if you need me, I'll come by and fix you something to—"

"I can manage, thanks," I said. "I've had plenty of practice lately."

"Uh-huh. Well, I'll call anyway." She gave me a fleeting glance, a cryptic smile, and vanished through the doorway, leaving the room a colder, bleaker place.

I slipped down into the blankets. Clearly she wanted more than an apology from me; a reaffirmation of love, of trust, a new commitment. I shivered, coming down from the emotional high induced by the argument, feeling sick and useless and vulnerable, realizing in a moment of startling clarity that I had been on the verge of capitulation, that my carefully nurtured defenses had been shaking, crumbling, settling around my head like crumpled parachute silk.

I shuddered. Dammit. Who was the injured party here? There was no doubt in my mind about what I had seen. If I had jumped to wrong conclusions, then so be it. Over the years men had been hanged on circumstantial evidence, cities sacked and razed, empires toppled.

I felt myself drifting toward sleep; I tried to pull back. I needed to ponder some more, to plan. I needed to get her back, and somehow I would.

It was a comforting thought; it put me to sleep.

/ *14* /

The next day, at midmorning, I had an unexpected visitor: Mrs. Phillip Arganian, looking cool and self-possessed in a white silk blouse and dark tailored slacks.

"Good morning," she said, as I swung open the door.

"Good morning," I echoed inanely, surprise holding me immobile for a couple of seconds—one second too many.

She tilted her head, eyebrows arching. "You look surprised, Mr. Roman. Didn't your wife tell you I was coming? I called yesterday."

I let my smile slide into a rueful grimace. "By golly, I guess she did, at that. I was half asleep, and I guess . . . I'm sorry—"

"Well, please don't apologize. I should have called again this morning. If I've come at an inconvenient time . . ." She let it drift, blue eyes shining.

"Oh no, no, of course not. Won't you come in?" I stepped back, feeling suddenly foolish, abruptly aware of my unkempt hair, baggy pajamas, and well-worn robe. "If you'll excuse me just a minute, I'll put on some decent—"

"No, no! You look just fine. After all, I understand you've been ill."

"Well, yes, a touch of the flu, but I'm afraid I've been taking advantage of that. I'm well enough to be up and about." I closed the door and ushered her into the den, then pointed her in the direction of the new recliner. "Could I get you some coffee?"

"No, thank you, Mr. Roman." She settled into the chair. I took a seat on the couch across from her.

At our initial meeting on her front walk I had come away

with the vague impression of a short, trim woman, probably thirty, pretty, meticulously coiffed and groomed, with a very faint Bostonian accent and dark blue eyes.

And now, up close, with time to study her as she talked, I discovered that my first impression had been essentially accurate. Even in the harsh light of day, the merciless revealing sunlight spilling through the patio door, she passed muster very well: pale smooth skin, unlined except for tiny creases at her eyes, even, regular features, and, as far as I could determine, no makeup.

We discussed my illness, the way Midway City was burgeoning, the growing traffic problems, the unbelievable price of housing, and then, with the smooth precision of a diplomat, she led into the reason for her visit.

"I do hope your trip west wasn't a contributing factor in your illness, Mr. Roman."

"Not likely. I understand this particular strain of virus has an incubation period of about three days. If that's true, I caught it before I left."

She nodded. "You probably are aware my husband is out of the state. I thought perhaps I might find out if you have anything of consequence to report."

"Your husband is on a trip?" I was sparring for time. I didn't know how much he had told her, if anything, and I wasn't about to volunteer anything until I found out.

"Yes. He has recently acquired interest in coal-mining operations in Wyoming, and he has been spending a great deal of time there." A furrow appeared on her brow. She wasn't about to be put off so easily. "Were you able to find any trace of Loretta at all?"

So much for secrets between husband and wife. I wondered how long it had taken her to finagle it out of him.

I shook my head, frowned, and sighed. "No. I'm afraid not. I had one lead—a Miss Wynters—but unfortunately she had an accident a short time before I arrived."

"An accident? She was badly hurt?"

"No, I'm afraid she was killed. A fall. She fell down some

steps in front of her house. I poked around a little, talked to the sheriff and to her father, but ..." I let it trail off and shook my head sadly.

"This woman ... Miss Wynters, was it? Perhaps she had some papers, letters, in her effects that may—" She stopped, laughed self-consciously. "I'm sorry, I'm afraid I read too many mystery stories. I'm sure you know your job."

I smiled at her. "There was nothing that could help us. As a matter of fact, the trail ended in Chatsworth, California. I was going to call your husband today and tell him that, but since he is out of town—"

"I can tell him if you like. I expect him home late tonight." She hesitated, then smiled apologetically. "I don't mean to butt in."

I shrugged. "No, that will be fine. Obviously your husband changed his mind."

She looked startled. "Changed his mind about what?"

"Telling you about Loretta. He seemed determined to protect you from the family skeleton."

She smiled and made a breezy gesture. "Oh, that. He can't keep anything from me."

"I can understand that."

She laughed and sat back in her chair. "It is a rather warm day, isn't it? I—if you wouldn't mind, I might have something after all.... A beer would be fine." She looked toward the kitchen. "I would be glad to get it."

"Sounds good," I said, and pushed to my feet, "but I'll get it; I need the exercise." I flicked the ceiling fan on low as I passed the wall switch. It was a little early in the morning for beer, I thought, and the room seemed perfectly comfortable to me. But what did I know about the drinking habits of the upper crust, and maybe having all that money kept the body temperature elevated at all times.

I brought two cans of Coors and one glass.

"The can will be fine, thank you." She gave me a small crooked smile. "I will take a napkin if you have one handy."

"You bet." I took the glass back to the kitchen and brought

her a paper napkin. "Sorry," I said. "I don't have any idea where Susie keeps the cloth ones."

"This will do nicely, thank you." She wrapped the napkin around the bottom half of the can. "Susie? Is that her picture there on the mantel?"

"Yes."

"She's very lovely."

"Thank you. I'll tell her you said so."

She took a sip of beer, eyeing me over the can. "On the phone . . . she sounded very . . . young."

"Yes, she sounds like that sometimes," I said, my voice a little rougher than I intended.

Her eyebrows shot upward. "Please, Mr. Roman. I hope I didn't offend you. I would be the last one to— I'm sure you must have noticed the obvious difference between my husband's age and my own."

"No offense taken," I said. "But I suppose I am a little touchy about it. She's sixteen years younger than I am."

"Is it a problem?"

I thought about it for a while, sampling my beer. "Only for me, I think."

"Then it's not a problem," she said emphatically.

I returned her look steadily. "Are you saying that my feelings are all that matter, that what others think—"

She lifted a hand. "Please, Mr. Roman. I wouldn't presume to advise you, but one thing I will say. The 'others' you mention shouldn't enter into it. Your feelings, and hers, should be the only consideration." She paused, smiling faintly, a touch of color rising into her pale skin. "Worrying about those others you talk about will not fill an empty bed, will not bring love into an empty life." Her eyes met mine squarely. "I've had two wonderful years with Phillip. It might end tomorrow, but no one can take those years away, can they? If we hadn't gambled, we wouldn't have had them, would we?"

"Then you admit it was a gamble?"

"Of course! Isn't everything? Name one thing of value in life that isn't. Even life itself. The very fact that you and I are here today is the direct result of countless numbers of minor random miracles through the ages."

I grinned in response to her enthusiasm. "You make life seem a pretty chancy thing, Mrs. Arganian."

She grinned back. "Well, isn't it?" I decided that she had a very nice grin, bright and sexy and lavish.

"Just think," she went on, "out of millions of cells you were the one lucky enough to find your way, the only one out of all those millions of potential lives in just that one ... group." Her grin widened, pleasantly contorted her entire face. "Sometimes I get to thinking about that, and it boggles my mind!" The blue eyes flashed roguishly, a somehow bawdy look that contained an element of flirtation.

I laughed; her exuberance was infectious. "The mathematical permutations would be astronomical," I said solemnly.

She laughed, upended her can, and drank a bit more of her beer with a dainty feminine flourish. She looked at her watch, a veil of composure creeping across her face.

"Oh, my," she said briskly. "I must be going. I'm sure I've tired you too much as it is."

"Oh, no. I've enjoyed it very much."

"Well ... thank you," she said shyly. "I enjoyed it myself." She rose to her feet and extended a hand.

"Thank you, Mr. Roman. You have been very gracious and considerate. I apologize again for imposing on you."

I struggled to my feet and swallowed her hand in mine. "Absolutely not. You brightened a boring morning for a poor ailing man."

"Well, thank you again. I do hope you have a swift recovery."

"Sorry I didn't have anything to report."

She nodded and took back her hand. I followed her to the front door.

She stopped on the porch and turned to look at me. "I'll tell my husband, Mr. Roman, but I'm sure he'll want to talk to you himself."

"Fine. I'll be here."

I watched her walk to her car parked in my driveway,

low-heeled shoes clicking faintly on the pebbled walk. For the second time I felt a twinge of empathy for Phillip Arganian. If all the stats were right, she would soon be entering the full flower of her womanhood, and if I was any judge, he was already on the back side of the downhill slope.

/ 15 /

That same day, around noon, Homer Sellers came by to see me. A big bear of a man, he had keen blue eyes perpetually distorted behind thick bifocals, large blunt features to go with his outsize body and a heavy mane of mud-colored hair that never seemed to lie in the same direction twice.

A captain on the Midway City police force, in charge of Homicide, he had been my superior officer the last few years I worked for the department.

He had been instrumental in getting me interested in police work in general and onto the Midway City force in particular. Born and raised in the same small Texas town, we were about as different as two men can be and still remain friends.

The law had been his life for most of his adult years, and he was quietly proud of that. Still strangely naive in the way only men from small towns can sometimes be, he firmly believed in honor and integrity and the inherent decency of Homo sapiens, had an abiding faith in motherhood, the flag, and the Dallas Cowboys. He had been a widower for fifteen years, and if he had a social life beyond our occasional poker games, hunting trips, and infrequent melancholy drunks together, I wasn't aware of it. Our friendship had been sorely tested when I abruptly left the police force. He considered it not only a personal failure but an act of disloyalty on my part.

But the cement of time had repaired the rupture, the bond now even stronger than before.

We drifted out onto the patio, each carrying a beer. We sat in the shade, sipped our brew, and watched the antics of my three resident squirrels busily engaged in harvesting acorns and pecans for the coming winter. We sat in silence for a while, the comfortable, almost cozy silence that comes from the trusted rapport of old companionship. It was one of those quiet moments in life you remember because they are rare.

Homer chuckled quietly as Rowdy, my neighbor's German shepherd, sat calmly watching the squirrels' activity, feigning a monumental indifference, yawning, only his pointed ears stiffly erect, his bright alert eyes betraying his eager interest, his frustration at the intervening chain-link fence.

"He'd give up his Alpo for a month to get at them little critters," Homer said. "But he's got too much pride to let us see it." He shifted his bulk on the redwood lounge and pointed to a small bundle of reddish brown fur clinging to the bole of an oak. "How'd that one lose his tail? Rowdy get ahold of him?"

"Born that way," I said, and waited for his skeptical grunt. "It's the truth. Either that or some old bull tried to nip his balls and missed and got the tail instead. At any rate, he came out of the nest that way."

He snorted and gave me a disbelieving look.

"I read somewhere else, or maybe the same place, that a squirrel couldn't run and climb in the trees without that tail as a counterbalance. Old bobtail there zips around better than the other two. So much for expert opinions."

"Experts. Yeah. We got some of them mothers down at the courthouse." He grunted and cut his eyes at me. "Speaking of experts, you get anywhere on that Arganian thing before you got sick?"

"Sure. I got all the way to a dead end in California. Why?"

He shrugged thick shoulders. "Cliff was just wondering if I'd talked to you lately, if you might've found out anything."

"Why would he be so interested?"

"Him and Arganian are friends, I guess, the way he talked. He's just curious."

"Curious? Cliff doesn't have a curious bone in his body. He's got an angle somewhere."

He gave me a quick, belligerent look. "Come on, Dan. Give him some slack. Cliff's been a damn good chief. A lot better'n the last one. What've you got against him? You guys used to be good friends." He hesitated. "I know something happened, I just don't know what. I ain't sure I want to, but one thing I would like to know. Was it you who busted—"

"Knock it off, Homer. Just let it lay."

He shrugged again and peeled the cellophane off a plastic-tipped cigar. He waited until he had it going, then abruptly changed the subject.

"Pulled that file on Cyrus Arganian, Phillip's daddy. It was about like I remembered. He was shot in the right side of the head, and there was some question about it not being a contact wound. Autopsy report estimated that the gun must have been two or three inches away from his head. They based it on the pattern of gunpowder burn around the wound. Sid Croft—you remember Sid, he retired a couple of years after you came on the force—well, anyhow, Sid wasn't happy with the suicide reading, and he put the Arganians through the wringer. As much as he could, anyhow, before the brass took over and stopped him. Nothing came of it. Phillip was forty or so and happened to be at home. He and the girl were in bed, and the old lady was in the kitchen with the cook when they heard the shot."

"So, it ended up a suicide?"

"Yep. Sid ran a gunpowder residue test on the dead man, and that came out positive, so that kind of took the wind out of his sails."

"How about the girl?"

He shrugged. "She passed out, went into a fit or a coma or something. Spent about a week in the hospital."

"Virginia Adams told me she went to live with her sister after that."

He turned to look at me, his shaggy brows lifting. "Hmm. I never knew that. That strikes me as being a little odd."

I took a sip of beer and sighed. "According to Virginia Adams, she felt her mother didn't love her, and she hated her brother. She was only eleven or twelve. That could be reason enough."

He shook his head and went back to watching the squirrels.

We talked for a while longer, discussing the possibilities of the upcoming deer season, the need for a trip to my four hundred acres in southeast Texas to check out the cabin, the tree stands, and the water level in my three-acre lake.

It was something we did each September or early October, along with Tom Jeffers and Lee Swain, our hunting buddies. One of the rituals of fall, a day in the field with good companions, cold beer, bad jokes, and irreverent laughter. A rejuvenation of primordial instincts: men preparing for the hunt, stones and clubs and cunning replaced by shiny instruments that could kill from a quarter of a mile away.

Pending the approval of Jeffers and Swain, we decided on the first Saturday in October, a little over a month before opening day of the season.

That decision made, Homer swigged the rest of his second beer, ordered me to take care of myself, and heaved to his feet. He hitched up his pants, an odd look on his broad florid face. "How's Susie doing?" he said casually, biting down on the plastic-tipped cigar, an inch-long ball of ashes flooding the front of his shirt.

"Fine. She's back at SMU. Hitting the books, I guess. Seems to like it okay." I had a feeling he already knew all about it.

"She coming back, is she?"

He tried to maintain the light tone, but something had crept in, disapproval or accusation. I couldn't tell which.

"You'll have to ask her," I said, mimicking his rough rumble. "And anyhow, Homer, it's none of your damn business."

He came to a stop in front of me, reflected sunlight turning the bifocals into burning opaque discs. "How come, when I called over here the last two nights to see how you was, she answered the phone?"

"I imagine because she was here," I said. "You ought to know, it was your idea."

He stood looking down at me. Silently, intently. It went on a little too long. I felt a worm of annoyance raise its head, stretch.

"What's on your mind, Homer?" I said coldly. "If you got something to say, say it."

He shook his head slowly, looking suddenly uncomfortable. "You've answered my question. She ain't living here. I just didn't know what was going on, is all." He jammed the cigar between his teeth. "She's just a kid, Dan. Sometimes I don't think you treat her right."

"She's a woman," I said softly, almost hissing the words. "A very capable woman. We're having some problems right now, but with a little luck we'll be able to get past them. I always had a sneaking feeling that you didn't approve of me for Susie, but we're married, and that's a fact, and one of these days soon she'll be coming home." I gave him a sour grin. "How does that grab your nosy, boy scout ass, Homer?"

He stared at me again, blinking slowly. Then he took a step around my chair and cuffed me behind the head. "That'd be great, you dumb-ass," he said, and turned and trundled across the patio to the den door. He looked back, grinned, wriggled his fingers, and disappeared.

I sat around for a while longer, cooling down, watching the squirrels, watching Rowdy finally get up and stalk away from the bobtailed one chattering angrily at him from the top rail of the fence.

I understood how he felt, the tug of war going on inside him, deep instinctual urges giving way to reason and logic and futility.

The sun rose higher, and I was finally driven inside by the heat. Restless, jittery, I went into the den looking for something to read, wondering if Susie would come by after her last class of the day.

I had mixed feelings about that. A part of me wanted her to come, and still I dreaded it. "Damn!" I muttered aloud, and pawed through the magazines in the rack. Nothing there I hadn't read. I cast around the room and saw Lacy Wynters's diaries stacked neatly on the mantel where Susie must have put them.

In desperation, I sorted through them, found the final two I had ignored before. I fell into the rocker-recliner with the last of my beer, a cigarette, and a sinking defeated feeling.

I was halfway through the book, drowsing over the petty quotidian experiences of Lacy Wynters's life, when the name Nancy Taylor leaped screaming off the page.

I sat erect, electrified, losing my place and scrambling frantically to find it again, half believing I had imagined it, conjured it up out of deadly boredom, inserted it amid the trivial pursuits of Lacy Wynters's dreary days.

But it was there. In her fine precise hand. The first entry on the day she had received an invitation to Nancy's birthday party in Chatsworth. It was followed by a violent declaration that she would die first, would die and go to hell before she would demean and humble herself by seeing Nancy with that son of a bitch director who had stolen her away.

Then the second entry a day later, calmer, cooler, more logical: Maybe it was a sign. Maybe she was growing tired of him—that sounded like darling Nancy. Maybe she had realized at last her terrible mistake. Maybe she was yearning to return to the one who cherished her above all others, the one who loved her more than life itself. . . .

In the next two entries, Lacy Wynters grew more and more convinced the invitation was a signal of distress, a tender message of love.

Of course she would go! It was clear that her beloved Nancy was calling out to her. Oh, God—to have her back again!

The pages representing the next three days were blank.

And then the entry for the day after the party, the day after Osgood had been killed.

It was confused, disjointed. I had to piece it together from the chaos of a traumatized mind: the long frustrating afternoon, her attempts to get Nancy alone foiled at every turn.

Finally, in the twilight of early evening, she had managed to get her to take a walk through the orange grove. They were near the highway, ready to turn back before it finally sank in that Nancy's invitation had been an act of friendship, of compassion, that she had no intention of ever coming back.

Crushed with despair, she had dropped to her knees in front of Nancy, pleading, had dragged her to the ground, intending to prove her love the only way she knew.

And suddenly Osgood was there, cursing, raging, believing in the twilight that they were making love. He attacked Nancy like a wild man, striking her with his fists, a stick he found. He had picked up a rock and would undoubtedly have killed Nancy if the Indian hadn't suddenly appeared out of nowhere. He and Osgood fought, and Osgood produced a gun. The Indian got it away from him as they struggled and shot him twice. Nancy screamed and grabbed the gun, but Osgood was already dead. Nancy fainted then, and the Indian picked her up, carried her to his car, and drove away.

Lacy, totally disoriented, had made her way back to the house and quietly joined the party, torn by indecision, fearful of the consequences of not reporting the incident, but fearing even more the possibility of somehow being implicated in the killing itself.

Miraculously, no one but Osgood had seen her leave with Nancy, and when Osgood's body was discovered later that night, she was not singled out for special attention by the police. The gun had been found with Nancy's fingerprints, and with her disappearance, the police hadn't bothered to look elsewhere.

I flipped rapidly through the remaining pages in the book, but there was nothing more about the murder, nothing more about Nancy Taylor. As far as Lacy Wynters was concerned, she had ceased to exist.

I settled back in the recliner and lit a cigarette.

Joe Lightfoot. She hadn't named him, but I was convinced

he was the Indian in her narrative. So, Joe had lied about not seeing Nancy again.

Enlightenment hammered at me like a bony fist. Joe Lightfoot had lied; Nancy Taylor's trail hadn't vanished with the death of Osgood. . . .

Joe Lightfoot knew where she was, or where she had gone after that night. . . .

The chain wasn't broken. Not yet. The only problem was, I wasn't at all sure I wanted to keep pulling on it.

/ *16* /

The doorbell caught me halfway down the hall to my bedroom. I was heading for my afternoon nap, a habit I had fallen into with amazing ease during my short illness. I no longer felt ill, or weak, but it was going to be a long day, and habits are hard things to break.

I halted in midstride, wavering, weighing sloth against curiosity, debating the pros and cons while I waited to see if it would ring a second time. I had a NO SOLICITORS sign on my door so it probably wasn't a salesman, unless, of course, it was a Bible salesman. They seemed to think they were immune to the limitations imposed by mere mortals, believing no doubt, and perhaps rightly so, that theirs was a higher mandate.

It rang again, and I shuffled back down the hall and opened the door.

She was old. Old and withered and shrunken, with hunched shoulders and the big-boned forearms of a much larger woman. She was no more than five-five but it was obvious that she had at one time been taller, with a firm and supple body to go with the strong face that still remained. Her piercing green-speckled eyes stared into my face with the ruthless scrutiny of an X-ray machine.

"Mr. Daniel Roman?" She swayed, leaned into the tall thin man standing beside her, his arm firmly grasping hers. He wore a dark suit, bow tie, and the kind of billed cap associated with movie chauffeurs.

Beyond them, sedately gracing my driveway, I spotted the unmistakable outlines of a Rolls-Royce.

"Yes, ma'am, I'm Dan Roman."

"I'm Marissa Arganian, young man, and I'd like a word with you if you don't mind." Her voice was strong and implied that she didn't really give a damn if I minded or not. She took a short jerky step forward.

"Yes, ma'am," I said, and gave way, watching the thin man wince with either disgust or concentration as his long arm snaked around her waist and guided her unsteady feet through the door.

"Just go on into the den," I said. I flicked on the light and closed the door and followed their halting progress through the short entry hall, not sure if I should offer to help, not sure that I wanted to.

Inside the den, the thin man stopped and looked at me with raised eyebrows, his pale narrow lips curved in the merest ghost of a smile. It took me a second to understand what he wanted.

"The recliner," I said, "best seat in the house."

"No!" she said sharply. "I need firm solid support for my back. Don't you have something firm?"

"The brown velvet," I said, and watched the thin man's lips work themselves into a sardonic smile, one eyelid closing in a companionable wink. I wondered at his audacity; she appeared to be looking right at him.

"You may go, Sylvester," she said as soon as she was seated. "Wait in the car. I'm sure Mr. Roman will be so kind as to let you know when I am ready to leave."

"Sure," I said. "But there's no need for him to go—"

"Yes," she said quietly, folding her long thin hands in her lap.

"He could wait out on the patio," I said. "It's cooler—"

"No."

I looked at Sylvester. He was already on his way to the door, looking at me over his shoulder, his narrow features reflecting mild contempt. She was definitely looking right at him this time; I wondered again.

"Could I get you something to drink, Mrs. Arganian? Tea, or a soda, or—"

"No, thank you."

I nodded and moved down the length of the couch and sat down across from her.

"I know you must be a busy man, Mr. Roman, so I'll come right to the point of my visit. I understand from my daughter-in-law that you are giving up your search for my daughter." She was facing a quarter turn away from me, speaking toward the other end of the couch where I had been standing. I cleared my throat and her head swiveled toward me, and I suddenly understood Sylvester's rudeness. She was blind.

"Not exactly giving up," I said. "I hit a dead end in California. But as a matter of fact, I—"

"You mustn't," she said fiercely, harshly. "You must find my daughter, my little girl. You must not allow yourself to fail . . . like all the others."

"Others?" I felt a turgid stirring in the pit of my stomach. "What others?"

She sighed and lifted one hand. "Phillip didn't tell you, I see. Well, I suppose he didn't want to discourage you before you even got started. There have been a number of others over the years. Men like yourself who specialize in this sort of thing. . . ." Her voice faded, and she sighed again. "With no success, as you know." The hand moved up to poke and tug at a corona of loosely curled gray hair that, along with a knee-length red skirt and a white peasant blouse, gave her the appearance of a wizened cheerleader. I wondered who bought her clothes, who had dressed her in such a ludicrous fashion. Second childhood?

"No," I said, managing to keep a growing smear of anger from staining my voice. "He only mentioned a man named Murdock."

"Yes, he was the first. That ended tragically. Mr. Murdock was a good man. I picked him myself." She hesitated. "I say I picked him. That isn't entirely correct. He was recommended to me by the same man who recommended you, as a matter of fact."

"Cliff Hollister?"

She shook her head, the grooves deepening across her forehead in a frown. "No. Senator Lucas Drumright. The Bannisters and the Drumrights have been friends forever it seems. I place great trust in the senator's recommendation."

"I know the senator. I did some work for him. But you've lost me. Who are the Bannisters?"

Her head lifted, the pointed nose and sharp chin forming a wrinkled concavity behind which colorless lips parted in an austere smile. "I am a Bannister, Mr. Roman. I am the last of the Bannisters. That is why it is so important that you find my daughter, my only blood, my only living child. The Bannister fortune must not fall into alien hands. It was my father's lifework, his father's before him, my life's work."

"You have a son."

The smile thinned even more, became humorless. The pale eyes stared at me as if they could see. "No, Phillip is not my son."

"I understand that. But he is your husband's son. You raised him. Surely—"

"No!" The word burst from her like a malediction, harsh enough to scratch her throat. "He is not my husband's son. Cyrus and his first wife adopted Phillip when he was born." She paused dramatically, as if to lend credence to her next words: "He was illegitimate."

I shrugged, then realized she couldn't see me. "A lot of men have been born bastards. Some of them turned out pretty good."

"That is not the point. The point is that Cyrus lied to me. I

93

did not know that Phillip wasn't his child until years after his death. Five years, to be exact. Far too late to find out anything about Phillip's parentage."

"Does it really matter? You raised him. You know what kind of man he's become."

"Of course it matters. That's precisely the point. Phillip is a decent, lovable man, but he is also weak. He has no business acumen at all. He has done only what I have told him to do over the years. If not for that, the Bannister holdings would have long since been dissipated."

"You mean the Arganian holdings?" I was being argumentative and a little snide, but this cast-iron old lady was beginning to get under my skin.

She smiled. "Cyrus Arganian owned hardly more than the clothes on his back when I married him. The name changed, but all the rest of it remained the same. Bannister money, Bannister business sense that made it grow."

I lit a cigarette, thinking suddenly of Phillip Arganian's belief in his half-sibling status with Loretta.

"Phillip doesn't know about his origin?"

She shook her head. "No. I saw no reason to tell him. He takes great pride in the Arganian name, quite possibly as much as I do in my own. I won't rob him of that." She paused. "I understand that what we discuss here is confidential, that we have a detective-client relationship like that of doctor-patient."

"Not exactly," I said dryly. "Technically, I'm working for your son."

She dismissed that with an imperious wave of her hand. "You are working for me. I want your word, Mr. Roman, that you will never reveal anything I have told you here in confidence." She paused, and when I didn't answer, went on: "The senator assured me that you are the soul of discretion."

I thought about it for a while, letting the old biddy stew. I puffed on the cigarette.

"Well," she said impatiently after a minute of silence. "Do I have your word?"

"For what it's worth," I said.

She smiled, an uncomplicated open smile that revealed a trace of what once might have been great beauty. "I'm certain your word is your bond."

I returned the smile, then let it die, feeling foolish, realizing for the first time in my life how difficult it must be for the unsighted, with the spoken word as the only medium of communication.

"You will proceed, then? I am sure you can see that I am very old, Mr. Roman. I am ill, blind, and do not have much longer to live. That is why it is imperative that you find Loretta, that I know—God forbid—if she is dead. I realize that's a possibility. I must soon make final disposition of my holdings. Phillip will not be cheated, but I want the bulk of my estate to go into hands that have my blood flowing through their veins." She stopped, her sightless eyes holding mine like living things. "Is that so strange?"

"I guess not," I said, finally feeling a trace of empathy, a flash of understanding. I cleared my throat. "Will it matter if those hands are not so . . . so clean?"

She smiled again. "Not in the least. I realize it was partly my coldness that sent Loretta away from us. I feel a great deal of guilt about that. The least I can do is not be judgmental." Her chin lifted, and she turned her head away. "I want nothing from you, Mr. Roman, except Loretta's whereabouts."

"All right," I said. "I can't promise anything, but I do have one more slim lead to follow up."

"Thank you," she said quietly. "And if you will be so kind as to call my smart-ass chauffeur, I'll get out of your hair."

I chuckled all the way to the door.

Along about midafternoon I ran out of cigarettes. I backed the pickup out of the garage and drove to a small shopping center at Highway 157 and Airport Freeway.

While I was there, I decided to do some much needed grocery shopping and joined the throng of harried, wild-eyed housewives wandering the aisles with squeaking carts and hand-held calculators, desperation written on stricken faces as they watched their weekly food allowance barely cover the bottom of the basket.

I picked up some steaks, lamb chops, an overpriced ham, and the butcher came rushing out, bowing and obsequious, obviously mistaking me for one of the landed gentry come slumming.

With two cartons of Carltons my bill came to almost sixty dollars. I carried the small bag out of the store in my left hand, wondering if the reports of the death of inflation hadn't been grossly exaggerated. I had a sneaky feeling it was still alive and well, hidden, perhaps, in the esoteric permutations of some malevolent bureaucracy.

When I got home, I found a message on the answering machine from the younger Mrs. Arganian, requesting my presence at one o'clock the following day. She said that she was calling for her husband, who very much wanted to meet with me.

I ate my dinner in a silent house and wondered where Susie was having dinner—and whom she was having it with.

/ 17 /

I noticed immediately that Lee Arganian was wearing makeup. That, and a simple strapless dress that seemed to be sustained only by a great deal of optimism and the swell of her breasts.

She held the door open for me, one slender hand fluttering nervously at the hollow of her throat as she talked.

"My husband asked me to extend his apologies, Mr. Roman. He was just this minute called away. No more than ten minutes ago; something about an explosion in the boiler room of one of his plants in Austin. I tried to call you, but I suppose you had already left."

"That's quite all right, Mrs. Arganian. No harm done. It's a nice day out; it was a pleasant drive." I smiled and nodded and turned to go.

"Oh, no, Mr. Roman, please." Her small hand flew out and rested lightly on my arm. "I will not have it," she went on gaily. "I've slaved all morning in the kitchen baking a lovely ham for our lunch. I will not have it go to waste."

"Lunch? I'm sorry, but . . ."

"Oh, and my husband did leave something for me to give to you. He said it may be of some help in your search for Loretta."

I nodded again and stepped inside. She closed the door and swept by me, and I discovered that the dress, midcalf length and full-skirted, came together briefly just under her shoulder blades then descended on each side at an impossible angle to her waist.

I followed her, staring in fascination at the smooth expanse of skin, wondering what in God's name was holding the damn dress up.

I noticed that she had also changed her hairstyle: parting it in the center with short bangs in the front and deep waves almost to her shoulders. Unlike the times before, it had a natural-looking sheen and bounced as she walked.

I was right, I thought, a little judicious use of makeup, the right hairstyle, and she was a knockout; her body's seductive possibilities had always been obvious.

She led me on a rambling journey through the house's hallways and out again through an enormous set of French doors to a wide glassed-in expanse of concrete that ran the entire width of the building. Round white metal tables were scattered at random throughout the area, one of them laden with food, enough food for a fat ladies' bridge party.

"Here we are," she said. "Now isn't this nice?"

I stared at the ten-pound boneless ham, the enormous bowl of potato salad, another of coleslaw, carrots, two or three different salads, a huge glass bun warmer stuffed with fist-sized buns, tea and coffee, and a carafe of wine.

"This should do me nicely," I said, "but what were you and your husband going to eat?"

Her laugh was immoderate and a little too long, entirely out of proportion to the humor in the timeworn joke, and I suddenly realized that she was nervous; I decided not to mention that I had already eaten a hot dog.

She sat me down and stood over me, passing bowls until we could find no more room on my plate. Only then did she sit down across the table and decorate her plate with a wafer-sized piece of ham, a spoonful of potato salad, and a carrot.

The food was delicious, and despite the hot dog I had already eaten, I managed to put away a respectable amount. She ate very little, talked a lot, and watched my gluttony with obvious enjoyment.

"I love to see a man eat well," she said. "Phillip eats so sparingly."

I finished my tea and sat back, acutely aware that I had overeaten; my stomach was sending distress signals.

I smiled sheepishly. "I'm afraid I made a pig of myself. I haven't eaten like that since high school."

"Nonsense, you've hardly eaten at all."

"The food was delicious. You're a very good cook."

Her eyes twinkled. "But you really believe I have a cook hovering somewhere in the background."

"No, but I wouldn't be surprised if you had. Do you do all your own cooking?"

"Yes, and most of the cleaning. I have a maid two days a week, but I'm young and healthy, and I like to keep busy. I enjoy cooking for Phillip. He's so easy to please. My only complaint is that he eats so little. My father, now . . ." She hesitated, smiled. "Now, there was a man who loved to eat. He was a large man and had an appetite to match." She looked out toward the pool, a fleeting shadow crossing her face as if the words evoked painful memories.

"Boston," I said, "or environs. Somewhere around there."

She smiled. "You have a good ear. I thought I had removed all traces."

"Almost. Just now and then the hint of a broad *A*, on a few words. You did a good job."

She winced ruefully. "I worked hard enough at it."

"You shouldn't have bothered. I love to hear a crisp Bostonian accent. And English. Certain types of British accents I find fascinating."

She nodded. "I agree. I love to hear the British talk. They are so direct and . . . earthy, somehow."

"Just like their songs."

"Oh, do you like English rock, Mr.—may I call you Dan? But only if you will call me Lee."

"Sure, Lee. To answer your question—no. I don't really care for rock music. A few songs. The same with country-western music. I like some songs, a few singers . . . the ones with the mellow voices; Eddy Arnold is probably my favorite."

"That's exactly how I feel. I have Roy Clark, Merle Haggard, Eddy Arnold, oh, a half-dozen others. Elvis and Tom Jones were the most enduring rock singers, I think." She laughed her deep laugh again. "When you were courting, who was your favorite?"

"No contest. Frank Sinatra. Even the girls who said they didn't like him began to pant a little when he really got low-down and torchy. I'd bet there have been more seductions to his voice than to any other singer in history."

She rolled her eyes. "I don't know, some of Elvis's songs . . ."

"Yeah," I conceded. "Maybe."

"And your wife," she said teasingly, "What does she like?"

"I think Susie likes most any kind of music as long as the volume is loud." For the third or fourth time since we had finished eating, I reached for my cigarettes, then let my hand fall empty. This time she saw me.

"Please, Dan. Go ahead and smoke. As a matter of fact, I think I'll join you, if you don't mind."

"I didn't know you smoked." I held a light to her cigarette, then lit my own.

She blew out a small puff of smoke and made a wry face. "I don't, not anymore. Phillip doesn't approve." We exchanged the conspiratorial, companionable grins of the dwindling smokers of the world. Then she leaped to her feet. She took my arm and tugged.

"Come on. I want you to see my record and CD collection." Her eyes twinkled. "You won't believe it."

She led me to a room, almost square, perhaps twenty by twenty, the walls completely covered with shelving, floor to ceiling, the shelves filled to overflowing with records, neatly filed and cataloged according to type, with subdivisions by artist. In the center of the room, eight leather-backed chairs were grouped in a loose semicircle around an expensive-looking stereophonic system with four turntables and an elaborate CD system.

"There are eight sets of headphones," she explained. "That means that two people can listen to the same system, or eight people can listen to as many as four recordings at once."

"Nice. You folks must like your music."

She shook her head. "I like it. Phillip doesn't care for it especially. He's into guns, hunting. He's an excellent marksman, by the way. Handguns. He won some kind of handgun competition while he was in the army and also the state championship here in Texas a few years ago. When it comes to music, he humors me. It's not a very good music room actually. With all the shelving and the flat ceiling, the acoustics are terrible. But it's the only room in the house that's large enough except the game room. And that's Phillip's, of course."

"Of course," I said, a blip of sarcasm slipping into my voice before I could stop it. She either didn't catch it or chose to ignore it.

"What would you like to hear?"

I sat down in one of the deep leather chairs. "Surprise me."

She walked to a section of shelving behind me. "I love to have company when I listen to music," she said. "It's so much more satisfying to share, don't you think?"

She came back into view carrying four or five singles and as many albums. I found an ashtray stand in a corner and placed it between two of the chairs. I arranged them so they were almost facing and sat back down. I lit two cigarettes, and when she finished stacking the records on the turntable, I gave her one.

She accepted it with a brittle smile and a strained look, the words of her thank-you drowned in the velvet tones of an early Sinatra, and I suddenly knew with a light thudding shock and a flash of insight that she was going to seduce me, or try to, which could in theory amount to the same thing.

Puffing nervously on the cigarette, leaving a vanishing trail of blue-white smoke, she moved to the wall and turned a rheostat, and the light dimmed to a pale rosy glow. She seemed to drift on her way back to stand in front of me, her face in the semidarkness soft and formless and alluring, body contours changing, hips outthrust in the unmistakable language of a woman on the prowl, exuding a swaybacked sexiness that incites lust the way ice cream electrifies a cavernous tooth.

"Would you dance with me, Dan." It was more statement than question, and she held out her hands, palms up, body already moving in a sensuous mating dance that no man— ignoble clod or unsophisticated savant—could misunderstand.

I lumbered to my feet. "I'm not good at this."

"You won't have to be," she murmured and came into my arms, as light as a bundle of thistles, as limber as a willow wand.

Without understanding why, I felt a deep instinctual tug of resistance forming, some primitive, inexplicable escape mechanism making itself known.

Our feet scuffed soundlessly through the carpet, bodies slowly welding from thigh to chest. The number ended and clicked into another with hardly a pause; we danced on.

Her hand drifted to the back of my neck, and I decided things were getting out of hand. The longer I let it go on, the more embarrassing it was going to be.

I stopped, put my hands on her waist and pried gently.

Mistaking the gesture, she sighed and rose on tiptoe and kissed me, her eyes closed, face flushed, breath warm, and lips that felt already swollen. Excitement shortened her breathing and brought a lazy sensuous indolence to her pliant body.

I responded to her soft wet lips and supple probing tongue; predictably, with a reaction that has little to do with reason and logic.

She murmured in appreciation, locked both hands behind my neck, her body molded to mine, rotating gently, a low throaty hum piercing my armor, chipping away at my feeble resolve.

I wavered, rising passion luring me in one direction, undifferentiated emotions tugging me in another. Then, my resistance building, I dropped my hands and stood motionless, feeling foolish and cowardly—Don Quixote without a lance.

Sinatra crooned his final note, and I felt her body stiffen. The tender tongue withdrew; the succulent mouth departed. She stared up at me, bewildered.

"What's wrong?" she whispered.

"Nothing," I said. "Nothing that makes much sense."

"I wasn't wrong, was I?" She dropped one slim hand to my nether region to check. Her eyes gleamed.

"Not about that, you weren't," I said with a feeble laugh. "But it can't see, can't hear, and don't know right from wrong. It's totally self-starting."

She leaned her head against my chest and laughed, her shoulders shaking, her hands clinging to my upper arms. The laughter died, and she hung there for a moment, slowly rotating her head.

"Is it your wife? Please be kind and say it's your wife." She raised her head to look at me, humor in her face, her startling eyes beseeching; no trace of reproach, the rancor of a woman scorned.

"It's my wife," I said without hesitation, realizing with a kind of sad comprehension that it was the undeniable truth, understanding in that same instant that in rejecting Lee Arganian I was making a commitment to Susie that could never be abrogated lightly, if at all.

We stared at each other, the moment stretching, crystallizing around her awareness of my belated epiphany, the budding knowledge that must have shown clearly in my face.

"Then I forgive you," she said softly, rising again on tiptoe to brush my lips with hers. "She's a lucky woman, I think."

"I'm not so sure about that. I'm no paragon of virtue. When we began dancing, I had no clear idea how it would end. Scruples have a way of fading when it's a matter of passion."

She smiled, pleased. "Then I did arouse passion in you."

"Just a tad."

"It wasn't a total loss, then," she said cheerfully, hooking her arm through mine, easing me gently out of the room and down the hallway toward the door.

I left it at that, not telling her the second—and perhaps equally important—reason why I hadn't allowed my body to overrule my head: I was working for her husband, and common courtesy proscribed taking a man's money and his wife at the same time.

We stopped at the front door and smiled at each other.

"Could I ask you a question?"

She nodded silently.

"Why? Why me? And if you tell me it's because I remind you of Paul Newman, we'll both know you're begging the question."

"You have such marvelous eyes," she said instantly. "Blue eyes, and they do remind me of Paul Newman, by the way. They're very exciting."

"Hmm. I'll have to check that out the next time I pass a mirror."

She laughed gaily. "There are other reasons, Mr. Dan Roman. At fifty-eight, Phillip is not as ... robust and aggressive as he might be, and—" She broke off, her face coloring. "And that's all I'll say about that."

I nodded and smiled, as if it all made perfect sense. "Thanks for the lunch. It was excellent." I hesitated a moment. "As was the rest of it."

She looked up into my eyes and smiled. "You know what they say about best-laid plans. Good-bye, Mr. Roman."

She was still standing there when I turned onto the street, her red dress a crimson blur at that distance. I was halfway home before I remembered that she hadn't given me whatever it was Phillip Arganian had wanted me to have. And then I recalled the ambiguity of her parting words and wondered suddenly, illogically, if maybe she hadn't tried after all.

/ 18 /

I found Susie hitting the books, papers strewn all over the small dinette table in the apartment she shared with Janey Petroski. She gave me a cool welcoming smile, a noncommittal peck on the cheek and offered me a Pepsi.

Dressed in prefaded jeans, jogging sweater, and Adidas, hair swept back severely from her face, she looked every bit the serious college student. She also looked cool and beautiful and somehow aloof, and all of a sudden the giddy plans I had made in the euphoric aftermath of my demonstration of high moral integrity with Lee Arganian seemed ill-conceived and puerile, doomed to the failure they deserved.

"It's about time you came to see where I live," she said, handing me a frosty can of Pepsi I didn't want and dropping into a gaily colored chair that matched the gaily colored sofa I was sitting on.

"I have to go back to Las Vegas," I said, hearing a tremble in my voice, feeling a shiver ripple up from my stomach and tickle my throat. "And I thought you might like to go with me. I'll only be gone one day."

She stared at me strangely for a moment, then stretched one side of her mouth in a wince. "Gee, Danny, I'd love to—any other time. But I missed a couple of classes when you were sick, and I can't afford to miss any more right now." She smiled ruefully. "Boy, your timing is sure bad."

I nodded and lit a cigarette. I took a drink of Pepsi and almost gave it up. This wasn't the way it was supposed to work, dammit! Where was her womanly intuition? Couldn't she tell by my crawling skin, my frozen smile, my shaking hands, my utter confusion—

"Come with me," I said, abandoning pride, like a precative politician.

She stared at me, transfixed, her face as still as stone, not one jot more revealing. Utter bewilderment swam in her eyes.

"What do you mean?" she whispered.

I tried to think of some witty way to say it, something sophisticated and urbane—Come with me to the Casbah, Come be my love again—something we could chuckle over and tell our children and our children's children, something memorable and rich with meaning. But in the end, in the throes of my second apocalypse of the day, there was only one way I could say it.

"I love you," I said. "Come back to me."

Joe Lightfoot opened the door almost immediately. He stood swaying, a glass of clear liquid in his right hand, the whites of his eyes shot with blood, the long black hair pushed behind his ears and held in place with a bloodred headband.

"I've been expecting you," he said after a while, lifting the glass in an elaborate salute and stepping back, his dark face expressionless, his eyes slightly out of focus.

"Then I guess you're not disappointed," I said, closing the door and following his unsteady gait to the area of the large room we had occupied before.

He shrugged and dropped into a chair, bad leg extended. He downed the rest of his drink, set the glass on the table beside him, and stared at me without changing expression, his dark eyes as unreadable as chips of anthracite.

"I ain't been worth a shit since you were here before. You came in here stirring things up—memories I ain't got no business remembering." He rubbed his leg just above the knee, wincing, his stone face relaxing. "Now you're back. I guess that means you found her."

"No," I said. "You know damn well I haven't found her. The trail ended on Osgood's ranch outside Chatsworth. The night Osgood was killed."

Something surfaced in his eyes, flickered, and died. "You told me you knew all about Chatsworth."

"Only that Osgood died and they were looking for Nancy as his killer. I didn't know about your part in it. You failed to mention that. I guess you forgot."

The edges of his mouth lifted in the suggestion of a smile. "Dumb Indian. What can you expect?"

"Cut it out, Joe. I'm not interested in Osgood's death. All I want is what happened to Nancy after you carried her out of that orange grove."

He tilted his head and squinted one eye. "How you know about that?"

"There was an eyewitness, remember?"

He nodded slowly. "The lesbian woman. It was pretty dark in the grove, but I thought I recognized her. She came over from L.A. once with Nancy. She was hiding behind a tree, but I thought . . ." His voice faded. "She finally come forward, huh?"

"She's dead. Fell down the stairs in front of her house. I found it in her diary."

He laughed, a harsh guttural sound like the rasping cough of an angry coon. "There goes your case. Nobody else knows about me even being over there except Nancy. Man, she'd never tell."

"I'm not building a case. I'm looking for Nancy. Where'd you take her, Joe?"

106

Our eyes met, locked. Time passed, and I fought down an urge to blink.

Abruptly he looked away, expelling his breath in a gusty sigh. "I brought her here. Where else?"

"Here? To your home? Weren't you afraid they'd come looking for her?"

He shrugged. "I wasn't thinking much of anything. I figured I was a goner, and I wanted to get her out of it. The next day I took her to my grandfather's hogan on the reservation. He was dead. Nobody went there anymore. That's what they believe, part of their religion. It wouldn't have mattered anyway; nobody would have told the cops anything."

"How long did you keep her there?"

"Two weeks, maybe a little longer. I had to have time to figure something out. Besides, I kept looking for them to come after me. They never did." He brought back the meager smile. "I wondered about that. I finally decided the lesbian woman didn't recognize me."

"And after that, where did she go?"

"Back home to Texas."

"Where?"

He sighed. "A friend of mine came through here. Well, not a friend exactly, a guy I served with in Nam. A nice guy and a damn good soldier. I'd trusted him with my life more'n once, I figured I could trust him with Nancy. He lives in Tennessee. He was on his way home, a new van, plenty of room. He spent a couple of nights here, and I asked him to do me a favor. I asked him to drop her off in Texas at her home."

"Did you ever hear from her? Or him? Do you know if he did what you asked?"

He shook his head wearily. "No, not for certain. I never heard from either of them." He stared at the floor for a moment, then looked around at me. "Why? Why wouldn't he?"

Maybe the same reason you killed a man for her, I thought. I lit a cigarette.

"What was his name?"

"Scott," he said, his face twisting as if the name evoked painful memories. "Richard Scott."

"You know where he lives in Tennessee?"

He nodded. "On a mountain. His folks owned the whole mountain. Rich, I guess, lots of horses, cattle, even a coal mine or two. Good guy, even so. Close to a little town— Big ... something ... rhymes with candy—Big Sandy. Yeah, that's it."

I mashed out my cigarette and rose to my feet. I stood looking down at him.

"Something I'm wondering, Joe. You knew his address, why didn't you ever try to get in touch with him, see if Nancy made it home okay?"

He stared dully at the space between his outstretched legs, hands kneading his thighs, shoulders hunched, as if expecting a blow.

Finally, he said: "You got what you came for, white eyes. Get out of my life, okay?"

"Okay," I said, and left.

I stopped at the floral shop in the hotel and bought flowers. Since I wasn't sure what her favorite would be, I bought a mixed bouquet, roses and mums and carnations, some others I couldn't identify. It was a large bouquet, multicolored and expensive, and I made my way to our room feeling profligate and self-conscious, fielding an aged bellhop's knowing leer with an inane grin as I fumbled for my key outside the door to one of the honeymoon suites.

Resplendent in a shimmering green satin robe, luxuriant raven hair spilling in disarray across her shoulders, eyes lustrous and gleaming, Susie reacted predictably, using the same four words that women have used since the first caveman brought home a fistful of water lilies from the local bog.

"For me? How beautiful!"

"Naw, they're for the maid," I said, picking her up, flowers and all, kissing the laughing mouth, lips soft and full and magical in their passion-igniting capabilities.

She clung to my neck with one arm and tried to protect her flowers; she giggled, but her dark eyes watched me steadily, knowingly, filled with an infinite wisdom far beyond her years.

Winded, knees shaking, I finally sprawled across the bed, laughing immoderately, allowing her to fall free, to bounce and roll on her side facing me, the flowers still clutched protectively in her arms.

Our eyes met across the mound of riotous color, and the laughter bled out of me, taking the nervousness with it, leaving warmth and certainty and quietly pounding blood.

"I'll have to get a vase for the flowers," she said, her voice oddly muted, curiously childlike.

I nodded silently, smiling, not at all sure what kind of smile it was.

"We've already crushed some of them," she went on, a plaintive note creeping into her voice, patches of color edging her cheekbones as our eyes continued their mutual caress.

I nodded again.

"But," she said, making a throaty sound, lifting the flowers and dropping them beside the bed, "that can wait." She moved against me, light winking on her wedding band as her hand came toward my face. "I've been waiting and waiting," she murmured, the plaintive note back in her voice, lips pursed in a delicious-looking pout.

I took her face in my hands and kissed her. "An hour. An hour out of our young lives. How can it matter?"

She returned the kiss, our lips meshing as if they were precision-mated parts, as if we had been doing this all our lives, in previous lives back through the ages.

"We'll see," she whispered. "I'll ask you that again an hour from now."

/ 19 /

The flight from DFW to Memphis International Airport was short and uneventful. I pushed my way through fellow passengers and harried airline employees with fixed smiles and remote eyes, and found the number-three car rental agency that promised no-hassle contracts, smiling service, and cheaper prices.

The tired-looking brunette behind the counter came through with flying colors, and as a consequence, thirty minutes later I was booming along Interstate 40 in one of last year's miracles from Detroit. A plain-vanilla Ford, it did have cruise control, and I puttered along at the speed limit until I got tired of watching other people's exhaust and goosed it up. I still saw a lot of exhaust, but I passed one now and then and gave them a look at mine.

Tennessee. The Volunteer State. Home of Davy Crockett and Sam Houston. Approximately forty-two thousand square miles of contrasting terrain, more than one half of its total area forested. From the majestic peaks and ridges of east Tennessee to the relatively level plateaus of west Tennessee, it was a beautiful land, a hunting and fishing paradise, home of one of the largest man-made lakes in the country. Rich in history as well, it was the site of more bloody Civil War battles than any state except Virginia.

I knew Tennessee well. My parents came from there, the Great Depression and the unforgiving soil of east Tennessee forcing them to flee slow starvation, to migrate to Texas to the relative security of my uncle's modest horse ranch. There they had labored long and hard and eventually prospered in their own right. But they had never forgotten their roots in the land of the majestic Unaka and the Great Smokies. They had bemoaned the malevolent fate that had driven them away, but even in the good years, the years of prosperity, they had never gone back. Not once, not even to visit. I had often wondered about that.

I was a pretty big kid before I understood that I was a Texan and not a Tennesseean, and for a time I felt a nagging sense of loss, a feeling that I had been born at the wrong time and the wrong place and really didn't matter much. It was a desolate feeling, but short-lived. Youth is a time of resiliency, of adaptation and change, and in time I loved Texas just as fiercely as they professed to love their own birthplace.

The useless feeling returned, however, after my mother's death at the beginning of my last year in high school. I watched helplessly as my father, a secret tippler for years, dove headfirst into the bottle, a long slide that would end in his death four years later, drunk and frozen a few yards from the door of a hunting cabin he and I had built during my fourteenth summer.

At the time of his death I was a captive warrior in a useless war, the unwilling guest of little brown men in Vietnam, a helpless pawn in a game I didn't understand, didn't like, and had never wanted to play.

By the time I was rescued and finally contacted by the Red Cross, he had been long buried, and the best I could do was stand over his grave and cry bitter drunken tears, swear righteous oaths, and make promises I knew I wouldn't keep.

He had left me four hundred acres of marginal woodland—all that was left of a once-prosperous ranch—the cabin, and a deep-seated fear of genetic susceptibility to all things alcoholic.

He had bequeathed me one other thing of value: a high regard for the law and the justice it was meant to represent. From the first day in a police uniform I had had the passion of an oracle for the law, a sense of self that was the exact opposite of the way I had felt as a kid: the certain knowledge that this was my time and my place and where I counted.

But there is often an enormous gap between expectation and reality, and the reality of the law in the 1970s was Miranda, probable cause, the specter of illegal search and seizure, the round-robin system of justice that had the perp back on the street before the arresting officer.

That was one of the reasons I gave myself for quitting. There were others not quite so easily enunciated: feelings of impotent rage and frustration, a sinking defeated feeling that what I was doing was not important after all, that nobody really gave a damn, a game of numbers, of good busts and sliders, of trades and deals and greedy palms crossed with greasy dollars.

And now, tooling along Interstate 40 East, hurtling blindly toward another undoubtedly fruitless quest, I felt a resurgence of old familiar feelings, futility and defeat, a nagging dichotomy: home and Susie and newly renewed happiness tugging me in one direction, the haunting puzzle of Loretta Arganian willing me relentlessly in another.

The temptation to quit was almost irresistible, to pack it in, to fly back to my wife and bask in the radiance of her love, to worship at the shrine of her youth and beauty.

The thought suffused me with warmth, flooded my mind with exquisite imagery.

But in the end Loretta Arganian/Nancy Taylor won. I had the rest of my life for home and hearth and Susie; I had only one shot at solving the mystery of this will-o'-the-wisp heiress to one of the larger fortunes in Texas, this enigmatic child of destiny who had chosen to live her life among the losers.

Big Sandy, Tennessee, a small wart on the southwest claw of the giant frog that is the Kentucky Lake, a man-made monstrosity that stretches across Kentucky and most of central Tennessee. One hundred and eighty-odd miles in length, it was the result of a massive flood-control effort by the Tennessee Valley Authority. Concluded in the 1940s, it brought recreation, prosperity to some, the mixed blessing of electricity to others, and buried forever countless acres of fertile river bottomland.

I located the sheriff's substation and checked in to let them know I was in their county. An affable, garrulous man in a dirty khaki uniform and a spotless Texas-sized western hat studied my ID photostat carefully, officiously, and gave me a friendly smile until I told him whom I was looking for. The smile died a painful death, and his eyes were suddenly hard, veiled.

"You a friend of Dickie Scott's?"

"I've never met him in my life."

"Business, then?"

I nodded slowly. "In a matter of speaking," I said cautiously. "I have reason to believe he may know something about a girl, a runaway I'm trying to find."

"Might at that," he said, his expression noncommittal. "He always seems to have a girl or two hanging around. Although girls don't usually run to Big Sandy, they run away from it." He allowed himself a bleak wintry smile.

"It was a long time ago. I'm not hoping for much."

"What was the girl's name?"

"Loretta Arganian." I produced the snapshot in the waitress uniform. "Later on she used the name Nancy Taylor."

He glanced at it briefly and shook his head. He gave it back to me and began drawing a map on the back of a blank arrest report.

"The last five mile's a bastard," he said. "But it's been dry lately, and I reckon you can make it." He walked to the window and looked out at my rental Ford. "Four-wheel drive would help." He came back and handed me the map. "You can make it even so." His voice was flat again, toneless.

"Thanks."

He nodded and glanced at his watch. "If you left now, you could probably make it in and out before dark."

"Right. And thanks again for your courtesy."

He followed me to the door. "You armed?"

I studied him for a moment, but his thin face told me nothing.

"Yes," I said evenly, "I have a .357 Magnum locked in my suitcase. It's not loaded."

He nodded again. "Get it out soon as you're out of town. Load it." He smiled faintly. "Check back when you come out, Mr. Roman."

I studied his expressionless face again. "Is there something you're not telling me?"

"No. Not really. Some of the folks who live out that way, 'specially the Scotts . . . well, they're different. If you must go, be polite."

I tried to find his eyes and made my smile as cool as his own. "Believe it or not, Deputy, we're not all loud-mouthed oil tycoons. And some of us even had mamas to teach us manners."

His stingy smile came back. "Not exactly what I meant." He lifted his hand, went back inside, and closed the door.

/ 20 /

I edged carefully through a hubcap-deep creek with a rocky bottom and clear swift-running water, the third one I had crossed in the same fashion since leaving the comparative luxury of the twisting gravel county road. Safely on the other side, I stopped and took another look at the map the taciturn deputy had given me. So far, so good. Three creeks and there had been no intersections, no branch roads to lead me astray.

I gunned the car up the rutted rocky bank, over the crest, and into a billowing sea of reddish brown dust. The light Ford fishtailed right, then left, skidded in a clinging wash of sand that had the consistency of mud. I thought fleetingly of broken axles, perforated gas tanks, and dust-clogged carburetors.

Low-hanging branches whipped the windshield and snapped at my face through the open window. I kept going. Then abruptly the terrain changed; I came into a washboard section of road that made the front end of the car chatter like a hung-over wino's false teeth, flung it willy-nilly into an incline, a deeply rutted trail that zigzagged up the side of a mountain in a series of narrow switchbacks that gave me no alternative but to go forward. To back down would be impossible, and any attempt to turn around in the narrow lane would be sheer suicide.

I looked out my window into a sheer fifty-foot drop and chuckled with a nonchalance I was far from feeling. "Must be almost there," I reassured myself aloud, licking dust-coated lips and fumbling for a cigarette.

And I was right. The Ford topped a rise, dropped into a washout, slewed sickeningly, then righted, and I found myself purring along on level hardpan, dusty and smooth.

I let my pent-up breath out in a gusty sigh and lit the cigarette, watching the straightaway give way to a long sloping curve that brought me into a relatively level plateau.

To my left, a field choked with sagebrush and weeds extended half a mile to a dark line of towering hardwoods. Directly ahead, through a scattering of tall stately white oaks, I could see buildings, a red-roofed wooden farmhouse that seemed to be leaning into the wind and a decrepit barn that showed evidence of recent repairs to its corrugated metal roof.

The house was a simple clapboard rectangle, old and dilapidated, with a waist-high porch extending completely across the front. Built into the slope of a hill, it was fronted by a high bank with wooden steps but no driveway. I parked across the road under the low-hanging limbs of a giant red oak.

I sat for a moment, finishing the cigarette, wiping my face and hawking the dust out of my throat. I could see movement out of the corner of my eye; I heard the clatter of a screen door closing.

I climbed out, beat dust out of my jacket, then looked toward the people silently lined up on the porch watching me. Two men, two women, and a boy, staring quietly, like a row of blackbirds on a limb.

I brushed ineffectually at the accumulation of dust on my Levi's as I climbed the wooden-plank stairs and crossed the littered yard. Remembering vividly the deputy's admonition to be polite, I stopped ten feet away from the porch and looked up at them with my friendliest smile.

"Good afternoon."

One of the men, who looked older and balder, nodded his head, his pinched features expressionless.

"Howdy, how're you?" His voice was soft, a quiet friendly quality that was encouraging.

I shook my head ruefully. "A little bit shaky. That road makes you start wondering if your life insurance is all paid up."

The woman next to him, thin and gray-featured, with a curious lump on her jaw, leaned forward and spat an amber stream of juice into the dust. She straightened and resumed her silent scrutiny.

"It's kinda rough the first time, I reckon," the older man said. "You get used to it." He looked across the road. "That's a purty nice car."

"Yes, it is," I agreed. I glanced at the other man. Too young to be Richard Scott. "This *is* the Scott farm? Richard Scott?"

He nodded. "That's right."

"Whatta you want with Dickie?" It was a fat-faced man, his tone abrasively belligerent. He moved a step nearer to the slender blond girl next to him. She was clutching a doll in one arm and wore a shapeless rose-colored dress that reached to her ankles. The other arm was crooked behind her back. She was pretty, about twenty, I guessed: I wondered if she could be his wife.

I kept my voice meek and friendly—be polite, the deputy had said. "I would just like to talk to him."

"What about?" His tone was even more belligerent; he

116

stepped closer to the blond girl and put his arm around her waist protectively. I studied his pale face for a moment, then looked back at the older man. He was watching me impassively, fists hooked in the bib of his faded overalls. He inclined his head.

"What did you want to see Dickie about, mister?" His voice was still gentle.

I brought back my friendly smile. "I'm sorry, I should have introduced myself. My name is Dan Roman. A few years ago Mr. Scott gave a ride to a young girl near Las Vegas, Nevada. She was supposed to be going home to her folks in Texas, but she never got there. I thought perhaps he could give me some information as to where she may have gone instead."

The old man was shaking his head before I finished. "I wouldn't know nothin' about that. My son Dickie don't live here anymore, mister."

"Could you tell me where I might find him?"

The young man cursed. "He's the goddamned law, Pa!" He brought his arm from behind the blond girl's back and stepped away, turning again with surprising agility, swinging the twin bores of a double-barreled shotgun in my direction. He pointed it at my stomach, his thick knobby thumb nudging the safety.

I lifted my hands. "Hey! Wait! You've got it wrong. I'm not the law. I'm just a private detective. . . ."

He cursed again. "See! Detective! I told you, Pa."

The old man shifted uneasily and looked at the younger man. "I don't know, Buck. I don't know what kind of law that is."

"He's a detective, Pa. That's the worst kind. They're worse than the sheriff even."

He jumped off the porch and began circling me cautiously, fat face contorted in a lugubrious mixture of rage and fear.

"Hey, wait a minute!" I circled with him, my hands in the air. "I'm a *private* detective. I don't have . . ."

He jabbed the gun at me. "Shut up, bastard! I don't care what kind of law you are. You come poking around here, that's your funeral. Throw out your gun."

"I don't have a gun. I'm telling you I'm not here to bother anyone. I just want to ask Richard Scott—but if he's not here, I'll just be going." I took a step toward the road, and he leaped in front of me. He shoved the gun barrel against my stomach.

"C'mere, Roy! Search this bastard." His voice was high, edged with shrill excitement. Saliva laddered at the corners of his mouth, his pale eyes twitching out of control. My stomach muscles crawled.

"Easy, boy," I said softly. "Just go easy with that thing. I'm not giving you any trouble."

His laugh was wild, near hysteria. "You goddamned better not, either, you bastard! I'll blow a damn hole in you that you . . ."

"Easy, Buck, just take it easy. I'll search him." The voice came from behind me, thin and calm and young. I felt hands at my waist, in the pockets of my jacket, then lightly down each of my legs. "He ain't got no gun."

"Well," Buck said. He looked around uncertainly, as if not sure what to do next. "Well," he said again. Then he stepped back a pace and motioned with the gun. "Get his pocketbook, see what it says about him."

"Left rear pocket," I told Roy. I tried to catch Buck's skittering eyes. "Let's just calm down, huh? If you'll let me explain . . ."

"Shut up," Buck said almost absently, and jabbed the gun barrel into my stomach again—hard enough to hurt. His eyes tried to focus on Roy behind me. "C'mon, dammit, what does it say?"

"It says he's a private investigator," the boy said quietly, "I don't think that's the regular law, Buck."

"Hell it ain't! He said he was a detective. The sumbitch is down here after—" He broke off and narrowed his eyes at me, apparently the only way he could keep them still. "What are you after?"

I felt the billfold being stuffed back into my pocket. "He's like that guy Magnum on TV. He's not like regular police, Buck."

"Shit on that stuff! TV ain't real. Everybody knows that. This sumbitch is the law, and I'm gonna keep him till Dickie gets back." He straightened his shoulders and glared at me menacingly. "Dickie might wanna waste his ass." Had it not been for his crazy eyes and white finger on the trigger of the gun, it might have been funny. But I didn't feel at all like laughing.

"Get some rope, Roy."

"Look, this is stupid. All I wanted—"

He sneered. "Who gives a shit what you want? Go get some rope, Roy, dammit!"

I turned my back on him. "Mr. Scott, I think this has gone far enough. You better tell your son here to put down that gun before he gets all of you in a lot of trouble."

The old man shuffled his feet, then moved back a step and spread his hands. "I can't do nothin' with him, mister. Besides, he knows better what to do than I do. You shouldn't come messin' around where you ain't wanted, nohow." His tone was defiant, but apprehension crawled across his puckered face and flickered in faded eyes.

I switched my gaze to the woman. She stared back at me impassively, then leaned forward and sent a stream of tobacco juice plopping into the dust an inch from my foot. "Fix him, Buck," she said, a nasal vindictive whine as cutting as a band saw.

I turned my attention to the young girl. "Miss, you'd better talk some sense into your folks here. So far, no damage has been done, but they're getting ready to commit felony kidnapping. If you don't try to stop it, you'll be an accomplice. You can go to jail."

She smiled at me, a flashing smile that lit up her face. "Uh unt thuk," she said, taking a halting step backward, the doll clutched in both arms, the big eyes above the smile bright and empty.

Realization hit me like a cattle prod behind the ear. I wrenched my eyes away from the pretty, vacant face.

Buck was staring at me, the gun drooping, his lower lip

hanging slack. He swallowed noisily, saw me watching him, and jerked up the gun. He motioned toward a dirt path that led around the corner of the house.

"Okay," he said importantly. "We're gonna have to put you in the motor home till Dickie gets here. Just don't give me any trouble and maybe you won't get hurt."

"Now look," I said. "If I've caused you people any inconvenience, maybe I could just pay you for your trouble and go about my business."

"You'd like that, wouldn't you?" Buck snarled. "Then you could go bringin' in the law on us. . . ."

I held up my hands, palms out. "I promise you. No law. We'll just forget what's happened so far. How about a hundred dollars and no questions asked?"

His eyes stilled for a second; he stepped in and jabbed with the gun. But I had learned to read the signals; I sucked in my gut, and the gun thumped almost harmlessly on my belt buckle.

"Just keep your damned mouth shut! You ain't paying us no money, and you ain't going anywhere, neither. Not till Dickie comes. Right now we're gonna put you in his motor home. Move!" He gestured toward the side of the house. I stepped out into the dirt path, then stopped again at his command. "You go first, Roy."

Silently, the boy walked past me and we followed him single file around the house.

The motor home was parked twenty yards behind the house, relatively new and sparkling clean. I wondered fleetingly how they had managed to get it over the narrow switchbacks.

The boy, his pale thin face expressionless, opened the door and stepped back for us to enter.

He had long blond hair like his sister's and the same pale washed-out eyes as his father. I tried to meet his gaze, but he turned sideways, avoiding eye contact and staring off across the mountaintop as if he had nothing to do with what was happening.

Buck poked me with the gun. "Git on in there."

I whirled on him. "You do that one more time," I said savagely, "and I'm going to make you eat that thing."

Startled, Buck stepped back. Then he twisted his head sideways and crimped his mouth.

Roy touched my arm. "Please, mister. Don't push him." He tugged gently, took my elbow, and leaned forward as if he were helping me. "Don't!" he whispered. "He'll shoot you." And for the first time I felt the cold tingling chill of fear.

/ 21 /

I twisted on the bunk as far as my bonds would allow and looked down the narrow corridor. Roy was standing in my line of sight, and I said sharply, "Get out of my way."

He jumped sideways, revealing Buck's profile on the couch in the rear of the trailer. He was pawing through my wallet, extracting pictures, staring at them intently, then crumpling each one and dropping it to the floor, face flushed and excited—Barbara, Tommy, Susie—

"Hey, you crater-faced son of a bitch! Stay the hell out of my—" I broke off as he rose abruptly and came down the aisle. He stood over me, his face drained of color, the pimples on his chin like drops of blood.

His eyes were jerking again, mouth twitching. He licked his lips, and his eyes steadied, became bright, shining . . . and it was enough of a warning for me to twist my left leg up to take the brunt of the blow he aimed at my groin.

The gun butt raked from my knee to my hip and agony exploded in my brain, bright red and blue streamers of pain that brought a wall of darkness peppered with tiny blinking stars.

I made a choking sound, and the boy pushed between us as Buck raised the gun again. Roy talked swiftly, softly, his tone pleading, almost whining, unintelligible through the roaring in my head.

Blinking through a red haze, I watched the man allow the boy to calm him, saw the deep shuddering breaths, the brutish face relaxing.

"I'll watch him, Buck. You don't worry about it. I'll stay right here and watch him. You see if you can find Dickie. Okay? You go on now. I'll watch him for you, Buck." He was talking quietly, crooning the words, patting the older man on the shoulder.

Slowly, carefully, Roy removed the shotgun from Buck's hands. He laid it on the small dinette table, then led Buck to the door.

"Why don't you try the Claypools, Buck? I know he was going by there. And the Lewisons. Old Dickie'll be at one of them places. He's gonna be proud of you, Buck. Just go on now. I'll look after things here. Okay, Buck?" Roy stood watching as Buck clumped down the steps and out of sight. Then he came back and slumped in the dinette booth and wearily buried his face in his hands.

I relaxed and lay flat on my back. "I owe you one," I said. "Thanks."

He nodded. He slid the shotgun against the wall of the motor home. "He ain't just right sometimes. When he gets mad, he goes crazy. I'm the only one he'll listen to, me and Dickie." He went out of sight up the aisle and a few moments later came back with my billfold in his hand. He leaned over and shoved it into my pants pocket. "I put your pictures back in there. I'm sorry he messed some of them up." He hesitated. "He don't show much sense sometimes."

"I'll go along with that."

"He's mostly like a big kid," the boy said gravely. "We used to play together all the time. It's like . . . like I just outgrew him."

"How old are you, Roy?"

"Fifteen."

"Has he always been like that?"

"Since he was about eight, Dickie says. He fell out of the hayloft and drove a rusty spike in his head. He like to died. Dickie says he never growed much more in his head after that."

"Your Pa can't handle him?"

"Pa couldn't handle a fly. Ma takes a broom handle to him once in a while. Mostly they just let him alone, let him have his way. It's less bothersome that way."

"Why did he get so upset when he thought I was the law?"

He shrugged. "We used to make moonshine. Dickie and Buck mostly. They caught us one day, and they beat Dickie up pretty bad. One of them kicked Buck in the ... the privates. He's hated all law ever since. To him they're all the same."

"Where is Dickie, Roy?"

A faint smile crossed his face. "Out chasing pus—women most likely." The smile died. "I hope Buck can locate him."

"What does Dickie do for a living?"

His eyes were suddenly veiled. "I reckon that's his business," he said sullenly.

"Of course it is," I said quickly. "I was just making conversation." I squirmed, trying to find a more comfortable position. I was spread-eagled on the bunk, my hands tied to the top corner posts, my legs to the bottom. Roy had left a small amount of slack in the ropes and I could almost turn my torso sideways.

"Don't you think you should untie me?"

Roy stirred uneasily. "I better not."

"Why not?"

He shook his head and looked out the window.

"Well, then, do you suppose you could light me a cigarette?"

"I guess so," he said. He fished my cigarettes and lighter out of my shirt pocket. He put a cigarette in my mouth and held the lighter. "Call me when you're through. I'll put it out."

I worked the cigarette to the corner of my mouth, held it between my lips. I tilted my head to keep the smoke out of my nose.

"Thanks, Roy. By the way, did Dickie ever mention a girl he met in Las Vegas? Nancy, Nancy Taylor."

A closed look came over his face. "I don't know nothin' about no girl."

"I thought you and Dickie were buddies. I thought he talked to you, told you things. Surely . . ."

He picked up the shotgun and abruptly walked to the door. The motor home vibrated as he went down the steps.

"Hey," I yelled after him. "Come on back. We won't talk about Dickie anymore. We'll talk about the weather, the—" I broke off as the door opened and the motor home vibrated again. I caught a glimpse of blond hair and then a face came into view, a smiling angelic face: the girl from the porch. She came in slowly, walking with a limp, a cane made from a cutoff pool cue in her right hand, the doll clutched in her left. She limped up the aisle and stood over me.

I smiled. "Hi."

She stared at me, unblinking, the smile frozen on pretty pink lips. She nodded her head. Up close she appeared older, tiny lines radiating outward from her eyes; twenty-five, I guessed.

"Uh," she said. Her voice was thick, guttural. I looked into her clear blue eyes and saw only glacial emptiness.

I smiled at her again. "What's your name?"

"Uh," she replied. She turned and placed her doll on the dinette table with great care. She laid the cane beside it, then brought her vacant eyes back to me.

"Uh unt thuk," she said, and stood waiting, the smile fixed, the serene expression unchanging.

"I'm sorry," I said, "I can't understand you."

A frost line furrowed her smooth forehead, bunched pale shaggy eyebrows. The smile turned down at the corners, then disappeared.

I shook my head. "I'm sorry, honey, I don't know what you

want." My own smile was beginning to falter, but I kept it in place. "How'd you like to untie me? Think you could do that? I'll bet Dickie would like that."

She stared down at me silently.

"Hey, I've got an idea," I said, my voice as sweet as any pervert's on a playground. "I'll bet you could use a new dress. Fifty dollars. That'd buy you a really swell dress. How about it, sweetheart?"

"Uh unt thuk," she repeated again, the furrow in her brow deepening, her voice an octave higher.

I shook my head. "I don't understand. Why don't you go get Roy? I'll bet he'd know what you want." I smiled and turned my face to the wall to impress on her our lack of communication.

I heard a grunting angry sound and caught a glimpse of movement. I turned back in time to see her take a limping step toward me, the cane upraised above her head. Before I could move, she brought it slashing down across my thighs.

Pain rocketed and shrieked in my head, around and around like a steel ball in a revolving drum . . . and someone yelled.

Through the blinding red haze I saw the girl turn and lay the truncated pool cue on the table. She stood looking down at me for a moment, then reached down and grasped the hem of the long shapeless dress and lifted it above her head. She changed her handhold, tugged again, and it was off . . . and there was nothing underneath. In spite of the pain, my breath snagged in my throat.

"Jesus Christ," I said hollowly, comprehension descending like acid rain.

Smiling again, she leaned down and began tugging at my belt buckle.

I twisted sideways toward the wall, peering over my shoulder as she made a clucking sound of exasperation, the tiny frown creasing her brow again, blond hair bouncing as she shook her head in disapproval.

"Oh, Jesus," I said.

She turned and reached a slim hand to pick up the cane, then looked down at me, clicking her tongue in reproof, the expression on her face unchanging, peaceful, sweet. She raised the cane. . . .

"Oh, hell!" a rough male voice said, and the motor home rocked as feet clattered on the metal steps, then thudded on the carpet.

Bearded face contorted with effort, a tall blond man reached her in time to thwart the swinging cane, taking much of the force of the blow across his biceps. The cane thudded to the floor.

I discovered I was holding my breath. I let it out in a quick explosive hiss of relief.

"Come on, honey," the man said. "Come on, Angel, put your dress back on, honey." He turned her and slipped the dress over her head, then helped her work it down her slender body.

He looked at me over her shoulder and grimaced. "I'm sorry about this." He took the girl's face in his hands and kissed her forehead. "Go to the house, honey. I'll be in later." He spoke slowly and distinctly. She nodded happily, her face glowing. She picked up her doll and her cane and, without a glance in my direction, slowly left the motor home.

The man watched her go. He turned and glanced down at me. He produced a pocket knife and stooped at my feet.

"I'm sorry about all this," he repeated.

"So am I," I said. "I take it you're Richard Scott?"

He nodded. He cut the rope on my right wrist and reached across and sawed at the other. I sat up and massaged my wrists.

"Are you all right?" He had tightly curled blond hair and thick wide sideburns that merged with a heavy blond beard.

"Yes, thank you."

He shook his head. He turned and sat down in the dinette booth. He spread large hands in an expressive gesture of regret.

"I don't know what else to say. If it will make you feel any better, Buck won't be able to sit down for a week."

I stared at him incredulously. "You spanked him?"

He revealed white teeth in a smile. "I whipped him. With a

hickory switch. He's a child. He understands that. If I used my fists on him, it would kill him."

"You know he's dangerous."

He nodded. "That's why he never leaves the place. By the way, that shotgun wasn't loaded. Empty casings. I keep all the ammo locked in up here."

I stared at him again. "Jesus Christ!"

The smile widened into a sardonic grin. "Frustrating, isn't it?"

"Did Roy know the gun wasn't loaded?"

"Yes, he knew."

"But he seemed so . . . sympathetic. He tried to talk Buck out of it. He kept him from beating me half to death here in the motor home."

He spread his hands again. "After it got started, he was afraid of what you might do to Buck if he told you." He paused, then shrugged. "Roy is . . . well, he has his own problems, too."

"Angel," I said slowly. "Is she. . . ?"

"Angel was born pretty much the way she is, Mr. Roman. And so was Buck."

"The boy told me Buck was injured, something about a fall. . . ."

"Roy's fantasy. He has one for Angel too . . . she was horse-back riding, the horse tripped and fell." He shrugged. "He knows the truth, but he won't admit it even to himself."

He glanced away from my inquiring look, toward the rear of the unkempt house, his eyes venomous. His big hands, clean and well kept, came together in the center of the table, clenched.

"It's them two. Roy knows it as well as I do. He just won't admit it."

"You mean your mother and father?"

"That bitch is not my mother!" His voice rang in the small enclosure, thick with sudden anger. Then, with a clearly visible effort, he controlled himself and went on in a calmer voice, "My ma died when I was five. A year later she came to live with us. She's . . . she's Pa's half sister. I can barely remember, but I do remember her kicking me out of Pa's bed. A year or so later Buck was born. Then, when I was eight, Angel . . ." He raked a kitchen match across the bottom of the table and lit a small cigar. He puffed a small cloud of smoke. His blue eyes seemed darker, and the corners of his mouth lifted in a sardonic smile.

"Roy was born while I was in the army." His eyes squinted at me through the smoke. "Some family, eh?"

"Buck and Angel. You don't think they'd be better off in an institution?"

He waved his hand impatiently. "I can't afford a private place. Have you ever seen one of the state institutions? Well, I have. I wouldn't put my worst dog in one. They can't help the way they are, and besides they never leave the place." He paused, his eyes glittering. "And nobody ever comes up here . . . not anymore."

"I can understand that. That road would discourage anyone from coming twice."

"That's not the reason." He rolled the cigar in his fingers and stared down at it moodily, a small vein in the center of his forehead pulsing gently. "You saw how Angel is. . . . While I was in the army, she grew up. Some of the bastard boys around here discovered her . . . how sweet and innocent she was. Roy was too small to know or care what was happening; Buck was too stupid . . . and Pa, well, I guess he was too busy trying to scratch a living out of this rock to even know what was going on. The bitch didn't care. Anyhow, they got to her, taught her about sex. Brought her candy, trinkets, stuff like that. . . ." His voice was coarse, heavy. "I came home on leave, caught her with four of them down by the old sawmill. I put two of them in the hospital and scared the other two so bad, I don't think they've been out of Big Sandy since. I told them to spread the word. Anyone coming on this mountain again, I'd kill them when I got home." He smiled faintly. "They must have believed me. But the damage had been done as far as Angel was concerned. She don't bother Buck for some

128

reason, but Roy . . . she pesters him all the time. And me."
He rubbed his hand slowly down across his face. "I don't
know what to do about that."

I made a sympathetic sound.

"The woman helped her," he went on slowly, staring out
the window toward the stand of timber across the field. "She
taught her to read lips some. She was three before she went
completely deaf, and she could talk some . . . well, you heard
her . . . and we can pretty well understand her most of the
time. But the woman taught her to read lips, how to take care
of herself, keep clean, fix her hair, that kind of thing." He wet
his lips. "Jesus, she was patient. Hour after hour, she sat with
Angel, going over and over the words, calming her when she
got upset or angry and mean. She could really handle her . . .
better even than me." He was talking to himself, lost in
another time. "But even she couldn't do anything about the
sex thing. Angel has a short attention span about most things,
but I guess her body never forgot about the sex."

"The woman," I said, "was she Nancy Taylor?"

He nodded without surprise, without looking up. "Yes," he
said quietly. "Nancy Taylor." He turned his head and glanced
around the motor home. "I bought this for her. She wouldn't
stay in the house. I couldn't blame her for that. It's a pigsty."

"You brought Nancy straight here from Vegas?"

He nodded. "I didn't want to bring her at all. I let Joe
Lightfoot talk me into it. I was supposed to drop her off in
Dallas—she come from somewhere around there—but by the
time we got to Amarillo, I knew I didn't want to lose her. By
then she had told me about the killing, that they were looking
for her. . . ." His voice faded, and he abruptly rose to his feet.
"What would you like to drink?" He went to a cupboard
above a small built-in refrigerator.

"I've got gin, vodka, and some bourbon." He looked over
his shoulder inquiringly.

"Bourbon will be fine," I said. "A little water." I moved to
the dinette booth and sat down across from him. We sampled
our drinks.

"How long was Nancy here, Mr. Scott?"

He looked out the window again, his lips moving slightly as if he were counting. A large oak leaf, brown and beginning to shrivel, fluttered by the window. He pursed his lips and whistled soundlessly. "It's going to be a long hard winter."

In one swift movement he emptied his glass and got to his feet. "I think I'll have another one," he said.

/ 22 /

"I persuaded her to come here with me. It wasn't very hard. She didn't have any close kin left around Dallas."

"She told you that, huh?"

He looked up, surprised. "Of course. She said her parents had been killed in a fire that burned their home. She had been staying with a girlfriend that night. I think she was on a guilt trip about that."

"She didn't say anything about a brother, sister?"

"No. She said she was an only child. Why?"

I shrugged. "I was just curious."

His eyes glinted, suddenly cold and pale. "Why are you looking for her? Is there some kind of reward or something?" His voice had cooled, and now it rang with an edge of contempt, a note of belligerence.

"All right, Mr. Scott. I'll level with you. Nancy lied to you. She has a living mother and an older brother. The brother hired me to find her. Her mother is terminally ill and wants to know if she's still alive."

He stared at me, then slowly shook his head and grinned. "Damn, she was convincing. I would've sworn she was telling me the truth ... tears and everything. She said her mom and dad ran a small grocery store south of Dallas, that they lived in an attached duplex next door. She said the whole thing burned, no insurance to speak of. She was left homeless, destitute. She said she got a job, then after a while drifted west to L.A." He shook his head admiringly. "She sure sold me a bill of goods. You sure about this?"

"I'm sure; as a matter of fact, her folks are extremely wealthy. She just took off. She and her brother evidently didn't get along."

He made the soundless whistle again. "That's hard to believe. Nancy could get along with the devil. She had Buck and Roy and the old man eating out of her hand. The old bitch was the only one who didn't like her." He paused. "Well, I guess she did have a stubborn streak. Once she made up her mind . . ." He swallowed audibly. "Like . . . like when she left me."

I sampled my drink while he wrestled with it; moments later he went on, "It's dull up here, nothing to do, you know, no place to go much. She hid it pretty well, but she was lonely. Even with all of us around her, the kids pestering her all the time, she was still the loneliest person I've ever seen. It scared me, sometimes made me react in anger. I'd try to start a fight, you know, to get her to show something besides that eternal patience and kindness . . . but she wouldn't fight back." He smiled wryly. "We'd just end up in bed." He coughed to clear the huskiness out of his voice. "Ever so often I'd crank up this thing and take her to Memphis, or Nashville— she liked the Grand Ole Opry. We'd stay a few days, and she'd be happy as a kid. Everything would be fine for a while."

"How in the world do you get this monster down that road?"

He smiled. "There's a pretty good road on the north side of the mountain. While I was in Nam, some company came up here and talked Pa into letting them drill for oil. They built a pretty fair road. Good enough if you take it slow."

I decided it was time to repeat my question. "How long was Nancy here, Mr. Scott?"

"About a year, I reckon. I—I tried to get her to marry me proper, but she wouldn't. She said she wasn't sure. . . ." He took a drink of bourbon. His convoluted smile turned apologetic.

"I begged her, Mr. Roman. I guess I knew what would happen someday if I didn't marry her."

I shook my head. "It wouldn't have mattered. You can't hold someone with a piece of paper."

"No, I reckon not." He sighed heavily. "I took her to Nashville, to this friend of mine's place. We were gonna spend the weekend, do some horseback riding, fishing, like that. There were other people there, three other couples and a man from Memphis." His face darkened and the vein popped out on his forehead again. "He was the bastard who . . . he got around her some way . . . talked to her. . . ." His voice died away, and he looked out the window and continued in a flat monotone. "She didn't even come back here with me. . . . She left me a letter." He wrenched his head around and finished his drink. "Just another broad. Right?" He waited belligerently for my confirming nod, then looked out the window again. "That's a lot of shit, and we both know it."

"Who was the man, Mr. Scott?"

He grunted and canceled the weak smile, his face flushed. He stared at me a moment, then reached into his hip pocket and withdrew his billfold. He extracted a single sheet of tablet paper folded into a small square. He unfolded it carefully and smoothed it on the table. It was worn and about to come apart at the folds. He scanned it slowly, but I had a feeling he knew it by heart.

"His name was Sammy McBain," he said.

I took a small notebook from my coat pocket and wrote it down.

"A damn mick," he said wonderingly, as if that explained it all.

"You don't know where he lives."

"Just Memphis. He was some kind of director—made commercials, things like that. That's all I know about the son of a bitch." His voice had turned hard and harsh, and the vein in his forehead was throbbing. I had a feeling that another drink or two, a little time, and he would be breaking things. I got to my feet.

"I appreciate your candor, Mr. Scott. And you can be sure anything you've told me will remain confidential."

He looked up at me, his face puzzled. "Confidential? Oh, you mean about Pa and the bitch and the kids?" He made a short explosive sound. "Don't worry about that. Everybody in the county knows it, probably half the state."

I lit a cigarette and moved toward the door. "If I leave now, I think I can be down before dark."

Scott stepped down behind me. "One favor, Mr. Roman. If you find Nancy . . . tell . . . tell her she's . . . she can always come back here, no questions asked. And . . . and maybe you could let me know, you know, a postcard or something. Just Big Sandy, Route #3."

I shook hands with him. "If I find her I'll do both, Mr. Scott. And thanks again."

He made a deprecating gesture with his hand. "Just sorry about what happened. If you'll follow the road the way your car is headed, it'll take you down the north slope. When you hit the blacktop, take a left. It'll take you into Big Sandy." He turned abruptly and entered the motor home.

I hadn't moved more than three paces before he was back. He leaped down the steps and took my arm. His face was chalky-gray, the pale eyes smoldering.

"Mr. Roman. I don't know how true . . . I can't say for certain, but I heard the son of a bitch put Nancy in some sex films, you know, pornography stuff." He was having trouble with his breathing. "I—I thought about going over to . . . to Memphis and finding out . . . but . . . guess I don't really want to know about that." He turned and walked back to the motor home. "I just thought it might help," he said. And then he was gone again.

There was an excited babble of voices on the front porch that died as I rounded the corner of the house. I tried not to look but did finally.

They were all there, the concentrated hostility in their faces almost like a physical blow, a malevolent force that followed me all the way to my car.

It was full dark before I made it down off the mountain. The north road was wide and relatively straight, and I drove through Big Sandy without a glance at the sheriff's substation. I drove halfway to Memphis before I pulled into a Holiday Inn.

I ate in the motel restaurant, inspected my bruises in the shower, and watched an old Orson Welles thriller on television.

I was asleep by nine o'clock, and I never did find out who the Third Man was.

/ 23 /

Locating Sammy McBain turned out to be relatively easy; I found him in the telephone book. There was an office listing as well as his residence, and I called the former.

"McBain and Associates, can I help you?"

"Sammy McBain, please."

"May I tell him who's calling, sir?"

"Dan Roman," I said.

"Just a moment, I'll see if Mr. McBain is free."

I barely had time to light a cigarette before she was back.

"I'm sorry, Mr. McBain is in conference. Could I take your number?"

"Just go back and tell Mr. McBain that I represent some West Coast people who are interested in buying his product—particularly the ones starring Nancy Taylor."

"Just a moment, sir."

The wait was somewhat longer this time.

"Just a moment, sir. Thank you for waiting."

"It was a pleasure," I said, but she was gone, an instant later replaced by a rough male voice. "McBain."

"Mr. McBain, my name is Dan Roman, I—"

"I got all that," the voice growled. "Who's this Nancy Taylor you're talking about?"

"Do you really want to talk about it over the phone, Mr. McBain? I'm in the lobby of the hotel across the street from your office. I could be there in five minutes."

"I don't know any Nancy Taylor."

"Oh, well, perhaps we've been misinformed." I let a shrug creep into my voice. "We heard you did some pretty good work with Nancy Taylor. Very well, sir, I'm sorry I bothered you. We'll just have to look elsewhere."

"Of course I can't remember every girl I ever worked with. If your people are interested in volume . . . who did you say you represented?"

"I didn't. But that's all right, we'll just go—"

"If you can make it in five minutes, okay. But I'm a busy man."

Because of the ancient elevator in his building it took me seven minutes to reach his office, but he didn't mention it.

Whatever I had expected from the gravelly voice, it certainly wasn't the tall thin pleasant-faced man with the wavy graying hair who shook my hand at his office door.

"Mr. Roman?" His teeth were as white and even as modern science could make them, his handshake was firm without being ostentatious. He wore an expensively tailored gray suit that matched his hair perfectly, a matching silk tie, and a pair of soft-looking shoes made from the skin of something that had once worn scales.

"You're McBain," I said brusquely. I brushed past him and stalked to a short suede couch against a wall. I sat down, lit a cigarette, and propped my dusty boots on a table made from a solid slab of oak or walnut. My boot heels made a scratching noise on the surface, which had the polished glaze of silk.

"About this dame, Taylor. How many films did you make with her, and how many prints can you deliver of each within a week?"

His face warred between caution and greed. "I'm not sure. . . . Which commercial did you see her in?"

I made a rude farting noise. "Cut the shit, McBain. I'm talking sex films, and you know it. You're not the only one who's busy. Now, how many did you make?"

But caution won out, and he walked around his desk, his expression as indifferent and self-righteous as a eunuch at an orgy.

"I'm sorry," he said stiffly, "I'm afraid you have the wrong man. I make commercials, sir, nothing else."

I grinned and shifted my boots. He winced.

"I'm talking big numbers, McBain. A thousand copies each if you made less than five. Maybe a little bonus for fast delivery."

His eyes widened ever so slightly. "I'm afraid I don't understand. How—"

I waved him silent. "Never mind how. I'm interested in when, buddy." I sat up straight and dropped my ashes on the thick-piled rug.

"We've got one copy, Sammy. We happen to know there's more. With a little time I could run them down, make my own copies. But we don't have the time."

"But so many . . ."

"That's our worry. Let's just say we have an out-of-the-country market, folks of the . . . dark persuasion who happen to like Nancy's peaches-and-cream complexion. Okay? You just worry about the copies. We'll worry about the market. Now, how many and how much?"

He hesitated, licked his lips. "How do I know . . . ?"

I jumped to my feet and stormed across to his desk. I ripped off my Levi's jacket and slammed it on his desk. I began unbuttoning my shirt.

"You think I'm wired, Sammy? Is that what the hell's the matter with you? You think I'm *law*?" I jerked my shirttails out of my pants and twirled in front of him. "Okay. You convinced now? You convinced I ain't no damned cop?" I shoved my shirt back inside my pants. "If you ain't, buster, you just say so, and I'll get the hell out of here. . . ."

He held his hands up in protest, palms out. "Please, Mr. Roman, I wasn't worried about that. It's just that what you propose is so preposterous." The smile transformed his face, gave him a rakish look that women probably swooned at on sight.

I shoved my arms into the sleeves of my jacket. "Okay, pal, forget it." I headed for the door.

"Wait! Mr. Roman, you misunderstand me!" He got up and came around the desk, his arm outstretched. "Let me make you a drink. We'll discuss it. I'm sure we can find an equitable arrangement that will suit both of us."

"I'm sure we can," I said.

/ *24* /

McBain's house was palatial, a southern mansion complete with towering white columns, a second-story porch that ran across the entire front of the building, cupolas and ginger-bread, and at least five gables: a pseudo-antebellum cliché.

Porn must pay, I thought, and rang the bell, wondering if somewhere deep inside, the chimes might be playing "Dixie."

McBain answered the door, shattering another of my illusions about the way rich lived; I thought they all had butlers, or at the very least, a maid.

"It's the help's day off," he explained as he led me across a huge vaulted room the Dallas Symphony would have loved for its size and acoustics. We went down a curving stairway into a basement room filled with pool tables, a Ping-Pong table, pinball machines, a bar, and a row of otherwordly electronic games against one wall.

"This is my game room," he said, then turned to look over his shoulder when I laughed.

"I had about figured that out."

He led me to one corner, where six plush-velvet–covered chairs were arranged in a rough semicircle before a screen the size of a bedsheet. "Have a seat, Mr. Roman." He waved at the row of chairs and walked toward the other corner.

"Everything ready to go, Charlie?" he asked cheerfully, and for the first time I noticed the short balding man at a small table fussing with a film projector.

He looked up and nodded silently, his heavy jaws working rhythmically at a wad of chewing gum. McBain turned and came back.

"How about a drink before we begin? Same as before?"

I found an ashtray stand and moved it near one of the chairs. I sat down and lit a cigarette and wondered if I knew what the hell I was doing.

McBain came back with the drinks and handed me a vodka gimlet. The glass in his own hand contained amber fluid with one ice cube.

"Have everything you need? Ashtray? Fine." He sat down two chairs away and lifted his hand. "Let her roll, Charlie, me boy."

He was in an expansive mood, his thin aristocratic nostrils filled with the scent of money, or maybe he just liked porn movies.

"You must remember," he said as the camera zoomed in on a closed door in the opening scene, "there are no plots to these movies. These are straight flesh films. Elemental stuff, really."

And he was right: they were elemental. As basic, as graphic as you can get. The door opened and two people came in: a young man and a woman. They were arm in arm. They looked into each other's eyes one time, kissed, and headed straight for the bed.

The woman reached it first; she sat in the middle and smiled at the camera while she lifted a flimsy negligee over her head. She had long black hair, dark eyes, and a pretty, if garish, smile, and I felt a small electric tingle as I recognized Nancy Taylor. A tingle and a sliding, sinking sensation that I finally decided was embarrassment.

She was still too heavy, but there was a suggestion of lush firmness and a certain grace of movement that kept her from being a pitiful farce.

The boy's organ was oversize to the point of being grotesque. Long and pendulous and corded, it was undoubtedly the ugliest thing I had ever seen.

"That devil's twelve inches long, one solid foot. I know, because I watched it measured." McBain's eyes glittered in the dimness, as proud as if the boy's member were a work of art that he alone was responsible for.

I made a clucking sound that he accepted as approval, and he sat back in his chair chuckling contentedly.

There were four of the films; each one approximately thirty minutes long. And in each the star was Nancy Taylor. Only the men were different. A lot of men; I counted twelve in all. But I had to give her one thing, whether by design or accident, there was never more than one man in the bed with her at a time. That's something, I thought weakly.

McBain insisted on explaining the intricate details of the camera angles and lighting on the difficult shots, and I didn't object: it took my mind off what I was watching.

Other times, I tried closing my eyes, but they seemed to have a will of their own and kept opening again. Despite my revulsion, I began slowly to feel a strange tingling numbness, a weak shivery kind of sick sexual excitement, a feeling that in some odd way had nothing to do with what was happening on the screen, but rather came from her, would have come from her even if she had been fully dressed sitting in a front row in church.

It was an inexplicable mixture of innocence and a debauchery that came through on the close-ups, a kind of merriment in her eyes, as if she were trying to share with the audience the sad sick humor of it all, trying to say: "Hey, don't cry, it doesn't really matter."

"She's lovely, isn't she?" McBain said. "I turned her out myself. She took longer than most, I'll admit, but they're all whores. Sooner or later they all come around if you know how to work them." He gave me a man-to-man smile and a self-indulgent chuckle.

I wanted very much to alter his aquiline profile.

"Did you know her long?" I lit a cigarette, grateful for the gloom that hid the tremor in my hands.

He shrugged his shoulders. "Six months, maybe a little less. I took her away from some hillbilly up near Big Sandy. Asshole didn't know what a gold mine he had. Wanted to marry her, if you can believe that. Man, I spotted it right away . . . there's a look about them. I knew she'd be spreading for me right away." He frowned, a thin wrinkle running down the center of his forehead. "Took me a little longer than I figured. I tried to bring in a couple of my friends, you know, to get her started. But she had this thing about only one man at a time, she said she had to love a man to screw him, said I was the one she loved. Bunch of bullshit. Love. What a crock. What did she know about love? Been screwing around the country since she was sixteen. Love! Bitch like that'll believe anything you tell her. Right?"

"Yeah. You finally got her turned out, huh?"

"Yeah, after three months she was costing me nothing but money. I had to slip her a little angel dust, round up a couple of boys." He leaned over and tapped me on the arm. "Even got a little footage out of it. Couple of blacks I'd been using, hung like ponies. I let them stay all night, let her wake up between them in the morning." His laugh was as thin as his nose. "She didn't give me no more trouble. Hell, it's just a matter of finding the right button to push."

"What ever happened to her?"

He made a graceful gesture with one slender hand. "She kept going down, man. I got these four films out of her, rented her out to a guy I knew in between times." He shook his head sadly. "She just didn't have no staying power. We went to work on the fifth film, and she just wasn't there, man. Fat as a pig and handled like a sack of meal." He chuckled ruefully. "All that money and time I put into her, too."

"Yeah, man, I know what you mean. What ever happened to her?" I was feeling light-headed, a high-pitched keening in my ears, my stomach drawing into a tight painful knot. The pictures had finally ended, and Charlie had turned up the lights.

He made that airy graceful gesture again, "Aw, who the hell cares? She's probably hooking down in Mexico by now. Guy I sold her to won't take no shit off her."

"Sold her to?" I ducked my head and lit another cigarette.

He laughed. "Yeah, five hundred, and a redheaded kid from Little Rock. That bitch didn't have five hundred left in her."

"Who was the guy?" But I couldn't keep my voice casual any longer, and I felt his gaze swing in my direction. I lifted my head then and let him see my face. His eyes did that delicate widening act, and his skin lost some of its artificial color.

"What the hell is this?" He glanced toward the back of the room, to where Charlie was busy rewinding film. We both stood up.

"This is what it is," I said, and hit him in the stomach, a short fast jab, hard enough to bring up the air, but not hard enough to do any permanent damage.

He made a sucking rasping squawk, and Charlie and I both looked up at the same instant. Our eyes locked across twenty feet of empty space.

"You in this, Charlie?"

He studied me for a moment, then looked at his boss. He slipped out of the white jacket.

"I guess so," he said. He was short and round, but he had arms as big as my thighs. He hitched up his trousers and started toward me.

I eased the Magnum out of the inside pocket of my jacket. I raised it and pointed it at his head and pulled back the hammer. It made a nice clear clacking sound. "You want to reconsider, Charlie?"

He grinned crookedly and stopped. "I guess so." He walked

back and picked up his coat and put it back on. "Just tell me what you want me to do," he said soberly.

"I'll tell you what, why don't you go over there and lie on the pool table?"

He nodded and did as I told him. "On your stomach, Charlie, hands in the corner pockets."

I picked up a tray of brandy goblets from the bar and placed them carefully in the center of his shoulders. They jingled merrily.

"There you go, Charlie. Don't move too much. I hear them glasses jingling, I may let off a nervous-type round in this direction."

"Don't worry about it. I'm comfortable. You just go on about your business, mister."

McBain was watching us, just beginning to straighten up, his face the color of Silly Putty. I lit another cigarette and looked at him thoughtfully for a moment.

"Tell you what, McBain. Let's make a game out of it. Let's see how many times you can take it in the stomach before you feel like you just have to tell me."

"His name is Buster Statler," he said quickly.

I shook my head sadly. "Too fast, McBain."

I stepped forward and hit him again. He went all the way to the floor, curled into a fetal knot, a thin stream of saliva dribbling out of the corner of his mouth.

"You see, old buddy, I've got this problem. If I believe what you tell me and leave, and it isn't the truth . . . well, you're not likely to give me another chance at you. You see my problem? You have to be hurting when you tell me, so I'll know it's the truth. Makes sense, don't it?"

"I—I swear . . . I swear to God it's Statler."

"Where's he from?"

"San . . . San Antonio . . . somewhere around there. God, I think you've ruptured my ulcer."

"What does he do besides deal in slaves?"

"I don't know . . . exactly."

142

I walked around behind him and toed him in the kidney. "I think if you try hard, you can do better than that."

"I swear, Mr. Roman. I don't know him that well."

"You son of a bitch," I said. "You knew him well enough to sell him a woman, didn't you?"

"She was just a . . ."

I raised my foot above his face and aimed my heel at his eye. "Say it, man. Go on, say it."

He shook his head quickly, and there was nothing delicate about his face now: it was twisted into a sweating mask of pain and fear so intense you could smell it. I placed the toe of my boot across his Adam's apple.

"Okay, McBain. This is it. I'm going to watch your eyes. If I just think you're lying, you'll be talking through a tube in your neck for the rest of your life. Now, tell me, what was his name again?"

"B-Buster Statler . . . San Antonio. I swear!"

"Buster's a nickname. What's his full name?"

"I don't know. Please . . . I don't know!"

I put the Magnum away and reached down and hauled him to his knees.

"If you're lying to me, McBain, you're a dead man. If you don't believe me, take a good look at my face."

"I believe you. But . . . but I'm not lying to you. I don't have any reason. I don't give a shit about Statler." He reached up to wipe the sweat, and I knocked his hand down.

"You don't give a shit about anybody, do you, McBain?" I patted his cheek. "I'm going to have to hurt you a little, old buddy, and I want you to know it's strictly personal."

"Hey, come on, I told you—"

"Sure you did. But it didn't cost you a thing, did it? Everything in this life has its price. Looks to me like you've been getting the best of it for a long time now. All the young girls you turned out, got started on drugs, whatever. Don't you think they suffered some? How many ended up down in Mexico hooking for refried beans? Come on, man, fair's fair."

"Please," he said thickly, a hint of blubbering in his voice, his eyes moist. "Please, I have health . . . problems. I have a bad heart."

I nodded. "Yeah, I'd say you do. And a lousy character to go along with it. They say pain is good for that, builds character."

"Please, I'll pay you. I have money. . . ."

"Nancy ever say please, McBain? When you had her going down on those buddies of yours? She ever ask you why? I have to fix your pretty face so you won't ever be able to do that to a girl again."

"Listen . . . look, I never did any of those—I was just bullshitting. . . . Look, I liked Nancy, loved her even. I was just bragging—"

I shook my head sadly. "I hear you, McBain. Why is it I don't believe you?"

"Oh, God." He was crying, real tears running in silent streams, his nose dripping. He tried to wipe it, and I knocked his hand down again. He rocked back and forth, hands clasped in an attitude of prayer.

Do it now, I told myself savagely, do it now, or you won't do it at all. I took a step backward, measured the distance to the defenseless face, saw his eyes snap closed, his face cringe, contort helplessly, lips writhing out of control. I glanced down and saw the slowly spreading stain on the front of his sand-colored pants.

Oh shit, I thought, and snapped a short quick punch that caught the end of his chin and whipped his head around. He went down limply, soundlessly, and if I hadn't glimpsed the way his eyes rolled back in his head, I might have thought he was faking.

I glanced at Charlie, lying quietly, his face turned away from us. I walked back to the projector and gathered up the four small reels of film.

I passed by Charlie on the way out. "How you doing, Charlie?"

"Just fine, mister," he said heartily. "I like it here. I might just stay here awhile."

"Ten minutes will do, Charlie. Ten minutes is all I ask."

"You got it, mister."

=====/ **25** /=====

There were three messages on my phone recorder when I got home. Tom Jeffers wanting to confirm our preseason trip to my land, a frantic plea from a woman who wanted me to find her missing poodle before it ended up in a vivisection lab, and a polite request from Phillip Arganian to call him when it was convenient.

I opened a can of beer and settled into the recliner in the den with the telephone. I was dialing Phillip Arganian's number when the front door rattled, crashed open, banged shut, and a cheery voice rang out:

"Where are you?"

"In here," I said, punching the disconnect button and dropping the receiver by the chair.

Susie bounded through the doorway, face alight, a stack of books falling from her arms to the couch as she rushed across the room and leaped at me, making happy sounds and wearing a smile that threatened to dislocate her dimpled cheeks forever.

"God, I missed you!" she said, landing in my lap and throwing a hammerlock around my neck in one swooping movement, hair flying, covering our faces like a silken mantilla as her lips found mine.

"It's been only two days," I said when we finally came up for air. "But I'll admit I missed you, too."

She grabbed my shoulders and pinned me to the chair. "Then show it, stone face."

I made a big-eyed happy smiling face, and she laughed, settling for that and another kiss that stirred dormant desire the way a kick electrifies a sleeping dog. When we broke apart a second time, her eyes were heavy-lidded, shadowed, a peculiar look of helpless innocence that somehow conveyed an essence of boldness and daring, as if passion were a raging current sweeping her headlong into some unknown yet delightful environment.

She nuzzled my neck. "I want to hear all about your trip," she murmured, hesitating. "But I think that can wait, don't you?"

"Indubitably."

She sniffed in my ear. "Quit trying to impress me with big words. Carry me into yonder bedroom and impress me with your usual sterling performance."

"You got it, kid." I rose to my feet like Conan the Terrible, tottered down the long hallway like a ninety-pound weakling. A hundred and fifteen pounds gets heavier every year. I paused between the bed and the bathroom, weaving and rocking on my heels. "Do we have time for a shower?"

She raised her flushed face from my shoulder, smiling. "If we do it together."

We had an early dinner of ham and scrambled eggs and biscuits. I scrambled the eggs, she cooked the ham, and between us we kept a watchful eye on the oven. Face soft and relaxed, lips puffy, she peered at me sheepishly from time to time, then finally brought it into the open.

"I'll bet you think I'm some kind of nympho, huh?"

"Why, because you enjoy sex?"

"No. Because I enjoy so much sex."

I laughed. "Isn't that what people are supposed to do on their honeymoon? Even second honeymoons? We're still on ours, you know."

"A honeymoon's supposed to last a year, isn't it?" She turned to look at me, eyebrows cocked, the tip of a pink tongue at the corner of her smile destroying the intended air of innocence.

"It lasts as long as we let it last," I said. "Or more correctly, as long as I last."

She hung on my shoulder a moment, watching me chase the eggs around the pan. "I'm certainly not worried about that," she scoffed. "You're a great lover."

"I know it," I said modestly. "But that don't have much to do with how long I last."

She forked the ham out of the frying pan in silence, a brooding look on her face. "I guess you had a lot of practice," she said soberly.

"Scrambling eggs? You bet. I've busted a lot of eggs in my time."

"You know what I mean. You've had a lot of practice at being a great lover."

"It's not something you practice," I said, avoiding her eyes. "You've either got it or you haven't." I dumped the eggs into a bowl and took them to the table.

She stood in front of the oven moodily watching the biscuits brown. I came up behind her, put my arms around her waist. "I've been married, Susan. I went out with other women . . . and we made love sometimes. I thought you understood that, accepted it."

"Oh, I know all that," she said turning to press against me, her face disconsolate. "I just never realized before how terribly personal making love is. I sometimes feel so . . . so inexperienced and inadequate."

"You're not inexperienced in the most important part. You know how to give love, and maybe what's even more important, you know how to accept it. The mechanics are easy. That's only a matter of communication, understanding, experimentation. And while we're on this subject, I can tell you, you don't have to take a backseat to anyone. Not anyone."

"Really?" she said, her dark eyes pleased.

"Really," I said, "and if you don't get those biscuits out of there, they're gonna burn."

* * *

"It's very nice to hear from you, Mr. Roman." I had to put my hand over my other ear and strain to hear Phillip Arganian's soft voice above the pounding of the stereo in our living room.

"I'm sorry we missed each other before."

There was a moment of silence. "Oh, yes. Yes, of course, my wife told me you were here."

"I haven't found your sister yet, Mr. Arganian. But all things considered, I'm doing better than I thought in the beginning."

"Yes, well, fine. I'm glad to hear it."

"I'm going to San Antonio tomorrow. I'm beginning to think I may be able to find her for you after all."

"That sounds good. Is there . . . there anything you think I should know? You do remember our conversation?"

"Yes. But if you don't mind, I'd like to wait before I make a report. All I could tell you now is some of the places she's been, the jobs she's had, that kind of thing. Nothing of consequence."

"I see. What kind of work has she been doing?"

"Oh, she's worked as a waitress, had a few bit parts in some movies, did some commercial work, even did some practical nursing for a year." Taking care of Angel would surely qualify as practical nursing, I thought grimly.

"I see. Well, thank you, Mr. Roman. I'm glad to know you're doing so well."

"I could hit a snag at any time. But I'm narrowing the gap, and I'll stay with it if you like."

"Yes, of course, by all means. My mother, I'm afraid, isn't doing any better."

"I'm sorry to hear that, sir."

He sighed. "She's old, Mr. Roman."

"If you'd like, I could contact you when I get back from San Antonio."

"Yes," he said. He no longer seemed interested. "That would be fine. I will look forward to your call."

"Oh, by the way, Mr. Arganian, this detective named Murdock, was he the only one you've sent looking for Loretta? Other than me, I mean?"

The line hummed emptily for a moment, a silence that seemed suddenly charged, pulsing. I let it grow, using the hiatus to light a cigarette. Finally he coughed lightly.

"Why, yes. Why do you ask?"

"Just curious. That's a detective's stock in trade, you know. Curiosity."

"I see." He cleared his throat.

"I'll get back to you, Mr. Arganian."

"Yes, of course. Good-bye, Mr. Roman."

I was preparing to leave for San Antonio early the next morning when the call came from Lee Arganian. Susie answered the phone and handed the receiver to me with arched eyebrows and an expressionless face, her dark eyes gleaming.

"How was your trip, Dan?" Her voice was almost as soft as her husband's.

"It was interesting, to say the least."

"I wonder if you might find time to stop by for a few minutes?"

I hesitated. "I was leaving for San Antonio in a little while, but if you like, I could run by before I leave."

"That would be fine. I'll expect you shortly."

"No more than fifteen minutes." I hung up, wondering at an inexplicable feeling of excitement as the memories of my last meeting with Lee Arganian crept into my mind. I looked around to find Susie watching me quietly.

"I thought you worked for *Mr.* Arganian," she said flatly, her face still empty of emotion.

"I do," I said cheerfully. "He found some later pictures of the girl he wants me to pick up." It was an obvious lie, but she nodded. She came and stood on tiptoe and kissed me, her lips cold.

"I'll see you when you get back. Be careful." She turned and went into the kitchen.

I stared after her, my mind a blank. Then suddenly filled with an unaccountable mixture of anger and guilt, I grabbed up the small overnight bag, the Styrofoam cooler, and stalked out of the house.

*　　*　　*

"I'm so glad you could come, Daniel," she said. She smiled and extended her hand. Her hair was upswept again, framing her pale face. She looked achingly lovely, and I felt a deep atavistic stirring as I held her warm hand, mouthed some inane pleasantry, and followed her to the music room.

I watched the sway of her slender body and wondered if a man ever became totally immune to feminine beauty, the bewitching allure of supple form and captivating smile, of the unknown.

A Cole Porter oldie was on the turntable, an instrumental; no Frank Sinatra this time, no dancing, and no having to fight for my honor. I couldn't suppress a faint twinge of disappointment. There's nothing like being asked.

"Would you care for some coffee, Daniel?"

"No, thanks."

The chairs were much the way I had left them, the two center ones facing each other. She chose one, and I sat across from her.

Her smile this time was uncertain, and her hands fluttered in her lap like two small birds fighting.

"Daniel, I don't want you to think I'm meddling in my husband's personal affairs, but this thing about his sister—" She broke off and leaned forward. "I'm not entirely sure it's a good thing you're doing."

"I'm not sure I know what you mean. It's just a job."

Her brow furrowed, one hand flipping outward in a self-deprecating gesture. "It's just that he's been so . . . so morose, so distant since this thing began. Apprehensive, I suppose is a better word. It's as if his whole world is on hold." She paused. "My husband is not a devious man. In most things he is straightforward and open. But he's very reluctant to discuss this matter with me."

"I think that's understandable. He's afraid of what I'm going to find out about her. He told me that." I smiled faintly. "He doesn't want you to know if what I discover is seamy. He

150

wants to protect you from that. If it weren't for his mother, I don't think he would be doing this at all."

She stared at me quizzically. "His mother?"

"Yes. She wants to see Loretta, or at least know whether she's dead or alive before she . . . well, before her illness gets worse."

"I see," she said. She studied my face, then lowered her head and inspected her hands, as if she had never seen them before. "He told you that?"

"Yes, when he hired me."

She was quiet for a long moment, her head still bowed. Finally she sighed. "Very well, if it means that much to him." When she raised her head, she was smiling, but there was something different about her eyes, something veiled, even haunted.

"I won't detain you any further, Daniel. I know you have a long trip ahead of you." She stood up.

I nodded, falling in beside her as she left the music room and walked toward the door.

"She went to San Antonio?"

"Yes," I said, and volunteered nothing more. I was beginning to find this small intrigue among Arganian, his mother, and his young wife a little tiresome. From the first her inquisitiveness had seemed to run deeper than simple wifely curiosity or concern, and more than once I had found myself wondering where her interests might lie.

Could it be the money? Arganian had said that Loretta and he would share the Arganian estate after his stepmother's death. I had received a different impression from Marissa Arganian. Could be the old lady had different ideas, and maybe Lee knew it. Loretta Arganian, porno queen, might soon be one of the richer hookers in Texas. She wouldn't be the first one.

Maybe Lee Arganian's flippant declaration that the money didn't matter was just what I had thought it was when she said it—hot air.

At the door she extended her hand again. "I hope you have a

nice trip." Her voice was pleasant and cool, her expression noncommittal.

"Thank you," I said, shaking the warm hand, suppressing an urge to blurt out the questions swirling in my head.

"Good-bye, Daniel," she said, and closed the door.

I stared at its glossy surface for a moment, feeling an inexplicable swell of disappointment.

I noticed the car the first time simply because it was a green Dodge Monaco, 1974 vintage, one of the last Monacos made, exactly like the one I had traded in on a 1978 Cutlass—without a doubt the biggest mistake of my automotive career.

Parked parallel to the street at the edge of a convenience store parking lot a hundred yards north of the Arganian estate entrance, it gleamed and sparkled in the sunlight, obviously well tended and well loved by an owner who appreciated elegance and comfort more than tire-screaming performance, high mileage, and a bone-jarring ride.

I saw it again ten minutes later when I came out of a 7-Eleven with ice for my cooler and a six-pack of beer. Parked at the curb, a dozen yards down the street, it was facing away from the direction I had come, and the bulky figure behind the wheel was almost hidden behind a folded newspaper.

Coincidence? Not damn likely, I thought. There were still 1974 Dodge Monacos to be seen occasionally, even sea-green four-door sedans with vinyl tops. But they were usually dented and dull, the vinyl tops muddy-colored and peeling. This car had

152

showroom quality, the paint bright and shining, no dents or scratches or abrasions that I could see.

I finished packing the cooler and drove south on Highway 157. The green sedan nosed into traffic four or five cars behind me. At the intersection with Highway 10 I passed through the light, drove another hundred feet, then whipped left into a huge K mart parking lot.

By the time I crept across the wide lot, found an empty space, and parked, the Monaco was drifting in from the highway, angling across behind me, puttering down an aisle four or five car lengths away.

I opened the overnight bag and took out the .38 snub-nosed Smith and Wesson with its worn clip-on holster. I hung it on my belt and got out. I spotted the white vinyl top sliding into a space down near the entrance to the store.

I dawdled for a moment, lighting a cigarette, but the man in the Dodge didn't get out. He was obviously content with the situation so far, intending to pick me up again when I came back to my car.

Inside the store, I angled quickly to my left, zigzagging along the crowded aisles, dodging carelessly driven shopping carts and irate mothers chasing runaway progeny.

I exited by way of the garden shop, passing through the checkout stand with upraised hands and a guilty smile, catching a look of consternation on the face of the male clerk that told me he had glimpsed the gun. I gave him a reassuring grin as I went out the door.

I moved quickly past the automotive bays and out into the open, head lowered, shoulders slumped, searching the rows of cars for a telltale glint of green and white. I found it two aisles off to my left, the dark bulky figure slumped once again behind a newspaper.

I straightened up and walked directly toward him, keeping my eyes on the round shaggy head. It didn't move. He heard nothing, sensed nothing, until I was stooped beside the open window of the car, my left hand bunching in his shirt front, the .38 pressed against the side of his nose. It was a truly magnificent nose, worthy of Aztec kings and Apache warriors. I had seen it once before.

"You make a lousy shadow, Chico," I said, jerking him upright and grinding with the gun, following the instinctive movement of his head away from pain.

"Hey," he said, then he rolled large black eyes in my direction, peering over the barrel, his face twisting with fear. "Hey, man . . . shit! I told them assholes I wasn't any good at this shit."

"Who's Groucho, Chico?" I yanked him back against the door and rolled the barrel across his left eye. "What assholes?" I rapped the crown of his nose and watched his eyes begin to tear.

"Dammit! That hurt!" He raised pudgy hands toward his nose; I slapped them down with the gun barrel.

"You've got five seconds, Chico. I won't kill you, but some plastic surgeon's gonna have a lot of fun putting this beak back together."

"Hey, man, I ain't . . . dammit, I'm just a bookkeeper—"

"Tell me, dammit! I thumbed back the hammer on the gun, jammed it against the wide expanse of his nose. "One second, Chico!"

"Sackett! Sackett and Boyd! Shit, man, I ain't trying to do you any harm."

"Who's Boyd?"

"Boyd—he was with me the other night. He—he's Sackett's foreman. Come on, man, we was just having some fun the other night. Doing a favor for Sackett. Hell, he's our boss. Whatta you gonna do? Your boss asks you a favor, you're gonna do it, right?"

"Why was he warning me off Loretta Arganian?"

The curly head wagged from side to side as far as the gun would permit. "Man, I don't have any idea. We didn't even know who she was. He told us what to say, is all, and we said it. That stuff about staying back in the dark was all Boyd's idea. He said it'd spook you probably."

"What's your name?"

"Norman, Norman Alldridge. I'm Mr. Sackett's book-keeper and—"

"That other clown, Boyd. First name or last?"

"It's Boyd Hall. He's the foreman, second to Mr. Sackett."

I released him and holstered the gun. "Let me see your driver's license."

He rolled his eyes. "Jesus, you a cop?"

"Your boss don't tell you much. Come on, let's see the license."

He nodded eagerly and rolled his rotund body to the right, reached behind his hip, and came up with a bulging wallet. He fumbled for a moment, then handed me a plastic rectangle.

The picture was right, the name Norman Alldridge correct. Five feet eight, two hundred and sixty pounds, black hair, black eyes. It all fit. I gave it back to him.

"Why are you following me?"

His face screwed up into a grimace. "Hell, man, 'cause I was told to. See where you went, who you went to see, like that. I knew I wouldn't be any good at it. It ain't as easy as it looks in the movies. Hell, I almost lost you twice already this morning."

"That night at Texas' Best. You follow me from home?"

His head bobbed. "Yeah, me and Boyd. We followed you to your girlfriend's place, then on to the restaurant." He puckered thin lips in a tentative smile.

"Good job. I didn't see you," I said, feeling a rivulet of outrage thread its way across my brain. Unseen eyes watching, invading my privacy; I didn't like it. I stepped back and trailed my fingers along the mirrorlike finish on the door of the Dodge.

"Beautiful car, Norman."

His face lit up. "Yeah, ain't she? I bought this beauty new. Ain't never spent a night out of the garage. I wax her once a month, wash her every week. Someday—"

"I carry a ball-peen hammer in my car, Norman. If I ever see you on my back trail again, I'm going to work this lovely lady over; redecorate it. You have any trouble understanding that?"

"My God! You wouldn't!" He stared up at me, horrified, black bloodshot eyes aghast under fine silky lashes.

"Yeah, I would, Norman. I'm mean. Didn't Sackett tell you that? I came within a hair of killing both of you the other night. If the lady hadn't been with me, I would have."

"Jesus Christ!" he whispered, his wide eyes seized with the thought of what might have been.

"You better stick to keeping books, Norman. I don't think you're cut out for the wild life. You'll end up getting yourself killed."

His head wagged jerkily from side to side, then bobbed up and down, covering all bases, as if my words contained arcane considerations he couldn't begin to understand.

"Go home," I said. "Tell your boss I'll be coming to see him. Maybe tonight, maybe next week. But soon."

He nodded, reached mechanically for the key, started the car and raced the engine, the sound bouncing off the nearby cars like the roar of a startled hibernating bear.

The green Dodge lurched backward out of the parking space, died, roared to life again, then sped off down the aisle.

I watched Alldridge leave the parking lot, then walked back to my station wagon.

I felt a burning need to talk to John Sackett again.

I glanced at my watch.

There was no time like the present.

John Sackett's house was only moderately ostentatious. A two-story brick-veneer, with modern lines, clean and functional, it was not much more than twice as large as my eighteen-hundred-square-footer. Set among pecan trees and stately oaks in a restricted subdivision near the north edge of town, it had its very own satellite dish and a large oblong patch of cloudy plastic on the south side of the roof that I took to be some kind of solar heating system.

A three-quarter-ton pickup like the one I had seen at the tract building site was parked along the edge of the curving driveway, and through the open doors of a three-car garage I could see a mint-green Cadillac and a blue Mercedes. The other stall was empty.

Sackett and Boyd Hall and the auburn-haired woman, I thought, stepping out of the car, feeling exposed and absurdly vulnerable to the glaring eye of a huge picture window that reflected the sun like a rectangle of fire.

I ambled up the walk, forcing nonchalance, the bulk of the Smith and Wesson Airweight on my belt both reassuring and slightly embarrassing here in this quiet affluent neighborhood, the habitat of the makers and shakers. Our mayor lived around here, our doctors and lawyers and businessmen, the elite. The thought of violence in this serene setting seemed ludicrous.

Nevertheless, while I waited for someone to answer the bell, I slipped my hand under my jacket and tested the pull of the gun—and got caught doing it, the door snapping suddenly open, dark eyes staring at me out of a face devoid of makeup, the yellow-green bruises stark and obscene against pale smooth skin, the heavy mass of hair pulled back and coiled on the back of her neck.

Coolly, as if I practiced fast draw on people's doorsteps all the time, I reseated the gun in its holster and withdrew my hand, raised it to touch the brim of the cream-colored Stetson I had dug out of my closet for the occasion.

"Good morning," I said cheerfully. "Mrs. Sackett?"

The sleek head moved slightly downward. "What can I do for you?" There was no apprehension in her voice that I could detect, no hint of caution in her eyes, no change in expression.

"I'd like to speak with your husband, Mrs. Sackett. My name is Dan Roman."

"I'm sorry," she said. "He isn't here."

"Isn't that his Mercedes in the garage?"

"Yes," she said, and offered no further explanation.

"Boyd Hall, then. I believe that's his pickup in the driveway."

"Yes, that's his pickup, but he isn't here, either." Her eyes met mine calmly, a glimmer of something in their depths that was difficult to look into, impossible to face down: quiet strength, burning passion—something. I had an eerie feeling suddenly that I knew her, that our paths had crossed before the brief encounter at Sackett's office—the kind of feeling reincarnationists must have when they unexpectedly come upon their karmic soul mates.

"Well," I said, somehow unable to defy her. "I guess I'll just go, then." I cleared my throat. "He isn't at his office, either."

She nodded without speaking, a fleeting touch of humor in her face.

"He knows what it's about," I said. "Tell him I was here, if you don't mind."

"I'll tell him, Mr. Roman."

"And Boyd Hall," I went on inanely. "It's important that he know I was here looking for him." I knew they were there, somewhere behind her. I could sense it the way you sense an intruder in a pitch-black room.

"I'll certainly tell them both." The humor had crept into her voice and into her eyes.

"How did you get the bruises?" It came out without conscious volition, out of some deep primeval need to know, some atavistic desire for justice, another marker on the down side when I finally dealt with John Sackett.

She smiled without flinching and answered softly without rancor: "I fell, Mr. Roman."

There was nothing more for me to say, nothing I could do; I said good-bye and left.

/ 27 /

"Henry Wadesworth Statler," Homer Sellers had said. "A.k.a. Buster Statler. Been busted four times here in Texas. Small-time stuff mostly. One felony theft, one assault with a deadly weapon. No convictions. Arrested twice in California for assault under a different name, one in Nevada—different name again. Nothing big, just sounds like an ornery cuss. Last known connection, the Cobra Club. That's somewhere outside the city limits of San Antone. Topless joint, with both men and women waiters walking around half-naked. Been closed down a couple of times for going too far. Topless dancers and a suspected cover for dealing and prostitution. What the hell do you want with him, anyhow?"

"Just a link in a chain, Homer."

"You still working on the Arganian thing?"

"Yeah."

"If she's connected with Statler, you might as well give it up, boy."

"Why's that?"

"He's part of a pipeline, a conduit into Mexico, and God knows where from there. If she worked for him, chances are she's in Hong Kong by now."

"Maybe not. She's not just a hooker, Homer."

He snorted. "If she's connected with Statler, she is. He don't know no other kind."

"We'll see."

"Why in hell does Arganian want her back? She must be nearly thirty by now. That's old age for a hooker. She'll be broke down and wore out."

"You're a cynical bastard, Homer."

"Time was, you were, too. You changing?"

"I hope so," I said fervently.

"Well," he grunted, "don't get too soft. And watch yourself down there. Them's some mean mothers down around San Antone." He hesitated. "You get your tail in a crack, yell for a captain named Hank Leroy. He's Vice. You can use my name, but not too loud and not very often."

"Yeah, I know, mention your name, and I'll get a better seat."

He had hung up laughing.

I was thinking about his advice as I wheeled the station wagon under a neon sign that displayed a huge coiled cobra with red unblinking sinister eyes. It was early afternoon, but the parking lot was already half-filled.

I backed into a slot at the end of a row with a clear shot at the exit—just in case. I slipped an old snub-nosed .38 into the pocket of my jacket where they could easily find it, and fitted a small flat .32 inside the strap sewn into the top of my boot. Not much good for distance, but up close, a hollow point out of the little automatic could do some nasty damage.

I waited inside my car until a pickup came into the lot. Two men in Levi's, western shirts, and cowboy hats got out and went into the club. I sauntered in behind them. At least I wouldn't be thrown out for not wearing a tie.

We were in a small dimly lit foyer. A bored blonde in a glassed-in cubicle took our five-dollar cover charge and stamped the backs of our hands with invisible ink. I followed my unwitting companions into dusky darkness filled with blinking flashing lights and raucous sound. I paused just inside the thick padded doors and eased to one side until my eyes became accustomed to the gloom.

I soon discovered the sound was canned rock music, and the lights were highlighting a dancing girl at each end of the large rectangular room. A horseshoe-shaped bar to my right featured another girl gyrating behind it on a raised circular pedestal. She wore a G-string, a rope of pearls, and red high-heeled shoes. I made for the bar.

I picked a seat as far away from the girl and the noise as I could get. My bartender made a courtesy swipe at the top of the bar in front of me. He was short and fat, with a bald head and a crooked smile that could easily have been mistaken for a sneer. But his tone was courteous enough.

"What'll it be, Mac?"

I gave him my order and turned to watch the girl behind the bar. A tall slender brunette with large breasts and nice legs, she was working her way through an uninspired routine consisting mainly of waving arms and a twisting torso. She had a young pretty face framed by ringlets of glossy black hair, but I seriously doubted that the eyes of the men who lined the bar in front of her traveled higher than the jutting breasts that bounced and quivered pleasantly with her movements.

The bartender came back with my drink; I waited until he brought my change from the bill I gave him: "Buster around?"

His little eyes sized me up. "Don't know. If he is, he's in his office."

"Where might that be?"

He pointed a stubby sausage finger over my shoulder. "Through there. Last door on the end." He grinned. "I'd knock if I were you."

I nodded and grinned back. "Simple courtesy."

He propped his short arms on the bar in the classic bartender pose. "Don't believe I've seen you in here before."

"Nope. First time. Nice place. Your girls are a cut above average."

"Yeah," he said disinterestedly. He cocked his round head. "You're from up north. Fort Worth, Dallas, around there."

I laughed. "Yeah, I'm one of them north Texas Yankees. How'd you know?"

"I don't know," he admitted. "Something in the way you folks talk. I ain't wrong very often." He bobbed his head, pleased with himself. He absently lifted my glass and swiped at the ring of water, then replaced it and stumped off down the bar. I'd made his whole day.

I smoked another cigarette and finished my drink. The door he had pointed out was behind me and slightly to my left. I made my way around a section of empty tables and stepped through it into a narrow, dimly lit hallway.

I passed two doors marked HIS and HERS, one inscribed EMPLOYEES ONLY, and four more that were unmarked. The one I wanted was at the end, a white door that had fresh-looking paint, a large metal sign that said PRIVATE, and the muted sound of a rumbling masculine voice that faded as I rapped politely.

"Come on in!" Somehow it sounded more like a command than an invitation. I went in.

There were two men in the room. The one I nodded at first,

a short stocky man with a burr haircut, cold eyes, and thick hairy arms, was seated on a threadbare sofa directly in front of the door, elbows propped on his knees, idly leafing through a girlie magazine.

He stared at me without interest, unblinking, his pale eyes flicking over me in one swift appraising glance. I nodded again, and he went back to his magazine with a slight roll of his shoulders that dismissed me like a vagrant thought.

"Come on in!" The voice boomed again; I turned to my left to face it. I closed the door and took the two steps that brought me to the mammoth desk that filled half the small room, to the even larger man who sat behind it.

Six foot six or seven, an easy three hundred pounds, he had long arms and big hands that matched his body, and a narrow handsome face that didn't. He towered over me as he rose and extended his hand, a huge scarred hand with a surprisingly limp grip. He wore dark blue Levi's with white-topped pockets, a white western shirt, and a ten-gallon hat. The Levi's rode precariously below a generous stomach as round and hard looking as a medicine ball.

His voice was affable, his smile disarming, but he didn't fool me for a moment: I could see it in the dark unsmiling eyes, the quick restless movement of his hands, the arrogant set of his mouth as the smile faded and died. It was violence, or at least the potential for it, sudden and destructive, barely repressed, seething just below a thin veneer of conventional behavior. During ten years of police work I had dealt with too many men like him not to recognize the signs. Not a man to be treated lightly.

I smiled broadly.

"Mr. Statler, my name is Dan Roman. I'm a private investigator. I'm looking for a young lady I have reason to believe may have worked for you a few years ago." I handed him the photostat of my license, and while he was looking at it, I leaned forward and laid a head-and-shoulders blowup of Nancy Taylor in front of him, one made from a frame clipped from one of the porno movies.

He handed the license to me without comment and picked up the picture. He studied it for a moment. "Alicia Dawn," he said, and I nodded. Alicia Dawn was the name on the film container promo. The male star's name had been Rod Starr.

"That's right," I said, but he ignored me.

"C'mere, Elmo. Look at this. Ain't this Alicia Dawn?"

Elmo brushed past me and took the photograph in one hairy hand. I caught a heavy scent of garlic. He looked at the picture briefly and tossed it back on the desk.

"Could be her," he said. He had a surprisingly high, almost sweet voice. His pale eyes appraised me again, lingered, a tiny flame flickering in their depths. He went back to his seat and picked up his magazine.

"What do you want her for?"

"Her mother died. There's a small insurance policy. The company would like to clear it off the books." Money, that was something he could understand.

He nodded. "Wish I could help you, boy. I'm sure she could use the dough."

"She did work for you, then?"

"About six months."

"Did she quit?"

He frowned, his thick fingers drumming the desk impatiently. "She's gone, boy. What difference does it make?"

I lit a cigarette and shifted my feet slightly so I could see both of them at once. I folded my arms. I could feel the bulk of the .38; it wasn't too reassuring.

"Is she still in this area? She didn't leave the country suddenly by chance—say, to Mexico?"

His fingers stilled; his eyes rose to mine, and he smiled thinly. "If she did, she went on her own." The smile widened, turned sardonic. "Ask Elmo. He was keeping her for a while. That right, Elmo?"

Elmo shrugged, leafed slowly through the magazine. "Why not? She was available. Nothin' special." He shrugged again. "I haven't seen her for years." His tone was casual, too casual.

"That so?" The big man winked at me. "I heard you was buyin' her groceries there for a while."

"You heard wrong." Elmo's voice had turned harsh, almost masculine.

He threw down the magazine and glared balefully at Statler, his face reflecting a current of animosity so strong it was almost physical. He shoved to his feet and stalked out the door.

Statler's giggle was very nearly girlish. "Elmo's my partner—junior partner. I kinda like to needle him along."

"I think I'd just as soon pull a gorilla's chest hair."

He waved his hand deprecatingly. "Elmo's a pussycat. You ever see one of them that wasn't?"

I looked at him blankly, and he laughed a booming explosive laugh.

"Elmo's queer," he said, and laughed again. "Actually I guess he's double-gaited. He was banging that Dawn dame after . . . after I fired her."

"Mind telling me why you fired her?"

He frowned again in one of his mercurial mood changes. "None of your damn business, boy."

I nodded. "You're right. I was just curious, since you had a considerable investment in her."

"Oh, I got my money back and then some." He placed his hands palm down on the desk and stared at them. "And then some," he repeated. He suddenly slapped his hands on the desk top. "Aw, what the hell?" He turned a framed photograph on his desk around so I could see it.

"That's Mama, boy. That there is my wife. She caught me banging Alicia right there on the couch." He chuckled indulgently, proudly. "She clobbered the shit out of me, man. That's when I fired that girl. Shame, too, she was a good piece of tail."

The woman in the picture was standing at the side of a palomino stallion, the top of her head at least a foot below the animal's back. She looked tiny, fragile; I tried to imagine her and this lumbering giant together. It was impossible.

"She come in here with that sawed-off pool cue from under the bar, man. She damn near killed me 'fore I could take it away from her." He was still chuckling, his great body shaking.

"How about Alicia, she do anything to her?"

"Hell, no! Mama knowed she didn't have any choice." He was getting decidedly hostile, his leathery face beginning to take on a copper hue. I wasn't sure what had upset him, but I was sure I didn't want to find out. He had moved to the end of his desk, clenching and unclenching his hands. He made a move toward me; I lifted my hand and stepped out and closed the door.

I moved down the hallway to the entrance into the club, not exactly hurrying, but not dawdling, either.

/ 28 /

It was shortly after midnight when Elmo came out of the club. He was accompanied by a tall slender man I vaguely remembered seeing behind the bar. They came straight toward me, to where I crouched in the shadows at the end of the employee parking area. I saw the brief flare of a match as one of them lit a cigarette and heard the trill of laughter as Elmo said something. They stopped fifteen feet away. Elmo looked casually around the parking lot, then pushed the slender man into the shadow of a towering pickup camper. I saw the sparks as he threw down his cigarette, and I watched their bodies merge into one.

One of the shadows broke away, and I heard the low-pitched hiss of Elmo's voice: "Dammit, can't you wait?" There was a low-voiced reply, and Elmo laughed.

I came up behind Elmo. I pressed the .38 into the small of his back and breathed into his ear, "Freeze!"

His body stiffened, and he grunted, but before the man in front of him could react, I placed my foot on his shoulder and shoved.

The slender man twisted as he fell backward, rolled, and came to his hands and knees facing us. I shoved Elmo against the camper with my left arm and held the gun out into the light where they could see it.

"You bitch!" I snarled. "You trying to steal my man?"

I cocked the gun, the sound loud and clear in the crisp autumn night.

"You slut," I snarled again. "Run!"

The man came to his feet whimpering, glossy patent leather shoes flashing as he scrambled between two cars and disappeared.

Elmo crowded against the camper, busily zipping up his pants. I swung him around and tapped him between the legs with the gun barrel.

"Goddammit!" He leaped backward, cupping his crotch tenderly in both hands. "What the hell you doing? That hurt!"

"Sorry to break up your fun, Elmo, but I think you and I need to have a little talk." I grabbed his shoulder and prodded him toward my car. "That was to get your attention."

"What the hell you want?" A plaintive note had crept into his voice.

"Just some answers, Elmo baby," I said. I opened the passenger door and pushed him inside, then climbed into the seat behind him. He turned around to look at me; I poked his cheek with the barrel of the gun.

"Face forward, Elmo. I'll ask the questions and you answer. If I don't like your answers, I do this." I rapped him lightly on the crown of his head with the gun barrel.

"Jesus Christ!" He lurched forward. "Dammit, that hurt!"

"No shit." I got a handful of his collar and jerked him back against the seat. "The next one will hurt a lot more, Elmo. And the next one after that still more. You give me enough wrong answers, and your brains will be so loose, you'll be afraid to blow your nose."

"You don't have to be so rough," he said reproachfully.

"It's a damn rough world, Elmo. Particularly for young girls who get sold into Mexico and end up in Singapore screwing sailors and Chinks the rest of their lives. What do you know about that kind of thing, Elmo?"

His shoulders hunched and he put his hand on his head. "I don't know nothin' about that. That was Buster's thing. And even he don't do it no more."

"Why not?"

" 'Cause Mama won't let him." I touched the back of his neck with the gun barrel, and he jumped. "Hey, come on! I ain't lying!"

"You expect me to believe that little woman makes that big lummox step around?"

"Shit, man," he said fervently. "She may be little, but she's mean as a rattler when she's mad. He's plumb scared to death of her. I ain't shittin' you, man. He tried slappin' her around once, and she just looked at him with them big black eyes and reminded him that sooner or later he was gonna have to sleep. He musta believed her. He never tried it no more that I know about." He scratched his head. "She's half-Mex, and she's got five mean-ass brothers. I reckon that helps some."

"How about Alicia Dawn? He told me he cut her loose because Mama caught him with her in his office."

He nodded. "That's about right."

"And Mama didn't do anything to the girl?"

"Hell, no! She knows how that sumbitch is. She gave her a month's salary and told her she better leave for her own good."

"Why her own good?"

"Well—" he hesitated and turned his head to look toward the club, frowning—"I reckon she felt like most of the rest of us. Alicia didn't belong here nohow. Oh, hell, I don't know. She was like all the girls in some ways. She'd put out all right if you were nice to her and she liked you. Even did it some for money, I guess. Shit, I don't know. When she did it, it didn't seem so . . . so commercial somehow. Hell, you explain it, I can't."

"She put out for you, Elmo?"

"Hell, yes!" He turned to look at me, and I didn't stop him. "I can do it with girls, you know. Some girls. If they're . . . you know, patient. Like she was. I could do it with her all right almost all the time. It's just that . . . well, hell, you know, I just like to make it sometimes with a man." His face turned toward the front again.

"Where did she go, Elmo?"

He shook his head gloomily. "I—I mean after she left me, I don't know," he said hastily. "I had her with me two months after that big ape fired her. She came to shack up with me. Man, I think we could have, you know, made it. I was . . . well, I was nuts about her. Maybe she wasn't nothin' but a tramp, even a whore, maybe, but she was the best thing ever happened to me. We liked the same things . . . music, man, she loved music . . . old movies, reading—all kinds of stuff. I didn't even think about wantin' a man. If I coulda just reached her, you know, but there was something . . . something—" He broke off, shaking his head, groping for a word.

"Elusive," I said.

"Yeah! That's the word. Something elusive about her. One moment she was there with you, happy and laughing and acting silly so you'd laugh . . . and the next . . . man, she was gone. You never knew what to expect. But it was kinda exciting, you know. In a way even that was fun. It was so damned nice when she came back."

"And you don't know why she left."

"She just didn't like me enough, I guess. I wasn't what she was looking for. And she was sure looking for something. I ain't too smart, but even I could tell that. It was like all this shit that goes on here didn't . . . well, didn't touch her, you know. These other girls, after a few years they begin to show the wear and tear. But not her. Man, I couldn't understand it then, and I still don't."

"How did she leave, Elmo? She just tell you she was leaving and then go? Or what?"

He turned to look at me. "I came home one night from the club. She left me a letter. Man, I nearly freaked out. I went out and picked up a couple of guys. . . ." He let his voice drift, turned away from me. "I beat up both of them before the night was over. I hated them, and I hated me, but I couldn't stop wanting her."

"You don't know where she went? Don't have any idea?"

He shook his head slowly, without flinching, my gun barrel forgotten. "I thought I saw her once. I was positive back then, but I ain't too sure anymore."

"Where?"

"Dallas . . . well, no, it was Irving. Texas Stadium. I went up to see a Cowboy game. It was afterward. I was walking to my car, and this big black job passed me. I saw this face for just a second. I was sure it was her. I got a better look at the man. He was old."

"How old? Fifty, sixty?"

"Naw, he was a lot older than that. Seventy-five, at least, maybe even eighty. Old, man."

"What kind of car?"

"Jeez, I don't know. I was trying to see for sure if it was her. I didn't pay much attention to the car. It was big, and black, one of them stretch limousines with the rear window down. That's all I remember about it." He hesitated, turned to face me once more. "No, there was something else. I saw the license plate. It was one of the special kind, you know, with a name on it."

"What name?"

"Jesus, I'm not sure . . . well, yeah, it was like the Stallone movie—you know, the tough guy . . . oh, yeah, RAMBO . . . RAMBO . . . no, let's see . . . RAMCO, that's it. RAMCO!"

"RAMCO?"

"Yeah. It had a number after it. One, I think."

"RAMCO 1?"

"RAMCO 1. Yeah, that's it. I'm positive."

"And you were sure it was her?"

"Man, I was. I was shaking, I was so excited. If I'd had my car close by, I'd a followed them, you can bet on that."

I sighed. "And that's everything you can tell me about her, Elmo?"

His head bobbed emphatically. "That's it."

"I believe you." I put the gun away and lit a cigarette. "Sorry I had to come on like John Wayne, but you keep some rough company, and you look pretty tough yourself."

"I'm a pussycat," he said, and smiled for the first time. It was a nice smile, made up of good white solid-looking teeth.

"How's your head?"

"My head's okay. It's my cock that's still sore."

"Sorry about that. No permanent damage, I hope."

"I don't imagine," he said dryly, "but I'm going to have a hell of a time explaining to Floyd."

It was one-thirty by the time I got back to my motel room. I broke the cellophane covering one of the plastic glasses, splashed vodka over ice cubes, lit a cigarette, and sank into the room's only chair. I stared into the blind eye of the television and wondered what in hell I was doing here.

I was mind-weary and bone-tired. Sick of chasing a phantom, of crawling through the filth of other people's lives to satisfy the arrogant pride of a dying old lady and the indulgence of a dutiful son who obviously couldn't care less beyond a morbid fascination with the sordid details of his sister's wasted life.

An empty token gesture, and I had been hurt, had hurt others, unleashed old ghosts, and exposed the woman I loved to lonely nights and needless anxiety.

I gagged down the rest of the vodka and went to bed; but sleep eluded me. I tossed and turned, filled with an uneasy sense of desolation.

The trail had ended, the spoor vanished. I placed no trust in Elmo's fleeting glimpse of a face that he had probably seen dozens of times before in neurotic fancies.

The imagination plays tricks on the senses. For months

after Barbara's death my heart had leaped crazily at the sight of flowing auburn hair, the familiar curve of a cheek, an upturned nose, a lilting husky laugh in a crowd.

End of the trail; there was a kind of grim satisfaction in that.

Whatever Nancy's life had been, she had chosen it, had lived it with a curious kind of grace and dignity, accepting things as they came, as they really were, dispensing kindness and displaying a keen understanding of the frailties of others, surrendering herself to their selfish demands with a kind of good-humored indulgence, at the same time impervious to the taint of their degrading influence.

Damn it, I thought savagely, she had asked nothing of them. The least they could do would be to leave her in peace, allow her to pursue her own dream in her own way, as mean and pitiful as it might be.

But I knew as I finally slipped into a fitful sleep that I would carry the search one step further, fruitless as it must be. If for no other reason than my own peace of mind, I would have to know who owned a license plate stamped RAMCO 1.

/ 29 /

I drove by the Midway City Police Department before going home. Homer Sellers, as usual, was out of his office. I left a note on his desk requesting that he check out the license RAMCO 1, then stopped by a convenience store and picked up a six-pack of beer.

Susie was in class, and the house was silent and empty, the air stale. I stored the beer in the refrigerator, then went around opening windows. I wound up back at the refrigerator plucking the tab off the last can of cold beer.

I was taking my first sip when I heard the sound of car doors slamming out on my driveway. I crossed to the dining room window and looked.

I saw a black pickup with an eight-foot stake bed, a circular emblem on the door that boldly stated Sackett and Son—and two men walking forward, making the turn into my concrete walk.

John Sackett and Boyd Hall.

I felt a light thudding shock, a heated rush of adrenaline, a sinking thrill of fear. For one bloated second I stood frozen, conscious of the humming refrigerator, my pounding heart, the scuffle of their feet on concrete, the whine of an electric saw—

Then one of them laughed, and the spell was broken.

I moved, began to breathe again, crossing the living room in giant strides, scoffing at my unseemly fear, psyching myself up, suddenly cold with outrage at this invasion of my domain.

My turf.

My *home*, for Christ's sake!

The gun was still warm from my body heat. I shoved it into my belt and slipped into my jacket just as the chimes chimed.

I let them ring twice more before I opened the door.

Boyd Hall was already turning away; Sackett's hand was once again reaching for the bell. He jerked it back and instantly raised both hands to shoulder height, palms outward.

"Began to think you wasn't home," he said, grinning.

I looked past him at the bearded man. "Step out where I can see your hands, Harpo."

The big man stepped to one side and spread his arms. "Name's Boyd Hall," he said genially, and if there had been any doubt in my mind that Norman hadn't told the truth, the deep rumbling voice dispelled it.

"What do you want, Sackett?"

"Wife said you came to call. Just being neighborly. Besides, I got a little business proposition to make. Figured we might squat on our heels, spit in the fire, and chew the fat a little."

I nodded toward Hall. "What's he, your gun bearer, water boy, or what?"

Sackett smiled. "Boyd's a junior member of the firm."

"Speak your piece."

Sackett spread his hands and looked around. "Out here? In front of all the neighbors?"

"Here or nowhere. And you can begin by telling me the purpose of this charade. Why did you send this clown and your dimwit bookkeeper to scare me away from Loretta Arganian?"

Sackett looked at Hall, then back at me, and grimaced. "That was probably a mistake, but you never know until you try, right?" He shifted his feet and pushed the brim of his hat upward with a forefinger. "Well, hell, you know why. I told you the other day—man, I told you I still loved her—"

"Bullshit, Sackett. Either lay it out straight, or take your stooge and get the hell out of here."

"Hey," Boyd Hall said, straightening out of his slouch, his chest expanding under the black cotton T-shirt. "You taken a real good look at me?" He glowered at me under his hat, his huge arms akimbo.

"You're a lot scarier when you're hiding behind a trash bin," I said. "That's your natural element. You're out of it here, so don't get antsy."

"Hey, come on, you guys. This violent shit ain't where it's at. Boyd, you hush up." Sackett turned back to me. "Okay, I'll level with you. Strictly a hard cash proposition. I don't know what Arganian's paying you, but I'm ready to offer you a hefty lump sum to tell him the trail petered out in San Antone."

"What do you know about San Antonio?"

He shrugged. "That's my little secret. I know about the Cobra Club and Buster Statler and—well, that's enough hard facts to show I ain't bluffing."

"It does nothing to explain your interest in Loretta Arganian."

"For five thousand dollars I shouldn't have to explain anything."

"Gee whiz. Five thousand dollars." I leaned against the doorjamb and took out a cigarette, giving him a withering smile. "You're going up against the Arganian millions with five thousand dollars?"

The curl on his lips stopped just short of a sneer. "Okay, seventy-five hundred. I know damn well he ain't paying you near that much."

"Why? I don't do anything without a reason."

He broke eye contact. "I told you the reason," he said sullenly. "I can't help it if you won't believe it."

"You love her, huh? Twelve years, and you're still dragging your tail over a sixteen-year-old chick who ran away from you. That's a mite thin, Sackett. As a matter of fact, you're insulting my intelligence. As a second matter of fact, you're insulting me, offering me a bribe. That's two. Three's a bell ringer."

Boyd snorted and puffed his chest again. "Don't scare us."

"All right," Sackett said, his voice rising. "Okay, you want to know, I'll tell you. I saw her. Not much more than three years ago. In San Antone, at that Cobra Club I was talking about. I was down there at a Builders' Association Convention. She was dancing at that club. I knew her almost right away." He hesitated and smiled weakly, color creeping into his face. "We kinda . . . well, we got together again. Man, it was just like old times, like nothing had ever changed."

"Golly," I said. "True love always finds a way."

"Come on, man," Boyd Hall said, dropping a hand on Sackett's shoulder. "He ain't gonna believe anything you tell him. Don't make a fool out of yourself."

Sackett shook off the hand. "She don't want to be found," he said earnestly, a note of pleading edging into his voice. "Man, she told me. She don't never want nothing to do with her family, her brother."

"What happened to her? After your reaffirmation of love, I mean?"

He looked away, his cheeks dull red. "I don't know. I went back down there a month later like we planned. . . ." He trailed off, lips tightening, the color slowly receding. "She was gone—nobody knew where. Shit, I—" He broke off and gnawed on his lower lip.

Boyd made an angry disgusted sound. "Let's go, John. We tried, man. We can't scare him, we can't buy him off. What the hell else is there?"

"He ain't said no yet." It was a petulant hiss, a gust of noisy breath; for the first time I smelled the rank odor of whiskey.

"Yeah, he has, man. You just ain't listening."

I looked down at the cigarette, experiencing, incredibly, a twinge of pity. Then I thought of his wife's mottled face and the feeling skittered away.

"He's right, John. You're making a fool out of yourself."

"We could whip his ass," Sackett said tightly. "Both of us, we could do it."

"Man, you ain't seeing too good, neither. That ain't no banana he's got stuck in his belt there. That's a *g-u-n*, gun. Wasn't for that, I could do it by myself."

"We could hire somebody—hire us a hit man."

Hall looked at me and grimaced. He dropped his hand on Sackett's shoulder again. "Come on, man, give it up. You made your play and you crapped out. I know you ain't stupid, so quit acting like you are."

Sackett let himself be led away. Halfway down the walk he whirled: "Don't come sniffing around my house again! You stay away from there, you hear me?"

I lit the cigarette I had been holding for five minutes. I watched them drive off and wondered if I had just witnessed a stellar performance or a Greek tragedy.

/ 30 /

It was late afternoon. I was watching the news when the telephone rang. Susie lay curled on my lap asleep, her head on my shoulder. My whole right side was numb. I shook her.

"Hey, get the phone for me, will you? I can't move."

She scrambled up and a few seconds later stuck her tousled head around the doorjamb. "It's Uncle Homer, Danny."

"Tell him to hold a minute. I'll take it in the bedroom."

I hobbled down the hallway, needles and pins stabbing my right leg as feeling came back. I lit a cigarette, found an ashtray, and sprawled on the bed.

"Hi, Homer, how's it going?"

He grunted sourly. "Not worth a damn. Can't do my job for doing yours."

"Aw, come on, Homer. All I wanted was a name. What'd it take, five minutes?"

"Five minutes here, five minutes there. It all adds up. What did you want it for?"

"Just a lead, Homer. A slim lead on the Arganian girl."

He grunted again. "Well, we didn't have a RAMCO 1. We had a RAMCO 3. Lincoln limo. Registered to a man named Samuel Ramsey. That name ring a bell?"

"Not a tinkle. Who is he?"

"Hell, I don't know. We don't have a sheet on him." He sounded truculent, but I could tell there was more, and he would eventually get around to it.

"Samuel Ramsey, huh? What year was the car?"

"This year's. Hell, you don't think a rich bastard like him would drive anything but the best."

176

I laughed. "So, you do know more about him?"

He sighed with exaggerated impatience. "Well, I know I'd have to do it anyway, so I checked with Terry Blanton, that friend of mine on the *News*, you know, the guy who writes all that social and financial crap."

"Yeah. What about it?"

"Well, Terry called him a modern Midas. Made a fortune out of plastic and electronics after the war. Old as God. Been a widower for twenty years. Likes young girls—what for, I don't know, since he's around eighty-five—still goes to all the society shindigs, gives millions to charity, sponsors scholarships in engineering and medicine. He's considered an eccentric by some, a dirty old man by most. He has a home in north Dallas, a ranch in south Texas, and another home in Palm Springs, California. He has a villa in Rome, a hacienda in Mexico City . . ."

"Okay, Homer. I get the idea. What I want to know is where he is right now. And how do I get to see him?" I asked the question to shut him up, not with any inkling that he might have an answer.

He chuckled. "Me and you gonna have to work out some kind of partnership deal. I do all the work, and you collect all them fat fees."

"Yeah, well, we'll discuss that over some of that scotch of mine you like so well. Well, thanks, old buddy, you know how much I appreciate it."

"Hey, I thought you wanted to know where you could see him?"

The line hummed for a moment. "You mean you know?"

He laughed. "Hell, you know me. I don't do things halfway. When I set out to do something, it gets done."

"Would a senior partnership and all the scotch you can drink be all right?"

"I'll take the scotch. You ever hear of a town called Holmesville, Texas?"

"Sounds familiar."

"Three or four hours out on Interstate 20."

"I can find it."

"Well, if you wanted to see him, I reckon you'd have to run down there tonight."

"Tonight? Why tonight?"

"Well, from what I read in the papers, they're gonna bury him around ten in the morning."

I sighed. "Cancel the scotch, Homer. You'll be damn lucky to get a beer."

"It ain't my fault the old fart died. Musta been all them young girls. What do you reckon he did with them, anyhow?"

"Who knows? Ask me when I'm eighty-five. I wonder if they're burying him on his ranch?"

"Nope. Right there in the town cemetery. Right beside Mama and Papa and between his two wives. Don't you ever read the papers?"

"Raised around there, huh?"

"Spent the first forty years of his life there, Terry said. Raised two sons and a daughter on a half section of land that wouldn't carry a cow on twenty acres. Then his grandpa died and left him a piece of land out in west Texas with a couple dozen oil wells underneath it. Somebody come along and dug them up, and he took it from there. Terry says he reckons a hundred million ought to about sum it up."

"That's a nice round sum. About the girls. I wonder how young? Think he might go for a twenty-eight-year-old?"

"I don't know. That should seem pretty young to an eighty-five-year-old man. Hell, that seems pretty young to me. Your girl tied up with him?"

"There's a chance she may have been. I wonder how hard it would be to get to the children?"

I could visualize his shrug. "Rots of ruck, buddy, I gotta go, I've got to get out of here."

"Okay, Homer, thanks."

"Don't mention it, but just don't forget it, either." He hesitated. "How does it really look, Dan? You think you're going to find her?"

"I don't know. I don't have much faith in this RAMCO thing. The guy who gave me the information is a little off the wall, but I think he really believes he saw her in a car with that number. But he's like all the rest of them. She left him with a kind of mystical feeling about her. Hell, I feel it myself, and I'm still three or four years behind her. Sometimes I get the feeling she knows I'm back here, that she's just waiting around the next corner, waiting to see if I'm going to find her. It's an eerie feeling."

He cleared his throat. "Yeah, I can see where it might get a little dicey. Twelve years. Well, stay with it, son. Let me know what happens."

"I'll do it, Homer. And thanks again."

Susie's birthday dinner was a success. Porterhouse steak and baked potato, tossed salad, and a couple of side dishes. I burned the steaks just right.

We had a few drinks later on and watched a rerun of Roy Clark in something called *Fifty Years of Country Music*.

Actually, we only watched part of it, snatches now and then.

I gave her a watch, the first really good one she had ever owned. A tiny platinum oval, with bits of diamonds around the rim, and a narrow black velvet band. It looked positively elegant on her small wrist.

I showered and put on my navy blue pajamas and matching robe, the ones that enhance the blue in my eyes. I brushed my hair a few times and sauntered back into the den. Susie wriggled her eyebrows in appreciation and dashed off to her own ablutions and whatever else it is that women do when they are expecting more than a good-night kiss.

She came back wearing something that took my breath away. Voluminous, flesh-colored, and filmy, it would have been transparent had it not been for the multitudinous folds and pleats and tucks.

We had another drink and made our way to the bedroom during the last twenty-five years of country music.

I went into the bathroom, and it was when I came out that I remembered something I had forgotten about my wife: three drinks were too many. She lay sprawled across the bed, lovely and alluring and passed out cold.

/ 31 /

It was a dreary day for a funeral. A cold drizzling rain fell out of a sky that looked like a dirty old woolen blanket, hanging low and sullen with occasional threadbare patches revealing unexpected glimpses of gray-blue.

Maybe the weather accounts for the turnout, I thought, as I turned into the entrance to the cemetery and headed toward a half-dozen cars parked along the road thirty yards below a small huddled group of people. The last car in line was a sheriff's cruiser; a short stocky uniformed figure climbed out as I braked to a stop behind it. He strolled toward me, his lips held tightly together under the low-crowned, wide-brimmed hat. He carried a plastic-covered clipboard with a ballpoint pen dangling from a string.

I rolled down the window. Obviously, he was going to check me out, and I couldn't see any point in getting wet unnecessarily. He understood my reasoning, and a scowl settled on his wide brow. His tone was cordial enough, however.

"Could I have your name, sir?"

"It's Dan Roman, and to save you the trouble of looking, I'm not on your list. I'm not a relative, and I'm not a friend of the deceased. I'd like to talk to one of his sons or his daughter if it can be arranged."

His scowl deepened. "What about?"

"Business."

His frosty eyes stared at me for a moment, and I thought he was going to let it go, but he decided not to. Rain gathered on the brim of his hat and ran through the window onto my arm.

"What business?"

"Mine and theirs," I said. Abuse of authority and unnecessary intrusion into the lives of private citizens had always been one of my pet peeves, even when I was a policeman. I had no desire to alienate the scowling man before me, but I had no intention of letting him cow me, either.

He glanced toward the gathering on the hill, a small war going on inside him. Authority won.

"I reckon if they knew you were coming, they would have told me. You'd best turn this car around and head on out, mister. These people are bereaved. They got no mind for business today."

"Don't you think," I said reasonably, "that should be their decision?"

His eyes lit up. He was on firm ground now. He had given me an order, no matter how oblique, and I had not responded with the required alacrity. Deliberately or unconsciously, his hand dropped to the holstered gun slung low on his right hip. His voice lost its cordiality, became crisp and authoritative.

"I gave you an order, mister. I don't hear the motor on that car."

"Before you do something we'll both regret," I said affably, "I think you'd better get on your radio and talk to Sheriff Breslin. The name's Dan Roman, in case you forgot."

He stared at me for a long cold moment before he turned and walked to the cruiser. He opened the door and reached inside, then stood in the open door and talked into the mike while he watched me, his right hand still propped lightly on the butt of his gun. After a moment, he snapped the mike away from his face and abruptly got into the car. I grinned at the back of his head through the blurry windshield. Score one for the masses. And for Homer's connections.

I was on my third cigarette when the group of people began to slowly break away from the gravesite.

I got out and walked up to the cruiser and rapped on the window. It came down slowly.

I smiled in at him. "Would you mind pointing out the Ramseys to me? I assume they're all here."

He grunted, and I stepped back so he could open the door. He walked off toward the head of the line of cars. I followed him. The rain had slowed to a fine blowing mist, just enough to be irritating to the eyes and aggravating to the soul.

Two men and two women stopped beside the second limousine in line, and the deputy stepped up to them and touched his hat respectfully. They all turned to look at me, and the larger of the two men shook his head emphatically. He made a short sharp gesture with his hand, and they got into the limousine and drove away.

I walked up behind the deputy. "Thanks. I only wanted you to point them out, not intercede for me."

He gave me a nasty grin and shrugged. "I told you, buddy. They don't want to talk business today."

"How about the girl?"

His eyes flicked involuntarily toward the gravesite, to where a lone figure in a raincoat and hat still stood. Two men in work clothes waited near a backhoe parked farther up the hill.

"Thanks," I said, and grinned. I ignored his blustery "Hey, now," and walked toward the girl. She had turned away from the grave and was coming down. I waited halfway up the rise.

"Miss Ramsey?"

She stopped a few feet away. The section of her face I could see under the rain hood was round and plump and pretty. Her eyes, red-rimmed and swollen, were a curious shade of slate-gray. They stared at me quietly, unblinking.

"Yes."

"My name is Dan Roman, Miss Ramsey. I'm very sorry to bother you on this sad occasion, but I was wondering if I could have a few minutes of your time. It concerns your father, and it's very important."

"Nothing concerns my father anymore."

"What I meant was, it concerns someone your father knew."

She eyed me steadily for a long moment, then nodded slightly. "Do you have a car, Mr. Roman? I only live a few miles from here. We could talk on the way if you like."

"That would be fine."

We walked back down the hill. I waited beside my car while she talked to the driver of the limousine, turning to look at the deputy standing at the open door of his cruiser. Surprisingly, he grinned and gave me a casual thumbs-up signal before dropping out of view behind his foggy windshield.

She lit a cigarette as soon as we got inside the car, producing cigarettes and lighter from a raincoat pocket.

I followed the limousine out of the cemetery and onto a winding blacktop road. The limousine turned right; she directed me to the left, and we drove for at least five minutes in silence before she stubbed out the cigarette and turned somber eyes in my direction.

"What was it you wanted, Mr. Roman?"

"I'm a private investigator, Miss Ramsey. I'm looking for a girl . . . a woman. She was last seen in your father's company." I fished the picture out of my jacket pocket and handed it to her. She glanced at it once, then handed it back to me.

"Janine Conroy," she said. "Yes, she was one of my father's friends." She punched the dash cigarette lighter. "One of many," she added absently, her voice flat and noncommittal. She pushed back the rain cowl and lit another cigarette.

"Could you tell me anything about her?" I cracked a window to let out some of the smoke.

"Not very much, actually."

"Anything at all would help. How long was she with your father?"

"Six or seven months, I suppose. Something like that. She was older than most. Twenty-six or -seven. Very lovely. A very sweet person. She was his bedmate."

I glanced at her. "You didn't mind?"

She gave me a startled look. "Mind? Heavens no. Why should I mind? That poor old man got little enough out of life the last few years. No, I didn't mind. I encouraged it, as a matter of fact." She unbuttoned the raincoat and let it fall away. She was wearing a dark gray turtleneck sweater and a black skirt, with no jewelry, no hint of adornment.

"Janine left your father after a few months, then?"

"Yes. Father was very upset, as usual. He began wetting the bed again. He always did that when one of his girls left him. He was somewhat like a child in that respect."

"These women . . . were they nurses, companions, or what?"

She laughed softly. "They were for just what you think they were for. They were for sex."

It was my turn to look startled. "But at his age? Surely . . ."

She laughed again. "Not in the usual sense, Mr. Roman. All he could manage was touching, stroking, drooling over them. My father was perfectly lucid right up to the end. He wasn't senile, at least not in a legal sense. Quite the opposite. That was one of his greatest problems. He lost his ability to command his body, but his mind remained sharp and clear. My dear brothers tried to have him declared senile and incompetent, but he bested them to the very end. He was a very lusty man, and his mind never let him forget that. He remembered how it was to have sex, but his body couldn't respond. Imagine the frustration! That was the reason for the girls, pure and simple. They were well compensated, believe me. Janine was one of his favorites. I think he gave her somewhere around a half-million dollars."

"Jesus Christ!"

She laughed. "It is an obscene sum, isn't it?"

"It's hard to believe."

"Janine was special. She did something none of the others would ever do. She slept in the bed with him, held him in her arms . . . and even when he wet the bed, she never scolded him. The others would never do that. They allowed him to touch them, you know, but they would never sleep with him or hold him. I can't say that I blamed them. He was nothing but skin and bones—" She broke off, a shudder in her voice. "I could barely stand to touch him myself." She mashed out the cigarette and immediately lit another. "It sounds terrible, doesn't it?" She gave me a white-toothed, mocking smile.

"Not terrible. Sad. Nobody should live to be that old unless they're able to navigate on their own."

She nodded. "Live hard, die early, and leave a good-looking corpse. I read that somewhere." Her face lit up again with the brief wide smile. "Not too young."

"You don't know where Janine might have gone?"

"Why do you want her?"

"It's a family matter. Her mother is near death, grieving for her wayward daughter, that kind of thing."

She was watching me again. "You don't look like a policeman. You're much too clean-cut."

"A private investigator is not a policeman."

"It must be an exciting job."

"Not always. Mostly I try to find people."

"What do you do when you find them?"

"Nothing. I contact the one who hired me. They take it from there."

"That's all you do? That sounds pretty dull."

"Mostly it is. Long hours, bad food, and a lot of questions. I ask a lot of questions. Like the one I just asked you. Do you happen to know where Janine went? Where she is now?"

"What will happen if you find her?"

"I'll notify her brother. It'll be up to him to persuade her to come home to see her mother."

"What if she's married? What if she doesn't want her husband to know anything about her past? What then?"

"I guess I'd have to balance that against an old lady dying without knowing what became of her only daughter. What would you do, Miss Ramsey?"

"You call me miss. How do you know I've never been married?"

I shrugged. "I asked around."

"We're almost there. Turn left at that line of trees just ahead." She lit another cigarette. "Don't you wonder why someone thirty years old has never been married, Mr. Roman?"

I made the turn into the gravel lane before I answered. "I wondered. But not very much."

She had a nice laugh when she worked at it. "You're a rare thing—an honest man."

I smiled wryly. "I wouldn't count on it."

"Oh, yes, but you are. You want something from me, and you could have pretended interest, curiosity at least. No, I think basically you're an honest man."

I pulled into a circular drive and stopped in front of concrete steps leading to a two-story modern brick house. I looked at it with surprised interest.

"Somehow I expected to see an old ranch house. This is a working ranch, isn't it?"

She laughed. "This is it, with a face-lift. Father turned this ranch over to me ten years ago. I remodeled. We dismantled the outbuildings and corral and moved them down beyond the hill. Only the inside is the same—at least partly. Would you like to see it?"

"I don't think so, Miss Ramsey. If you can't tell me anything more about Janine, I'll be going."

She stubbed out the cigarette with a quick nervous movement. "I'm too much like my father," she said without looking at me. "I like sex. But I have one problem with that: I like it with different people." She looked at me then and smiled coolly. "That's why I haven't married. I haven't found a man I cared for who would tolerate that. Is that what you wanted to know?"

"No," I said. "I only wanted to know about Janine."

She shook her head. "You can carry honesty too far, Mr. Roman."

I shrugged. "It's like anything else; it gets to be a bore."

"You're sure you wouldn't like to come inside for a while? I'm all alone here." There was almost, but not quite, a pleading note in her voice. "Perhaps later we could talk some more about Janine."

I studied her smiling face for a long time, until her cool composure began to fade along with the smile, until the color began to mount in her face.

"What you mean," I said quietly, "is that you know where

186

she is, and if I'll go to bed with you, you'll tell me?" I smiled to take the sting out of it in case I was wrong.

"Bingo, Mr. Roman."

"You're pretty honest yourself."

"Then you're interested?"

I shook my head slowly. "I'm afraid not. I'm not above a quick roll in the hay, particularly with an attractive lady like you. But I like to do the asking. Just something left over from the old chauvinistic days. I've been known to do a lot of things for my clients, but whoring isn't one of them."

She looked straight ahead through the windshield; her voice came low and sad. "This is a bad day for me, Mr. Roman. I loved that old man we put into the ground today. I'm the only one who did. I'm lonely, and I need someone. Maybe if you would just come in and talk and hold me ..." Her voice faded, and she turned puckered lips and a quivering chin in my direction.

But I was watching her eyes, and I grinned and tapped her lightly on the chin.

"Hey! That was pretty good. Is that how you got around the old man? I'll bet you ripped his heart out with that one."

"You bastard!" she said, her eyes flashing. But her voice lacked conviction, and in a few moments she sighed. "Give me one of your cards. The best I can do is talk to her. It will be her decision." Her mouth quirked. "I hope she tells me to tell you to go to hell."

"How soon?"

She made an exasperated motion with one plump hand. "I don't know, dammit! A few days. I'll call you—collect." She looked at me soberly. "And don't try any of your private eye tricks on me, or you'll never talk to her. I'm the only living person who knows where she is, and if I see you or anything suspicious, the trail will end here, period."

"No tricks," I said solemnly. I held up my right hand. "I swear on the canceled shows of my pals Magnum and Rockford."

Her eyes glinted. "You're a smart-ass too," she said mildly.

It had stopped raining. She got out and took off the raincoat and folded it across her arm. I watched her go up the walk.

Everything was there, in correct proportion, a tad overblown perhaps, but the face made up for a lot. I started the car and continued around the circular drive and into the lane.

I was experiencing a mild exhilaration, a gentle increase in the pulsing of my blood, a heady feeling that I knew from past experience would build slowly to intense anticipation now that I had scented my quarry, now that I knew she existed in the here and now, now that I knew with a reasonable certainty that I was going to come face-to-face with her at last.

But why, I wondered as I turned onto the narrow blacktop highway, why was I feeling underneath it all so damned apprehensive and melancholy?

/ *32* /

By the time I reached Interstate 20, it had begun to rain again, a steady drizzle that slicked the highway and slowed traffic almost to the speed limit. As a result it was midafternoon by the time I reached Midway City.

I was in a foul mood, tired and hungry, and the fact that Susie wasn't home added one more muddy smear to an already dirty day. Even thoughts of her fade-out on me the night before failed to raise as much as a sour chuckle.

I made a sandwich from greasy packaged bologna and ate it in the den with a cold beer and a tennis match on television. Two long-haired young men with the killer instinct in their eyes. I awoke later with a start to a cheering crowd on the TV, and Susie coming in the front door.

Moments later, she was standing over me with a warm

smile and an indulgent expression on her face. She dropped onto the arm of my chair and slid into my lap.

"Is my poor baby tired this afternoon? Is him having a little bitty nap?"

She kissed me before I could say anything nasty, and by the time she finished, I was out of the mood. She combed her fingers through my hair. I smothered a yawn.

She laughed. "Oh, boy. Am I boring you?" Her eyes twinkled mischievously. "You weren't so bored last night." There was a tiny thread of uncertainty in her voice.

I mustered up a grin. "How do you feel today?"

"Oh, I feel wonderful!" she gushed, her eyes still searching my face for a clue. "Did—how about . . . was it good for you?"

"It was terrific, sweetheart," I said, unable to stop my grin from growing.

"Danny! Why are you grinning?" Her face sobered. "I wasn't any good! I had too much to drink."

I hugged her. "You couldn't have been better."

"Really? Then why do you look so funny?"

"When I'm happy, I look funny. So, shoot me."

"That might be fun, too," she said tartly and slid off my lap. She stalked to the couch and sat down. She pushed the hair away from her flushed face and changed the subject, almost certain that I was putting her on, not sure why, or what to do about it.

"Did you find out anything, Danny?"

I nodded, managing to get rid of my grin.

"It was a good lead after all. The Ramsey girl said she knows where Nancy is. She said she'd set up a meeting."

She had been watching me intently and didn't miss the lack of enthusiam in my voice.

"You sound like you don't much care anymore."

I lit a cigarette and pushed back in the chair. "I guess I don't, strangely enough. She's not a poor little girl anymore. If the Ramsey woman can be believed, she has, or had, a half-million dollars two years ago. The old man gave it to her."

"What on earth for?"

"Because she gave such good back rubs, I guess. The point is, with that kind of money, she could set up a pretty decent life-style."

"Lordy, I can imagine."

I shrugged. "On the other hand, she may not have a dime. She's a pushover for a sob story or a smooth operator with a good line."

She smiled faintly, her expression enigmatic. "You talk as if you know her."

I returned her smile. "You're right, I do feel like I know her. Better than anyone else in the world, I guess—except you."

"Just keep it that way, buster," she said, her face softening. "I think I almost dread having you meet her, this mysterious lady you've been chasing for so long."

I nodded. "I've had a weird feeling for a long time," I said slowly. "As if there's something I should know and I'm missing. Something I should be aware of and I'm not. It's worse since I talked to Christine Ramsey this morning. I don't know, I have a feeling of . . . of reluctance, a strange compulsion to let it go and walk away. Sometimes I feel she's there in the darkness somewhere, watching, waiting—waiting to see if she's going to have to come out into the light, out of the shadows."

"Maybe it's because you're so close," she said quietly. "Maybe you're afraid the reality of her won't measure up to your romantic fantasy. And don't tell me you don't have one, Danny. I know you better than you think."

I stared at her thoughtfully; sometimes she displayed an annoying insight beyond her tender years. I shook my head. "Nancy is the one with the romantic fantasy. Most of her life's been spent chasing some improbable dream, looking for new answers, a new life, or maybe just a better way to live the old one. It'd be easy to romanticize her, I guess, but I don't think I could. I know too much about her now, the life she's led, the things she's done, all the men—"

"That's all part of it." She leaned forward eagerly. "Those things can repel, but they can attract, too. Why do men go to prostitutes? Women that have had hundreds of other men? Why do promiscuous women attract men in droves? Some of them aren't even attractive. History is filled with them. Cleopatra, Helen of Troy, Messalina, Julia . . . they weren't all pretty, but men ran after them like dogs. And not only in history. Even in high school we had girls—" She broke off, her face coloring. "Listen to me, the sex expert," she said lightly.

"Hey," I said. "Not only beautiful, but deep, too."

"Oh, hush," she said, her color deepening, but I could tell she was pleased. "Whom are you going to see next?"

"The younger son, Mark Ramsey. The sheriff said he was a pretty decent sort. He said the older one was a bastard."

"Why? If the Ramsey woman is going to fix it up for you to meet Nancy?"

"That may take days. Maybe Mark knows as much or more than she does. It's something to do while I'm waiting. I want to get this thing over. Get it done. I feel something's wrong about it, and it's bugging me."

"You can quit, Danny. Just tell Mr. Arganian you couldn't find her."

I shook my head. "It doesn't work that way. You're probably right. Meeting her may well turn out to be a sorry anticlimax. She may be fat and frumpy and married with a kid by now—solid establishment. Money can do that to you."

The half smile came back to her face. "Would that be so terrible? Fat and frumpy, I mean. I may be that way some day, you know."

"Not a chance. You may get fat, but you'll never be frumpy. That's a state of mind more than a condition."

"We'll see," she said darkly.

/ 33 /

Mark Ramsey's office was on the seventh floor of the Friedman Building. His secretary was a petite, slender woman with long straight red hair, glasses with lenses the size of saucers, and a large black mole on her chin. I looked at her wedding ring and wondered why in God's name her husband didn't have the thing removed. She had a pretty face, a pleasant voice, and a very nice smile, but I couldn't keep my eyes off the mole.

"Do you have an appointment, Mr. Roman?" she asked in a voice that said she knew damn well I didn't.

"No, ma'am," I said, "but if you'd just tell him my name and that I'd like a few minutes to talk about a girl named Janine Conroy, maybe he'd work me in." I smiled winningly and lifted a finger. "You might add that this is the same Miss Conroy who used to . . . to nurse his father."

"I'll try, sir." She absently rubbed the mole with the thumb of her right hand. "But he's awfully busy." She pushed a button on the interoffice console, then changed her mind, pushed another one, and got to her feet. "Just a minute, sir."

She went through a door marked simply: M. Ramsey, Private. She came back almost at once. She smiled sweetly and held open the door.

"He'll see you, sir."

I looked past her in time to see the slender man behind the desk get to his feet. He was nattily dressed in a dark blue suit and a pale pink shirt, open at the collar, and had black hair streaked with gray and a thin unsmiling face. He looked to be about forty-five. His hand was as limp and cold as a sock filled with wet sand.

"Mr. Roman," he said.

"Mr. Ramsey. Thanks for seeing me."

"Please have a seat. I understand you've come about a . . . a Miss Conroy?"

"Janine Conroy, Mr. Ramsey. I believe she worked for your father for a few months."

"Yes, well . . ." he said. He had deep worry lines across his forehead and heavy eyebrows above dark blue eyes that looked everywhere in the tastefully furnished office except at me.

"Yes, well," he said again, his wandering gaze finally coming back to me. "Well, Mr. Roman, I knew someone would come some day, of course." He picked up my card from his desk with thin white fingers.

"You're a private detective. I assume you're working for Miss Conroy's parents." It was a statement rather than a question, and he didn't look up.

"We tried to locate them," he went on, "but after a respectable amount of time . . . you understand, of course?" He coughed into his hand. "It was indecent to keep her any longer." His eyes began their drifting routine again.

I leaned forward in the chair, the first faint tendrils of chilling premonition creeping into my mind.

"Keep her where?"

His eyebrows flew upward like tiny startled birds. "Why—why at the mortuary, of course. We kept her for two months, Mr. Roman. I'm sure you'll agree that is . . . was a proper amount of time."

I took the picture out of my pocket and stared down at it. A wave of weakness swept over me; I felt a hard dry knot building in my chest, expanding into my throat, drying my mouth.

"You're saying she's dead?"

"Why, why—" he took a deep breath—"why, yes, of course. Isn't that . . . I thought you knew." He went on with a rush. "If the parents want her moved, we'll be more than happy to have it done. All expenses paid, of course. Please don't—"

I leaned over his desk and held the picture in front of his face. "This is the girl you're talking about?"

"Why, yes, I believe . . . yes, that's her. Only somewhat older and a bit thinner, I believe. I saw her only a few times. But, yes, that is Janine Conroy . . . I'm sorry, was Janine Conroy. She was killed in an accident. A riding accident on my father's ranch."

"Riding accident? Horseback riding?"

"Yes, of course. She rode quite often, I understand. Loved it, in fact, according to my sister."

"Your sister. Why would your sister lie about Janine Conroy? Why would she tell me she knew where she was, that she would try to get her to talk to me?"

He leaned back in his chair and pinched his nose between thin fingers. "She told you that?"

"After your father's funeral. I drove her home."

He nodded. "I'm afraid my sister is sometimes . . . irrational, Mr. Roman. She has a very macabre sense of humor. I don't know why she would say that, but I can believe she did."

"Dammit," I said savagely, "it doesn't make any sense."

He sighed. "Christine rarely ever does."

"The accident. How did it happen?" The knot in my chest had given way to frustration and an aching sense of loss.

"She was riding where she shouldn't have been," he said primly. "Along the north ridge. A very narrow trail, an animal trail really. There's a very steep ravine below. The horse evidently slipped or became frightened and fell. She was trapped underneath . . . all the way to the bottom. It—it tore her up rather badly, I'm afraid. They didn't find her until the next afternoon—it's terribly rough country out there—and I'm afraid the animals had been at them. It was terribly . . . sad."

"And you were sure the girl was Janine Conroy? Was the identification positive?"

"Oh, yes. There was no doubt. My sister identified her. Of course there was no one else on the ranch except a couple of ranch hands at the time."

"And you are sure this was the girl?" I held out the photograph again, and he took it silently. He looked at it politely for a moment, then handed it back to me and nodded his head.

"I'm terribly sorry, but yes, that is the girl."

"Was there an effort made to trace her, identify her legally?"

"Yes, of course. Sheriff Breslin checked her fingerprints, but there was no record anywhere that he could find. She had told Christine her parents were dead, but there seemed to be conflicting accounts at different times, and I'm not surprised to find that she was lying. I'm very sure that few of the girls my sister procured for my father gave their correct names. A large number of them were no doubt runaways. A very distressing business, at least."

"Distressing for whom?"

He gave me a startled look. "Why—why, my father, of course. And the girls, some of them."

"Why do you say that? I thought the girls were hired to take care of your father."

He uttered a short mirthless laugh. "Christine's version, I'm afraid. Ostensibly that was the reason. But in actuality, my sister hired the girls—for my sister."

"You're saying your sister is a lesbian, Mr. Ramsey?"

"Unfortunately, it isn't a very well-kept secret."

"But she—" I began, then cut it off and thought about it for a moment.

He smiled faintly. "She came on to you?"

"Yes, as a matter of fact, she did."

"She wouldn't have delivered. Christine has a rather virulent hatred for all men, I'm afraid. Now that our father is dead, my brother and I move to the top of her list."

"It wasn't obvious."

"Oh, she's a master at concealing it. She's had plenty of practice. My mother was fifty when she was born. A menopause baby. My sister was around six or seven when she finally realized that they neither wanted nor loved her. One could assume that is why she is the way she is."

"Yes," I said, "one could. Where were you and your brother?"

"Away at military school most of the time. Then the oblig-

195

atory years in the service. The sapling was already bent before we could be of any assistance."

"If you were so distressed, you could have taken your father away from the ranch."

"Oh, no, not at all. I think you misunderstood me. My father was all that my sister undoubtedly said he was. The girls were ostensibly hired as ... as playmates for him. But Christine did the hiring, the screening, that sort of thing. I'm sure they were amenable to her ... her persuasion, shall we say."

"Where was Janine buried?"

"In the same cemetery where my father was buried. As a matter of fact, she was buried in a corner of the family plot."

"That was charitable of you," I said, making no attempt to keep sarcasm out of my voice.

His face stiffened. "Our intentions were good. We felt that was the least we could do under the circumstances."

"But in hallowed ground," I murmured, and regretted it instantly. "I'm sorry, Mr. Ramsey. That was uncalled for." I glanced at my watch. "I must be keeping you past your closing time." I stood up. "One more thing. Who paid the girls?"

"Christine handled it, I'm sure, but the money came from my father. Some of the sums were quite substantial, I believe."

"You don't know?"

He shook his head, and the stingy smile returned. "My father maintained control of his affairs right up to the end. His mind remained remarkably clear. It wouldn't have mattered at any rate. Christine had power of attorney for his personal fortune. Dempsey and I were too straitlaced for him, you see."

He came around the desk and leaned against one corner. His face seemed to relax, and he smiled a frank uncluttered smile. "There was something so obscene about it. Those bony old hands ... all that young female flesh." His shoulders rippled in either a shrug or a shudder. "I'm sure the girls earned every penny. Christine would have seen to that. It was a regrettable situation but quite beyond our control. Dempsey and I handled the business, and Christine took care of the old man. A classic love-hate relationship if there ever was one."

"Yes," I said, and moved toward the door. I was learning more than I wanted to know. But I wasn't to escape so lightly. Mark Ramsey beat me to the door and stood with his hand on the knob.

"After money," he said, his voice suddenly thick and ugly, "women were his only interest in life. His family, my mother, meant nothing to him. Not just a woman occasionally, but lots of them, all the time. My poor mother . . ." Saliva leaked at the corner of his mouth. "No wonder poor Christine turned out the way she did. Unloved, unwanted, a whoremonger for a father, a mother who retreated to her prayer beads and her plaster saints." His thick eyebrows danced up and down over glittering eyes. "It's a wonder we all didn't turn out to be hopeless paranoids . . . paranoiacs, whatever." His eyes were glaring, but they were looking inward, into some burning cesspool of hate I couldn't begin to comprehend.

I smiled sympathetically and made a motion toward the doorknob still clutched in his white-knuckled hand. He opened the door and preceded me into the small outer office.

The pretty girl with the mole was gone, her desk neatly cleared, her typewriter precisely covered.

"When Christine was twelve or thirteen," he said huskily, moving his clenched fists in short uncontrolled circles, "that filthy bastard began taking her into his bed." He sucked in his breath in a hissing sob. "We all knew it, but nobody did anything about it. We were all afraid of him—him!—a runty, cocky little son of a bitch even I could have broken like a dead branch. But we were all afraid." His features were suddenly slack, his eyes empty. "God! I'm glad that son of a bitch is dead!"

I crossed to the outer door, and he didn't move. I opened it and stepped out into the corridor. I left him staring into the empty space where I had been.

/ 34 /

Phillip Arganian stared at me intently, his eyes fixed and unreadable. When I finished, he got up and walked to a floor-to-ceiling window that looked out over Fort Worth. He pushed back the drapes and peered into the neon-speckled darkness.

"You're sure of this, Mr. Roman? You're absolutely certain my sister is dead?"

"As sure as anyone can be without seeing her body. There was no way to verify her fingerprints, according to the sheriff. Evidently they were never recorded."

He came back and sat down at his desk. "You saw her grave?"

"No. I only learned about it after I came back home."

He nodded and placed his hands flat on the top of his desk, fingers widespread. "Very well. At least we know. That was what I asked of you." The fingers of his right hand drummed on the solid shining wood. "If you'd like, I can give you a check now, or you can submit your bill with your report."

"Later will be fine. I'll send you a bill." I hesitated. "The report, Mr. Arganian—I'm not sure you want to know all that I've found out about your sister. Some of it isn't very pretty."

His head shook emphatically. "No, Mr. Roman. I want to know. You will remember that was one of the conditions of your employment. I—I didn't know my sister well before she ran away. It's . . . I feel I owe it to her to at least know how she lived her life. I feel a great sense of responsibility for what happened to her. Perhaps if I had spent more time with her, tried harder to be a brother after we lost our father—" He broke off and shook his head again, slowly. "No, Mr. Roman. Please. I need to know. The bad as well as the good. Everything."

"I'll have your report for you tomorrow, Mr. Arganian." I smiled thinly. "Just the way you wanted. The whole ball of wax."

I tried to warm my smile a little, wondering at the sudden animosity I felt.

It could be his money—but that had never bothered me before. His young beautiful wife? That hadn't bothered me, either; I had a young beautiful wife of my own.

Maybe, I thought, it was because he displayed absolutely no grief at the death of his sister, didn't even bother to ask how or why.

When I got out of bed the next day, I found a note from Susie stuck to the refrigerator with a green metallic frog.

Janey and I have gone shopping, love. I'll see you when I get back. P.S. I hope your head is killing you!

It was too early for a drink, so I had a glass of milk, reread Susie's note and chuckled.

On my way back from Phillip Arganian's, I had stopped by Club 45, Midway City's favorite watering hole for off-duty cops, firemen, miscellaneous city employees, and a not inconsiderable number of minor hoodlums.

Homer Sellers was there, as usual, glowering glumly into his beer and proclaiming loudly to all who would listen that the citizens of Midway City were a sorry ungrateful lot—especially them city council bastards—and not deserving of a police captain of such sterling caliber as he.

I made the mistake of asking him what his problem was, and spent the rest of the evening ensconced in a back booth bending my elbows at regular intervals while he told me.

He was still telling me when we parted in the parking lot at one o'clock in the morning. I drove home slowly and carefully, only to find him parked in the center of my front lawn. Braced against the side of his car with his left hand, he was staring with drunken intensity at the amber liquid splashing off his left rear tire and onto my lawn.

"Dammit, Homer, you're killing my grass."

"I had to pee, boy. I didn't know where else to go."

"Go piss on your own lawn."

He stared at me, his eyes magnified owlishly behind the bifocals.

"I ain't there, boy, I'm here," he said reasonably.

He was admittedly too drunk to drive, as was I, and we sat on the grass for a while and had a drink from his emergency bottle while we discussed ways and means.

He emphatically declined to spend the night, or what was left of it, at my house. He explained at length that, as a dedicated police officer, he was on call at all times and, while the ungrateful bastards didn't deserve him, he was duty bound to keep himself available. That made sense to me.

We sat cross-legged in the grass, passing the bottle back and forth.

We were near the bottom of the bottle when he came up with the solution to our present dilemma. He climbed cautiously to his feet, staggered around in a small circle, giggled, put his finger to his lips for absolute quiet, and tiptoed to his car.

Speaking rapidly and with amazing clarity, he barked out my address and the call number for "policeman down and needs help."

He broke the connection and was still giggling as he slowly settled to the grass, stretched out comfortably, and passed out cold.

Having no particular desire to be shot by an overzealous rookie, I watched the proceedings from inside my house.

Within minutes three squad cars converged, sirens screaming, lights flashing, and lights began to brighten windows up and down the street. A crowd quickly gathered; a knot of blue-coated figures stood silently around the somnolent figure on the ground. One, a tall thin man with sergeant's stripes, leaned against Homer's car, one hand covering his face, his body shaking.

I never did get to see how it came out. My own lights came on, and I remembered turning to face an indignant Susie. I also remembered thinking fondly that she was looking more beautiful every day, when somebody somewhere pulled a switch, and all the lights went off everywhere. . . .

At noon I had a beer, ate a bologna sandwich, and watched the news. All upbeat stuff: five murders during the past twenty-four hours; more fraud in the Fort Worth school district; a mother and two children burned to death in a clapboard shanty in south Dallas; another dump site of poisonous chemical waste discovered in Tarrant County; one more rehash of the last pitiful Cowboys game, and to top it all off, my favorite weatherman newscaster had been scheduled to receive bypass surgery. Just the thing to add a little shine to a dull overcast day. I was reaching for the remote control when the phone rang.

I took it in the kitchen, grabbing another beer before picking up the receiver. I grunted something appropriate.

"Mr. Roman?"

"Speaking."

"Marissa Arganian here. I trust I'm not interrupting your lunch." Her voice seemed oddly subdued, almost childlike.

"Not at all."

"I just had a visit from Phillip, Mr. Roman. He told me you had—" She broke off. I heard the sound of a ragged indrawn breath. "Is it true, Mr. Roman? Is my daughter dead?"

There was only one way I could think of to say it. "Yes, ma'am. To the best of my knowledge."

The line hummed for a moment; another heavy breath, or a sigh. "I understand she died here in Texas. Do you suppose . . . perhaps it's possible she was making her way home?"

"Yes, that's entirely possible." I didn't believe it for a moment, but it no longer mattered.

"I will have her moved, of course. Don't you think that's best?"

"Yes. That's what I would do."

Silence descended again. I lit a cigarette and tasted my beer.

"Did she have a . . . a bad life, Mr. Roman?"

It was my turn to hesitate. Phillip would have the facts, but I very much doubted if he would pass them along to her.

"No, ma'am, I don't think so. I believe she mostly did what she wanted to do. Few of us can say the same. More important, I think she was happy."

"I hope so." She sighed. "You know I feel a great deal of guilt."

"Join the club, Mrs. Arganian. We're all human. It's our natural state."

She made a sound that could have been a sob or a quiet chuckle. "Thank you, Mr. Roman. You did your job very well. I shall instruct Phillip to give you a small bonus."

"No," I said, my tone more brittle than I intended. "My fee is adequate."

"Very well," she said, her voice regaining some of its normal strength. "Thank you again."

"You're welcome."

I hung up, stubbed out the cigarette, and upended the beer can to help ameliorate the bitter taste in my mouth. Mrs. Arganian, like her son Phillip, had not expressed any curiosity whatsoever about the circumstances of her daughter's death. And I found that extremely difficult to understand.

I flipped off the set, pulled another beer tab, and prowled restlessly around my backyard. It was a cold day, threatening to rain again, and I was soon back inside.

I stacked a random handful of records on the stereo and slouched in a chair by the front window, staring out at the empty lifeless day that added scope and dimension to my already burgeoning discontent.

I listened to sad songs about cheating wives and wandering husbands, about pain and losing, crippled children and truck-driving men—and one ancient Sinatra that made me remember another day in another room.

I finally turned the damn thing off and did what I knew I was going to do all along: I drove west to see the grave of Nancy Taylor.

/ 35 /

The rain caught up with me seventy miles southwest of Fort Worth, and by the time I reached the cemetery, it had settled into a steady blowing drizzle, the kind that soaks the earth and invades the soul.

A blue-and-white Scout sat where the hearse had been parked. It had wide fat tires; its sides and windows were streaked with mud.

I wiped the steam from my windshield and spotted the solitary figure at the top of the hill.

She wore a long raincoat with a black hood, and there was something sad and lonely and depressing in the slumped shoulders and bowed head.

I sloshed through the wet grass and puddled water to stand beside her.

It was a good five minutes before she acknowledged my presence. She finally turned to look at me. I felt a rumble of shock at the slack face, empty of emotion. Wordlessly, she turned back to resume her vigil.

"Where's the girl's grave?"

She lifted one arm and pointed a chubby finger. I walked in that direction. I found a flat metal marker tucked among the huge granite monstrosities on the surrounding graves. I stood looking down at it, not feeling much of anything. I had expected, at the very least, a flash of grief, pity—something. But nothing worked its way up through the scar tissue.

"She's not in there, you know." Her voice came from behind me, low and dull and close.

I whirled to face her. "Not in where?" I said inanely.

"Janine. She's not in that hole."

We stared at each other for a moment. Hot anger exploded inside me like spontaneous applause. I took two swift strides and grabbed her shoulders. The stiff rubberized material felt slick and slimy under my fingers.

"Don't lie to me, dammit! No more games! You understand?"

She gazed back at me placidly, her round freckled face expressionless. She shook her head. "I talked to her the way I said I would. She'll meet you."

I shook her. "You're lying again, Christine! I talked to Mark! He told me about you, your lies!" I was yelling in her face. Her eyes blinked, then slowly widened with something like wonder.

"Why don't you believe me?" she asked plaintively, her voice thin, childlike.

"Stop it, dammit," I yelled. I shook her harder, then harder still. I was so absorbed in my anger that I never saw the knee that exploded in my groin. I yelled, doubled over, and dropped to my knees in the puddles of rain, my hands scrabbling at my center, white waves of searing exquisite pain radiating upward, bringing murky darkness, then light filled with shooting stars.

I fell on my side, curled into a tight fetal ball and opened my mouth so the vomit could run out and not choke me. I hung suspended, encapsulated in a tiny world dominated by absurdity and pain.

Her voice seemed far away and dismal. "Why wouldn't you believe me?" I felt her hands at the pocket of my jacket. "There's the address and the time and everything."

I heard the splash of her feet in the puddles. I opened one eye and watched without much interest as she marched sturdily toward the Scout. She never looked back.

"Honestly, Danny, I don't believe this! Running around in this kind of weather! My God, you look like you've been wallowing in mud!"

"I fell," I said defensively, and sneezed. I was standing dejected and shivering in the bathroom, feeling the blast of warm air from the overhead register, Susie's fingers peeling away my stiff and muddy clothing layer by layer.

"You're going to be sick again," she said accusingly, and slapped away my hands when I tried to take off my own shorts.

She opened the door to the shower and half pushed, half lifted me into the pelting streams of hot water.

My God, I thought, she'll be a martinet at forty.

She stood watching me, amusement and concern warring for supremacy in her face. "What happened?"

"I fell," I said, lifting my face to the warmth of the stinging spray.

"You said that. Did you find her grave?"

I stared at her. "How did you know?"

She made a wry face. "I'm not dumb, Danny. I knew sooner or later you'd have to go. But I didn't think you'd do it in this kind of weather." She paused, then went on softly. "I was right, wasn't I?"

"About what, Susan?"

"Don't be coy," she said tartly. "You know what I mean. About you and Nancy. You were . . . you had a kind of thing for her, didn't you?"

I let the water rinse away the soapsuds; except for way down deep inside, the shivering had stopped. "I never met her. How could I?"

I could feel her eyes on me. "All right, Danny, if that's the way you want it." She picked up my jacket. "This thing is probably ruined. I'll try to have it cleaned. Is there anything in the pockets?"

"No," I said—then I remembered. "No, wait. The top pocket, the small one. See if there's something . . ."

She inserted her finger gingerly into the pocket. "A piece of paper, I think." She brought it out, a small square of white paper, folded several times. She started to unfold it, then her face tightened, and she held it out.

I laughed. "I can't read it in here. Read it to me."

"All right," she said indifferently, quickening eyes betraying her interest. She studied it for a moment. It says: " 'The Airport Mall, the Cotton Bowl at noon tomorrow.' Tomorrow is the fifteenth, isn't it?"

"Yes."

I sighed. Mark Ramsey's evaluation of his sister had been a massive understatement. The damned woman was a certifiable candidate for a rubber room. But, nevertheless, as I stepped out of the shower and rubbed briskly at the droplets on my pink skin, I felt a minuscule stirring of doubt.

"That sounds like an assignation," Susie said. She was sitting on the commode watching my progress with the towel. I turned my back on her.

"It is." I said. "I'm meeting a hot little tomato in the Cotton Bowl."

"That may be," she said, handing me a pair of clean pajamas. "But right now you're getting into bed before you catch pneumonia and die on me."

"Are you coming with me?"

"Not on your life. What you need is aspirin and sleep."

"What I need and what I want aren't necessarily the same thing."

She laughed. "They rarely are." She hesitated. "Are you going tomorrow?"

I shrugged. "I don't think so. Christine Ramsey's a dippy dame. Even her brother believes she's working a short deck."

"That doesn't make it true. Anyway, Danny, she didn't know you were going to come to the cemetery. She already had the information. She was probably getting ready to call you."

"Could be," I said, and sneezed.

"Okay, that's it. Down the hall and under the covers."

"Aw, Ma," I said, and let her propel me out of the bathroom, down the hall, and into the bed.

She tucked me in and kissed me quickly on the cheek. "I don't want to see or hear from you for the rest of the night." She paused at the door. "Unless you get sick."

"I'm already sick," I said. "And freezing."

She grinned at me through the crack in the door. "You'll have to do better than that. Cover up."

She closed the door.

/ 36 /

I was up early the next morning. I typed my report to Arganian, a slow business, since I was working mostly from memory. What few notes I had taken were for the most part illegible and, out of context, didn't make a lot of sense.

Slowly I wove the fabric of Nancy Taylor's life, gritting my teeth at times, forcing myself to lay it all out for him, the filth along with the good.

He wanted to know so, damn him, he would know.

Susie came in, tousled and sleepy-eyed, and watched me finish. I folded the thin sheaf of papers and put them with the movie reels in a large manila envelope. I sealed it, tossed it onto a corner of the desk, and massaged my face.

"Is that Mr. Arganian's report, Danny?"

"That's it."

"How about Nancy? What if she should be there?"

"She's not going to be, Susan. We both know that." I shrugged. "If she is, then I'll have something else to tell him, won't I?"

She nodded, yawned, then smiled sheepishly. "Boy, I didn't

get much sleep. I stayed up after you went to sleep and read."
She yawned again. "I finished another one of Lacy's diaries. I
only have one more to go."

"Interesting stuff."

"Some of it is. I feel sorry for her. She never got a single
thing she wanted out of her whole life."

"Yes, she did. She lived it the way she wanted to. Few
people get that chance. Maybe it didn't work out the way she
wanted, but at least she got a shot at it." I stood up. "How
about you fixing some breakfast for a poor sick man?"

"You find me a sick man, and I will." She slid off the desk
and under my arm. We walked toward the kitchen.

"You've made up your mind about going to the Cotton Bowl,
then," she said, peering up at me through disarrayed strands
of raven hair.

"I guess. I don't have anything else planned."

She laughed. "Don't act so uninterested. It'd take the whole
Cowboy team and a mad bull to keep you away from that
place, and you know it."

"What'll it take? Twenty minutes? Thirty?"

"Uh-huh," she said and pulled my arm tight around her
waist. She looked up again, her face solemn. "I've been thinking about what you've told me. I think you're right. She's not
going to be there."

"Maybe not," I said, and gave her a belated good-morning
kiss. "We'll see."

She was there. Sitting quietly in one of the imitation-leather
booths lining the outside wall of the restaurant. A tall, half-empty
glass of orange juice sat on the table in front of her. One slender
hand toyed with its smooth sides, while smoke from the cigarette
between her fingers wafted upward in small ragged puffs.

She looked up as I stepped through the door. Her eyes were
dark without the blue contacts, and she smiled hesitantly at me.

The change in her appearance without the colored contacts
was less startling than I would have imagined, but it was
enough—Nancy Taylor twenty pounds lighter, four years

after Memphis. A heart-shaped pretty face that used to be round and plump. A slender supple body. Only the smile remained much the same, and I wondered why I hadn't seen it before, wondered if maybe on some deep instinctual level I had known since McBain and I viewed the films.

I was looking at Lee Arganian.

Our eyes met and locked for a long empty moment; I felt my face tighten, felt the first faint stirring of anger inside me.

I held the eye contact a moment longer, then turned and walked out of the restaurant. I had nothing to say to Mrs. Phillip Arganian, but I damn sure had plenty to say to her husband.

The anger built steadily as I drove, and by the time I reached the Arganian estate, I was raging inside. The smooth, lying son of a bitch had suckered me.

Sister, hell!

It was his young pretty wife he was concerned with—her past that she had undoubtedly lied like hell about. Maybe he was tired of her and wanted a divorce. Or maybe his old man's pride demanded reassurance that a last spasmodic twitching of a fading libido had not deluded and tricked him into a reckless alliance.

Whatever his reason, I thought savagely, the bastard lied to me, sucked me in with his woeful story of an aged dying mother and an old man's belated repentance over his unfeeling treatment of a young willful girl.

I ground to a stop in front of the mansion, and even though the garage yawned emptily, I thumbed the bell and pounded on the heavy door.

Not too surprisingly, there was no answer; I gave the door one last disgusted kick and went back to my car and drove away.

By the time I reached the highway, the anger had begun to dissipate. I lit a cigarette and reluctantly accepted the fact that a great portion of it had been directed at myself and Lee Arganian. At Lee Arganian for being what and who she was and for her artfully orchestrated seduction attempt in the music room of her husband's home; at myself for my carefully nurtured delusion that I was searching for Phillip

Arganian's sister, when down deep around the edges of my consciousness, I must have been dimly aware for a long time that it was his wife's trail that I was following.

She was here all along, I thought bitterly. Five miles away. And he sent me scurrying all over the country, digging into the filth of her past, because he had to know whom he had so hastily chosen to share the Arganian name. No wonder he wanted all the gory details.

Well, he would get them, I promised myself grimly. All of them. Right down to the last sick gasping orgasm. And, almost immediately, I wondered how much of my vindictiveness was directed toward Arganian's duplicity and how much was inspired by Lee Arganian's now obvious attempt to bribe me with her body.

As far as Arganian was concerned, maybe I could forgive him for lying to me. Maybe I could even forgive him for using his mother's illness as a spur to prod me on my way. But I could never forgive him for using me as an unwitting tool to hurt Nancy, and from where I sat, that was the only possible reason he could have for wanting to know.

Susie came out of the den as I entered the front door, an expectant look on her face. I brushed past her without speaking and picked up the manila envelope from the desk. She watched silently while I slit the flap and extracted the report I had so meticulously prepared for Arganian. Finally, she made a soft exasperated sound.

"Well?"

My total fee and expenses had amounted to slightly over five thousand dollars. I drew a heavy red line through the figures and wrote in ten thousand dollars.

"Danny?"

"What?"

"Was she there?"

I nodded. I twirled the expense sheet into the typewriter, to the empty space halfway down the page.

"What happened?"

"Nothing happened. I didn't talk to her."

"Well, why not, for heaven's sake?"

"Nancy Taylor is Lee Arganian, not Loretta Arganian, Susie. She's Phillip Arganian's wife, not his sister."

She stared at me, her eyes wide with amazement. "His wife?"

I lit a cigarette and smiled grudgingly at her look of consternation.

"I think I've been had, babe."

"Good Lord, Danny, what do you think he'll do?"

"For one thing, he'll probably wet his pants when he gets my bill. I don't like being hustled just so some rich old man can dump his young wife without paying the tab. I told him in the beginning I didn't do divorce work."

"You think that's what he has in mind?"

"It's a logical assumption. Now, if you don't have any more childish questions, could I get some work done, please?" I softened it with a smile.

"I can take a hint." She walked to the door and stood until I looked up. She thumbed her nose at me. "How's that for childish?" she said as she disappeared from view.

I took a last puff from my cigarette, snubbed it out, and began typing:

You will notice immediately the increase in the total amount of my bill. The reason is simple; I don't like being hustled. I dislike it so much that my first impulse is to dump all the information I have gathered about your wife and charge it to experience. However, after careful consideration, I feel that would be doing her an injustice. If your character is such that it will allow you to lie and deceive in order to gain your objectives, then she is well rid of you. If you have any questions about the bill, I will be glad to discuss them with you in person.

I lit another cigarette and read it over, then read it again, vaguely dissatisfied that it wasn't more forceful, that it failed to express my anger and contempt. I was tempted to tear it up and do it over again, really tell the bastard what I thought of him.

"To hell with it," I said aloud, "I'll tell him in person."

Susie's head popped through the door. "They got you talking to yourself, old man?"

I glowered at her without answering. I took a fresh manila envelope from the desk drawer and inserted the films and my report. I sealed it and laid it in the center of my desk with a feeling of relief, of finality. I looked up at Susie and grinned.

"So much for the Arganians."

"All through with them, huh?" It was more a challenge than a question, a small crooked smile creeping across her face.

"You got it. All through with them."

"Uh-huh. Then I guess you don't want to talk to her?"

"No. Not particularly. Why?"

Her smile widened. "I'll go tell her, then. She's on the phone." She turned to leave, eyeing me over one shoulder.

"Wait. Susie . . ."

"Oh, then you do want to talk to her?" The smile turned crooked, mocking.

"Well . . . did she say what she wanted?" It was an absurd question, and we both knew it.

"No, but I'll be glad to ask her."

"Never mind, I'll do it," I said, trying to sound annoyed, and only partially succeeding.

"We both know what she wants, don't we?" Susie murmured as I brushed past her.

"What the hell does that mean?" I said over my shoulder, having no trouble sounding annoyed this time. I turned to look at her, but she was gone; I shrugged and picked up the receiver.

"Hello."

"Why did you run away?"

"I didn't run away, Mrs. Arganian. I left. There's a difference."

"Why, Dan?"

"I couldn't see that we had anything to say to each other."

"You looked . . . furious."

"Your husband lied to me."

212

"Did you . . . have you talked to him?"

"Not yet."

"Please, I—I need to talk to you first."

"You're talking, so talk."

"No. I mean I need to meet with you. There are some things . . . please?"

I laughed: a sharp, harsh sound without mirth. "If you're planning on taking me to bed in exchange for silence, Lee, forget it. We've been down that road, remember? That was as much a lie as the bullshit your husband fed me."

"I'm sorry."

"I'm not, Mrs. Arganian. Everybody likes to be asked."

She was silent for a long moment. "You can believe this or not . . . but I didn't do it for the reason you're thinking."

"Of course not. It was a purely conditioned reflex to my magnetic charm. Happens all the time. Women come up to me on the street even."

"I'm not sure that's very flattering."

"No, I guess it isn't. I did feel flattered there for a while, strangely enough. I suppose we all believe what we want to believe."

"I see." I heard the scratch of a match. "You don't like me very much, do you, Dan?"

"I don't see that it matters."

"I had the impression the last time we talked that you had some . . . feeling for Nancy Taylor."

"I did. Maybe more than I wanted to admit. In spite of everything she did. I could be wrong as hell, but I felt that in spite of all the filth that touched her, the human scum she was exposed to most of her life, the parasites that fed off her, abused her, used her—in spite of all that, I felt there was a . . . core of something . . . innocence, honesty, that none of it could touch, that nobody could reach and destroy."

"Thank you," she said softly.

"Don't thank me," I said savagely. "I'm talking about Nancy Taylor, not Mrs. Phillip Arganian."

"We're one and the same, Dan."

"Not anymore. Nancy Taylor died when Mrs. Phillip Arganian was born. Nancy Taylor would never have sold her soul to an old man for a name and money."

She made a noise that sounded like a sob. "Oh, God, Dan! There's so much you don't know ... please come to me. I want ... no, I need for you to know."

"So, tell me," I said harshly. "I'm not going anywhere."

"No. Please! Not over the phone. I need to face you—to make you understand."

There was no denying the genuine distress in her voice. I lit a cigarette and thought about it. Despite the anger and disgust I felt for Lee Arganian, there was a faint stirring in my blood, a slow acceleration of my heartbeat at the thought of meeting Nancy Taylor face-to-face, of looking at her with new eyes.

"All right," I said at last. "Where?"

"Any place you name," she said.

"Do you know the small park on North Main?"

"Yes—yes, I know it. When?"

"Thirty minutes," I said. "I'll meet you there in thirty minutes."

/37/

It was a cold sullen day, but she was waiting outside her car, pacing nervously in the grass at the edge of the narrow winding street through the park. I stopped behind her car; she tossed away the cigarette and gave me a quick smile before climbing in beside me. She stripped a glove from her right hand and held it out.

"Thank you for coming, Dan."

I gripped her cold hand briefly. "No big thing," I said.

"It is to me." She fumbled in the pockets of her coat; then said apologetically, "Could I have one of your cigarettes? I seem to have left mine in my car."

"I thought you didn't smoke." I shook two cigarettes out of my pack and thumbed the dash lighter.

She grimaced. "I'm afraid I'm acquiring the habit again." She gave me a wan smile. "Nerves, I suppose."

The lighter popped out, and I lit our cigarettes. I pushed it back into its socket. I leaned back and faced her, studying the lines of her face, the high cheekbones, the flat planes of her cheeks.

I nodded slowly. "I must have been blind. It's all there—the same face minus the fat. How many pounds did you take off? Fifteen, twenty?"

She smiled the wan smile again. "More like thirty. I was always pretty chubby."

"It makes a difference."

She nodded. "My hair. I cut it and changed the color. I guess that made the greatest difference of all." She puffed nervously on the cigarette, then carefully stubbed it out in the dash ashtray.

"And the contact lenses. They were such a dark blue, I wondered about them the first time I saw you." I cupped her chin and turned her eyes to the light. "Dark brown. In the pictures they looked black."

She returned my look solemnly. "This morning. When you saw me. You already knew. There was no surprise in your face. Only anger."

"I knew. I guess I've really known since the porno films in Memphis. Or at least I think I knew then that you were Nancy, but it made such little sense that I must have suppressed it."

She smiled briefly. "I could use another cigarette." She lifted a hand; it was shaking. She winced. "I guess I'm a coward."

I gave her one and lit it for her. I placed the pack on the dash in front of us.

"Whatever Nancy Taylor was," I said heavily, "she wasn't a coward."

"No," she agreed, "she wasn't." She looked at me quickly, then bent her head over the cigarette curling smoke from her fingers. "What was Nancy Taylor, Dan?" she asked softly.

I shook my head slowly. "I'm not the right person to ask that question. The kindest thing I can say about Nancy Taylor is that she was a free spirit—although I'm not even really sure what the hell that means."

She made a quiet chuckling sound. "But you must understand that there are reasons why people run away?"

I shrugged. "I'm sure there must be. Enough people do it. Especially the young ones. But it rarely ever solves anything." I turned to face her. "Look at you. I don't know what you were running away from, but I know a hell of a lot about what you ran to. And none of it was exactly a bed of roses. All of the people I know about that you knew were misfits, emotional cripples, every one—or worse."

"They may have been that," she said defiantly, "but they all had one thing in common." Her eyes blazed at me out of their dark wells.

"What was that?"

"They all wanted me," she said tightly, fiercely. "They all wanted me for myself."

"Even McBain?" I asked gently.

She glared at me for a moment longer, then I watched in amazement as her face softened, her eyes moist with unshed tears. "That poor man," she said.

"McBain? Sammy McBain? Are you sure we're talking about the same man?"

"Yes."

"Jesus Christ, Nancy! The man put you in porno movies. He sold you to another man. And you say 'poor man.' I don't believe you!"

She moved her hand in a negative gesture. "No. No. You don't understand. Sammy was just a weak little boy trying to

216

live in a grown-up world. He never made me do anything. He only thought he did."

"You wanted to be in those movies?"

She shook her head sadly. "No. But if I hadn't, something very bad would have happened to him. Sammy was a gambler, the way some men are alcoholics. He was way in over his head with some of the big-time gamblers in Memphis. That was the only way he could buy himself out. He didn't know I knew, but I did. So, when he asked me, I said yes."

"And the business with Statler?"

"Buster and I arranged that. Buster and I go back a long way, all the way to California. It was time for me to move on. Sammy really knew what was happening, but the way we handled it, he could pretend, act like it was his own idea. See?"

"I'm not sure," I said, remembering the way McBain had bragged, the way he had folded when I tapped him in the gut, remembering also that I had come close to rearranging his face.

She stared at me intently. "Now I have a question. How did you get from San Antonio to the Ramsey ranch? Nobody there knew where I went."

"A matter of luck. Good or bad depends on how you look at it. You remember a man named Elmo. High voice, double-gaited?"

She smiled. "Yes, I remember Elmo."

"He saw you in Irving at one of the Cowboy games. He remembered Ramsey's license number . . . or, rather, the name RAMCO 1. I traced Ramsey from that."

The smile had changed to a frown. "Elmo told you. I thought he was my friend."

"Don't blame him too much. I can be persuasive when I have to be."

But she wasn't going to be pacified so easily. The frown deepened. "And Christine, she helped you, didn't she? She called and told me you knew it wasn't me in that grave. She said she didn't know how you found out. But I knew she was lying. She had to be. She was the only one besides me who knew."

"How did that happen, Nancy?"

She shook her head. "I don't really know for sure. I was already gone when the girl had the accident. Christine had hired her to take my place at the ranch. She called me in Dallas a few weeks later and told me what she had done. She had identified the girl as me, and they had buried her that way. She said I could quit worrying now about the police from California looking for me. I was scared, Dan. I didn't know what to do about it."

"Who was the girl?"

"I don't know. Linda something. I'm not sure I even heard her last name. She came the morning I left. Christine had picked her up somewhere in Houston, I think."

"You and Christine were lovers?"

Her dark eyes looked back at me steadily. "Yes. It made her happy."

"How about you?"

She thought about it solemnly for a moment. "It was nice to be wanted, to be loved. But no, it didn't make me happy."

I shook my head. "Joe Lightfoot. Did Joe make you happy, Nancy?"

Her entire face softened, seemed almost to blur, and her eyes grew misty again. "Joe. Yes, Joe made me happy. I really loved Joe. Most of all, I think. I could have stayed with Joe my whole life . . . except I couldn't make him happy. I couldn't make up for what he lost in Vietnam. Not just his leg—something else. Maybe his manhood, I think."

"And Phillip, Lee, do you love Phillip?"

"Oh, yes!" Her hands came out and grasped mine convulsively, squeezed fiercely. "That's why I had to talk to you. He doesn't know. If he finds out . . . if you tell him . . . God, he wouldn't be able to live with it! It would kill him!" Her hands were chunks of ice throwing off a chill that went all the way to my bones.

"Maybe not," I said gently. "If he loves you . . ."

"Oh, he does, he does! I know that! But you see . . . he's a proud man. He couldn't take . . . God, if he knew—" She broke off, her face crumpling.

I looked away from her misery, riven by dichotomy, my need for reprisal against Phillip Arganian fading before his wife's distress. Maybe he didn't know. Maybe he really did want me to find his sister. I lit another cigarette and realized with a sinking feeling of defeat that I could not bring myself to increase her pain, could not add myself to the list of people in her life who had betrayed her in one way or another, intentionally or otherwise.

"You don't need to worry," I said after a moment, the words coming easier than I expected. "I haven't told him anything bad about your life beyond a few innocuous details. I told him his sister was dead. So be it."

She nodded and slipped across the seat and kissed my cheek. "You're a good man, Dan Roman." She moved back to the door and clicked it open.

"Sure," I said. "It's easy for you to say; you don't have to shave every day."

She smiled, almost laughed, then ducked out the door.

I lit a cigarette and watched her zip off down the street in her forty-thousand-dollar sports car and wondered where she had come from, who she had been before she became Nancy Taylor, girl vagabond. And what had happened to Loretta Arganian? Where had I lost the trail?

Maybe Nancy's life had been a true rags-to-riches story.

I hoped so. There weren't many dreams that came true anymore.

/38/

"I'll be damned," Homer said, shifting his bulky body in the creaking swivel chair. "He's had you chasing his wife's back trail all this time instead of his sister's?"

I nodded. "He was probably in a fever when he married her and didn't know a lot about her background. I guess after his blood cooled a little, he started having second thoughts. What I don't understand is why he lied to me."

Homer shrugged. "I do. Cliff told him you wouldn't touch anything but missing persons."

"There are other private detectives around. Some specialize and some don't. Most don't. He could have found someone else."

"Yeah, but you're the only one in Midway City. You're a hometown boy, and Cliff gave you a terrific build-up. Arganian stressed discretion, and Cliff told him you had a mouth tight as a virgin's twat."

"All the same, I wish I could call him on it. But I can't do that without messing up her life again. So, I'll paint a pretty little picture that'll fit the background she gave him and let him think I'm either inept or a scoundrel. He knows damn well she isn't buried in a grave on Interstate 20, and that's what my report will have to say."

He tapped a sausage-sized finger against the side of his nose. "What if he hires another detective?"

"He'll dead-end at a house in Chatsworth, California. Lacy Wynters is dead, and so are her diaries. Without the diaries there's nowhere to go."

"Yeah, that's so." He leaned back in the chair and laced his hands behind his head. "Whatta you reckon happened to the real Arganian girl?"

"No telling. Virginia Adams received a letter a short time after she left. She'd hooked up with some bikers' club in California. Some guy named Chance, Wade Chance. You know how that shit goes. They pass them around like—"

"Who?" He came forward slowly in the chair, broad face perplexed, eyes squinted, glassy behind the bifocals. "Who did you say?"

"Wade Chance. Belonged to some bikers' club called the Dust Devils or some such crap. Why?"

He shook his head, staring down at his desk blotter. His brow furrowed, creating a row of inverted *V*s down the center of his forehead.

"What's the matter, Homer? You got a pain?"

He shook his head again, then splayed huge hands on the blotter and shoved to his feet. He clumped across to a filing cabinet with a stack of case folders piled on top and shuffled through them, muttering something about lazy clerks. Then he grunted, slipped one out of the pile, and returned to his seat, still muttering, this time happily, a smug grin on his face.

"Mind like a steel trap," he said, and slapped the folder on his desk. "Never forget a face or a name or a good piece of tail."

"I don't believe that last one," I said, trying to read the name on the folder. "You've had so many." All I could see was the name Henry. His big thumb hid the rest.

"Had my share," he said, his blue eyes scanning the first page. He grunted, flipped that one over, went on to the second. I watched his eyes move along the lines, stop suddenly, then rise slowly to meet mine, squinted again in bewilderment.

"What is it?" I said.

His eyes stared through me, glazed, the way they sometimes looked when his mind was working under load.

"Something screwy," he mumbled, and turned the page around for me to see, one finger pointing to a name: Wade Chance.

I read it, pushed his finger away, and read the entire passage. I read it again, puzzled, groping for enlightenment. When I looked up, Homer was staring at me, his faraway look receding. Our eyes locked, comprehension forming in the air between us, like hoary breath on a frosty morning.

"Jesus H. Christ!" he said, his voice as hollow as an empty grave.

"Maybe," I said, licking dry lips. "Could be coincidence. But I just remembered something else." I had remembered the Cobra Club and San Antonio. The answer to the puzzle had been there all along.

I could feel my head begin to pound with anger.

He watched, grinning, while I dialed his phone, then cocked his head and listened intently while I talked, and slapped the desk and hooted when I hung up.

As I was going through the door, he called out: "Need any help, just holler!"

Still an hour and a half before dark, the sullen day had turned blowy and bitter. The park was desolate and empty, and this time she was waiting inside her car. She climbed out as I came to a stop behind her. She crossed in front of my pickup and came around to the door, her lovely features composed and resigned.

She opened the door and got in, the dark eyes briefly meeting mine before she settled in the seat and faced forward, hands clutched in their accustomed position in her lap, an absurd mixture of defiance and acquiescence in her face.

I waited in silence. After a few moments she sighed and turned to face me.

"All right, so you know. I don't know how you found out—"

"It doesn't matter," I said harshly, "but just for the record, I'll tell you. You said you and Buster Statler went back a long way . . . all the way to California. Only he wasn't Buster Statler then, he was Wade Chance. Loretta Arganian lived with Wade Chance in California, according to her letter to Virginia Adams. That qualifies as a long way back, and it's one hell of a coincidence."

She shook her head slowly, one hand coming up to maul her chin. "Wade Chance was his stage name. He wanted to be an actor, even got some small parts in the movies, extra, walkons, things like—"

"I don't give a damn about Wade Chance, Lee, or should I say Loretta? What I want to know is what kind of goddamned game are you and Phillip playing?"

She stared at me, eyes growing wide, a shocked look crossing her face. "Game?"

"Yes, dammit! Game! Pretending to be married. Sending me all over the country like a rookie mechanic looking for a left-handed monkey wrench. I'll admit it. I must be stupid. I can't figure it out. Is it the money? Is your mother involved in some cockeyed way? Or is this just some new kind of sport for the idle rich? Wind up the monkey and see him run?"

"My God," she said, her voice barely above a whisper. "You still don't understand."

"Dammit, I just said that!"

Her hand came out and gripped my wrist, fingers as cold as death, lacquered nails biting my flesh.

"Phillip and I—" She swallowed audibly. *"We are married."*

I stared at her, suddenly disoriented, trying to assimilate the meaning of her words, understanding, yet refusing to believe, my mind sluggish with shock, the chill from her hand creeping up my arm and radiating throughout my body, bringing numbness, a palpable essence of horror.

"Jesus Christ," I said huskily, knowing the horror had crept into my face, my voice.

"But Phillip doesn't know," she said, her own voice growing firmer, as she seemed to derive strength from my shock and confusion. "You see, Danny, Phillip really sent you to find Loretta."

/ 39 /

"Phillip doesn't know, doesn't suspect?"

She shook her head, cigarette smoke trailing from thin nostrils.

"God, no! There's no way he would be able to handle it if he did." Her right hand moved back and forth from her mouth to the ashtray; her left maintained its death grip on my wrist. Her face had regained some of its color, but the bones in her cheeks and forehead seemed more pronounced.

"How can you be so sure?"

"Because I know him," she said firmly. "Phillip is so straightforward and honest, it hurts. He's incapable of deceit, at least with me."

I shifted restlessly in my seat. "Dammit. How could he not know? You were sixteen when you ran away. Even *I* can see now the resemblance between you and that girl. Just from a photograph. He was your brother. It doesn't make sense that he can't see it."

She shook her head again. "I was eleven the last time I saw my brother. Not sixteen."

"Eleven? Was he away in the service?"

"No." She sighed and methodically crushed the fire from her cigarette in the ashtray. "I suppose you could say I actually ran away from home at age eleven. I went to live with my sister. That was when . . . when my father died."

She stared at me vacantly for a moment, then down at her fingers locked around my wrist. She smiled suddenly and tugged my hand into her lap, began massaging it gently with the tips of ice-cold fingers.

224

She bent her head, absorbed in what she was doing, firmly kneading the back of my hand, rolling my fingers between hers, probing between my knuckles with her thumbs; and it was all I could do to keep from shuddering at the death-cold of her touch.

"My father had big hands like yours," she murmured. "I used to love to touch them, to do this. He loved to have them massaged. And his head. He would get up in the morning with a . . . feeling bad, and I would massage his forehead." She laughed softly. "Sometimes it would put him to sleep again." She lifted her head; her eyes blurred.

"I loved my father very much," she said simply. She looked down again, quickly. "He was such a happy man. So big . . . and so handsome. Always laughing and jolly. He used to carry me on his shoulders, leaping and shouting . . . and I would be so tickled, and a little scared, too. It was so far to the ground." Her hands stopped working and lay loosely around mine. She gazed straight ahead through the windshield, at a boy and girl crossing the street in front of us, their arms wrapped tightly around each other. She followed them with her eyes until they reached a bench in the park and immediately went into a clinch.

She sighed. "He was an alcoholic." I felt a tremor ripple through her hands, and her face tightened.

"But it wasn't his fault. She was the one . . . she drove him to it . . . her, my mother. She was so cold . . . so cold. I don't think she ever loved me. I came too late, I guess. Phillip was twenty-eight, and my sister, Alice, was twenty-five when I was born. They were both living away from home. I—I always thought my mother hated my father because of me. She didn't want me . . . but he did. Oh, yes, my father wanted me. He loved me. . . . My father loved me very much." Her face crumpled, dissolved into soft blurry lines. Tears welled in her eyes and rolled over the edges, formed into rivulets and followed the curve of her cheek to her chin. But she made no sound except for the toneless drone of her voice.

"I guess she loved me, too . . . in her way. But she was so

cold and distant, so strict . . . and she never . . . never kissed me." Her hands had curled around mine again, but gently, and they had begun to warm up. She smiled at me tremulously. "I'm sorry. I'm getting . . . emotional."

I cleared my throat. "I don't mind," I said. I dug my handkerchief out of my pocket and handed it to her. "Here. This isn't too dirty."

She nodded her thanks and wiped her chin and blotted her eyes. She twisted the handkerchief into a ball and pressed it between her palms. The silence lengthened, and after a while I prodded gently.

"What happened when you were eleven, Lee?"

"That's when my father died. I wouldn't live there with her anymore. I went to live with my sister, Alice, and her husband."

"Why?"

She reached for the package of cigarettes on the dash, but her hand was trembling so badly, she spilled several on the seat. I took them away from her, lit two, and gave her one. She sucked the smoke deep into her lungs and exhaled with a soft coughing gasp.

"I was only eleven, Danny," she said, her tone precative. "I didn't understand what had happened. That night . . . the night he died, I was in bed. Something woke me up: a loud noise. I thought Daddy had come home drunk, had fallen downstairs. I got up and ran down the stairs. I saw them . . . standing over him. . . . There was a gun in Phillip's hand. And Daddy . . . Daddy was lying on the floor. I could tell . . . I could tell he was dead. I thought . . . I thought they had killed him. I didn't know—" She broke off and raised the cigarette, her hand shaking so hard, she had trouble finding her mouth. She puffed rapidly, fiercely, not inhaling, the smoke billowing around her head in a swirling cloud.

I watched her silently, finally taking the cigarette stub from her fingers just before the fire reached the filter. She stared at me and immediately reached for another one. I caught her hands and held them in mine.

226

"Tell me, Lee. Tell me about that night."

She took a deep breath, shuddered, and when she resumed talking, her voice was low and firm, almost didactic.

"I didn't understand then what had happened. Mother and Phillip were standing over Daddy on the floor. Phillip had a gun in his hand. I thought . . . I thought he had shot my daddy. I—I remember . . . screaming . . . running to Daddy, seeing the blood . . . the blood on his cheeks." She took another deep breath. "And I guess I blacked out, went into shock or something. It was a day or so later before I remember anything else. I woke up in a hospital, I guess it was. And Phillip came. He explained what had happened. He told me that Daddy had killed himself, that he and Mother had just come into the room before I got there. He said he picked up the gun from the floor without realizing what he was doing." I felt her hands ball into fists inside mine, and she shook her head fiercely.

"I let him talk . . . but I didn't believe him . . . not one damn word. He and my daddy had been arguing a lot about the business. Phillip had taken over part of the business down in Houston, and they argued all the time about the way Phillip was doing things. I thought they had fought and Phillip had killed my daddy and that Mother was helping him. I—I remember . . . when he finished talking . . . I began cursing him. I called him every bad name I knew . . . and later, when Mother came, I did the same thing to her. I wouldn't go home with her. They ended up sending me to my sister's to live." She was breathing rapidly, chest heaving, her face a taut white mask of pain. "That was the last time I saw Phillip until two years ago. I stayed with my sister in Irving until I was sixteen; then I ran away for good. I never wanted to see any of them again."

"And you believed all that time that Phillip killed your father?"

"Yes. And God, how I hated him. All those years. And Mother, too, I guess. But . . . but I know now . . . I know it happened just the way Phillip said it did. Daddy took his own life. My sister tried to tell me . . . something about the police checking for gunpowder on Daddy's hand. But I wouldn't listen. I couldn't believe he would do that . . . leave me alone with her . . . like that. But he did. A year after we were married Phillip told me all about it, and . . . I believed him implicitly. But by then I already knew that Phillip couldn't have killed him. By then I was already so much in love with Phillip that I—I don't think it would have mattered anymore if he . . . he had." Her eyes shied away from mine.

"I know . . . I know you think it's . . . it's sick, but God help me—I can't change the way I feel."

"I don't understand. Did you still believe he had killed your father when you married him?"

She nodded slowly, her face still averted. "Yes. I still hated him. I wanted to . . . I wanted revenge. All that time I wanted revenge on Phillip for taking my daddy away from me. It was always in the back of my mind, like a growing cancer. I-I suppose that's why I eventually came back to Dallas. I was only dimly aware of it, but I guess the desire to hurt him was always there, buried." She withdrew her hands from mine and turned to face forward, her fingers plucking aimlessly at the balled handkerchief.

"I saw it in the newspaper, Mother and Phillip's annual charity barbecue at a place they had down on Lake Granbury. It was open to the public. All you needed was two hundred dollars to get in. I—I decided to go. I'm not sure why . . . except that I suddenly needed to see them, Mother and Phillip. I'm not sure what I felt right then, hate maybe, maybe just contempt. But, at any rate, I went down there." She paused, studying her hands, her face slowly composing itself.

"I saw Mother first, standing with some people on the veranda. I passed right by her, but she didn't even look around. It wasn't until later that I realized her eyesight had finally failed her, that she was blind. I couldn't feel anything—not pity, not anything. I just turned away and went looking for Phillip. I didn't find him, not until later, and then it was he who found me. I was walking around with a plate of food looking for a place to sit—there were too many people for the number of tables—and he just came up to me and took my arm and said he had a place reserved at his table. I didn't recognize him at first, he looked so different. I thought he was someone . . . well, someone coming on to me. But by the time we reached the table and sat down, I knew. I heard someone call him Phillip, and I knew who he was, although he looked nothing like the man I remembered. For one thing, he no longer wore a mustache, and his sideburns were gone, his hair faded and thin.

"While we ate, he kept talking to me, laughing a lot, a funny look on his face, and for a while, I thought maybe he had recognized me, as unlikely as that seemed. But, after a while, it became apparent that he was . . . well, *interested* I suppose is the right word. Some of the other people at the table had noticed it, too, and it became embarrassing, then funny because he was being so open about it, and I guess that wasn't like him at all. He told me after we were married that he saw me come in alone and immediately decided he had to meet me, that he watched me wandering around until I was loaded down with my plate of food. He said he fell in love with me watching me eat spareribs and corn on the cob.

"I decided to leave as soon as I finished eating. It wasn't working out the way I had planned. I kept trying to bring up the hatred I'd felt all those years, but it wouldn't come. . . . I couldn't feel anything at all except anxiety, a need to get away from there, away from him." She stopped, restless fingers plucking shreds of thread from my handkerchief and dropping them into the ashtray.

"But it wasn't that easy. Phillip caught up with me before I got to my car. He said there was going to be dancing later and pleaded with me to stay. He was witty and charming, and I almost did. God knows why, but I found myself liking him, and I almost gave in. But I didn't. He walked me to my car, and I finally let him talk me out of my telephone number. I did it to get rid of him, I told myself, but I think the seeds of a plan were already forming, a way to get back at him. He called me Sunday afternoon and asked me to have dinner with him. I said no. He moved on to Wednesday. I said no again. We finally settled on the next Friday night." She stopped and sighed.

"I waged a war with myself for days. My need for revenge against my liking for him as a man. My hatred won. I decided this might be the perfect way to shatter him. I would make him love me, even marry me, maybe . . . and then . . . and then I would tell him." Her voice had suddenly grown thick and hard and ugly.

"I would tell him . . . tell him that he had been making love to his own sister, his own whore sister who had given herself to almost every man who ever wanted her, tell him about all the filthy ugly things I had done with all those men. Things that he wouldn't even know existed." She was panting, short, quick breaths that rasped harshly through dry lips.

"I knew it would crush him, smash him, maybe even kill him . . . that was what I wanted—to destroy his pride. To destroy him the way he had destroyed my father." With a visible effort she controlled her breathing. She turned dark glowing eyes on me.

"But my heart failed me. I waited too long. I kept telling myself the longer I waited, the sweeter would be my revenge. But it didn't work out that way. I discovered one day that I loved him—not as a brother but as a man, a man I wanted to live with the rest of my life, love the rest of my life, and the fact that he was my half brother meant nothing to me. He was kind and good and tender, and I loved him more than life, and that was enough. I knew there would never be children, so what could it hurt? Tell me, Danny, where is the hurt?"

I couldn't drag my eyes away from her dark hypnotic gaze. I cleared my throat. "None, I guess."

She nodded emphatically. "You're right. None. Not for me, not for Phillip . . . not as long as he doesn't know. I can handle it. But Phillip couldn't . . . not ever. It would kill him. That's why—" She faltered, her hands tearing at the handkerchief now, tiny balls of cloth she dropped absently into the ashtray. "That's why, if you're going to tell him . . . I need to know now. I want to leave. I couldn't bear seeing him . . ." Her voice faded, and she stared at the boy and girl on the bench, their arms and legs tied into knots as they tried vainly to absorb each other.

"I won't, dammit," I said gruffly.

She smiled and nodded, as if that was the answer she had expected. She reached for the cigarettes, thought better of it, and withdrew her hand.

"He doesn't like me to smoke," she said almost primly. She reached instead to touch my cheek. "You're a nice man, Dan Roman, a good man." Her eyes glistened, and she gave me her clear brilliant smile. "And that day in the music room . . . it wasn't what you think. I never thought for a moment you could be bribed. It was just something that happened, and I've never been sorry I tried."

I nodded mutely and returned her smile as best I could.

"I have to go. Phillip doesn't know where I am."

"One other thing," I said. "Where does John Sackett fit in all of this?"

She smiled ruefully. "I'm sorry about that. John told me what he was trying to do. I made him stop."

"He knows who you are, then?"

"Yes. I ran into him at the Cobra Club in San Antonio a few years ago. Then I ran into him again about a year ago. Even with the blond hair and the contacts, he recognized me. It scared me a little at first, but John is really a nice man. He's just a little mixed up."

"He's a flake," I said. "Are you sure you can trust him to keep your secret?"

"I think so. I really don't have much choice."

"Maybe you do at that. He offered me money to stop looking for you."

She brought back the rueful smile. "Maybe he's protecting the golden goose. I loaned him a hundred thousand dollars six months ago to keep his business from going under."

"Blackmail?"

231

"No, it was a legitimate loan, but I've found out since that his credit is no longer any good. No one else would lend him money."

"Sounds a lot like blackmail to me."

She frowned. "I don't know. He said he just wanted to help." She hesitated. "He said he still loved me." She made a wry smile.

"Help who? You or himself?"

"He called me the day after you went to see him. That's how I knew what Phillip had hired you to do."

"I wondered about that. Phillip seemed dead set on you not finding out about . . . you."

She nodded. "The story he told you about our mother. It isn't really true. She's blind and feeble, but she's not near death. It was guilt on Mother's part that started the entire thing."

"It took her long enough." I could see no reason to tell her about her mother's visit, but for one almost irrepressible moment I wanted to tell her about her husband's origin, that they weren't related after all. But as old Mrs. Arganian had put it, my word was my bond, and there was, after all, the detective-client relationship to consider. Not legally binding, perhaps, but morally supportable. Besides, I had a feeling it didn't really matter to Lee.

She looked at her watch, suddenly flustered. "I really must go. Phillip will be wondering where I am." She leaned forward and kissed me lightly on the lips.

"Thank you, Dan Roman, for giving me my life." Another quick flash of white teeth, and she had the door open and was gone.

I sat there for a while after she drove away, watching but not seeing the writhing couple on the park bench. Giving myself a breather, allowing my unraveled emotions time to knit themselves back into some kind of coherent fabric.

I smoked another cigarette I didn't need, buried some thoughts I didn't want to think, and fought back some memories I couldn't bear to remember.

232

But all in all, it was time wasted, a losing battle, and I finally started the pickup and drove off, gripped with a cold shivering disgust, the thought of Susie warming me like an unexpected benediction.

/ 40 /

She must have been waiting in the living room, watching for me; she met me at the door, beaming, so obviously happy to see me that I suddenly felt like crying. It was then I realized that my emotions were far more disrupted and disheveled than I knew. I felt vulnerable, fragile, exceedingly old and tired.

She stared up into my face, but before she could speak, I swept her into my arms and kissed her. Her lips were warm and passive, barely responding; when I finished, she gripped my arms and pushed back far enough to see my face.

"What is it, Danny? What's wrong?"

"Wrong? Nothing's wrong, my little flower." I walked her backward into the den, arms around her waist tightly, my feet swinging wide to avoid her toes. "All I need," I said huskily, "is some of that good old-fashioned loving you're so good at."

"Come on, Danny. You've been to see her. Something's wrong. Please tell me."

"Nothing's wrong, child," I said brightly, giving her my most innocent boyish grin, but it failed miserably.

I reached the leather recliner. I twirled her around, caught her at the waist again, and sat down. I tugged her onto my knees and kissed the back of her neck, then pulled her hair out of the way and kissed her below the ear.

"I'm just suddenly very lonely, Susan, and I have this overwhelming desire to make love to you." I began the sentence lightly, airily, but by the time I finished, my voice had thickened, hoarse with the sudden wave of passion that stormed unbidden into my body.

She heard it in my voice, felt it too; she squirmed around in my arms to face me, her eyes glowing, the unanswered questions forgotten.

She raised her lips to meet mine, the sweetness of the kiss almost taking my breath away, her eager trusting innocence making me want to weep again. In a burst of sheer exuberance I squeezed her until she squealed, her dark eyes shining with excitement and lustrous with emotion.

"I'll need a few minutes," I said. "Five, maybe even less. There's something I have to do first."

"It can wait, Danny." She placed her hand over mine and pressed it tightly against her breast. "Why can't it wait, Danny?" Her breast was warm and firm under my hand; she thrust upward, seeking more contact.

"It'll only take a minute," I promised. "I just need to call Arganian about the report. . . ."

"Oh, that." A slow smile spread across her face. "You can forget that, Danny. He came while you were gone. I gave him the report."

My heart skipped a beat, stumbled, and almost stopped. I stared at her in horror, shock scudding through me in sickening waves.

"What . . . what did you say?"

She stretched luxuriously, her eyes closed. "Mr. Arganian. He came by, I gave him—"

"Jesus Christ!" I lifted her out of my lap, scrambled to my feet, my mind racing, trying to remember what was in the report—enough . . . too much!

Everything! My God, everything was in the manila envelope, the movies, the report . . . my note . . . Jesus, my note! It would tell him beyond doubt that his wife and Loretta Arganian were one and the same. I slammed my fist into my palm, dimly aware of Susie's frightened gasp behind me. I whirled to face her.

"What time was he here?"

"My God, Danny, what's the—"

"Susan! Please! Answer me! What time was he here?"

"Just . . . just after you left. What—"

"Dammit," I yelled, grabbing her and shaking her by the shoulders. "How could you be so stupid?"

"What are you talking about?" she said, her voice rising to match mine. "I don't—"

"Shut up," I yelled. "Just shut up!"

And then I did something I had never done before. I slapped my wife—hard—across the face.

"I'll never forgive you for that, Danny," she said. "Never." And then she ran into the bedroom, slamming the door shut behind her.

But I was already moving across the den into the entry hallway. I grabbed my jacket and raced for the front door, a cold empty place already forming in my insides.

Outside, the rain had finally materialized, and I drove hunched over the wheel, peering through the twilight drizzle, the headlights of my pickup almost invisible on the wet black asphalt.

Traffic streamed bumper to bumper on the freeway. I bypassed it, taking side streets, twisting and turning, relying on my instincts to take me the shortest route.

Maybe, I thought, he didn't go straight home. Maybe he stopped for a drink, to pick up some groceries, the cleaning . . . anything to keep him from seeing the contents of that package. . . . How long had it been? An hour? Two?

Moments later, trapped and helpless at a red light, I lit a cigarette and drummed on the steering wheel, a sense of futility creeping in, sudden doubt assailing me like a clubbed fist.

What the hell was I doing charging through rain-slick streets like Sir Galahad on a mission of mercy? To what

235

purpose? There were no villains in the piece, only victims. Only losers.

Through no fault of mine, he was getting exactly what he had bargained for, the current whereabouts of his sister Loretta. The fact that the knowledge might well wreck their lives, as it certainly would their marriage ... well, it was their tempest, and they would have to weather it; I was nothing more than a random instrument of capricious fate.

But I found little comfort in my sorry rationalizations. A nagging conscience tugged at me, pulling me relentlessly through the intersection when the opposing traffic finally cleared. As long as there was the faintest hope of retrieving the manila envelope, I had to try. To still the niggling tendrils of dread, the faint premonitions of disaster, if for no other reason.

Finally the pillars of brick and the wrought-iron archway over their lane loomed through the drizzle. I drove the rest of the way at a reckless pace, the curving driveway wet and black and treacherous beneath my skimming tires.

The lower level of the house was dark and somber, but light glowed dully through drawn draperies in a second-story window. Her small sports car sat beside a dark-colored Rolls-Royce on the apron in front of the garage. I eased to a halt at the end of the walk and rolled down my window, my previous doubts snaking in to assail me again.

What right did I have to interject myself into what had to be the most traumatic moment of their lives? The answer came right after the question: none.

My part in this charade was finished, whether I liked it or not, whether or not I could accept the fact that I had failed her so miserably.

I was reaching for the ignition key when the sound came, one flat muffled explosion, almost an echo, unmistakable to ears that had heard the sound of too many gunshots before.

I cursed, snatched the .38 out of the glove compartment, and shouldered my way out of the pickup into cold blowing rain. I went up the concrete path at a fast-paced walk, breaking into a run as anxiety exploded in my guts.

The door was locked. I swore again and hit it with the flat of my foot; it cracked and clattered but held, and I had to do it twice more before it gave with the sharp splintering sound of breaking wood. But the glossy oak had exacted its toll: my right ankle throbbed and threatened to turn under my weight as I limped through the dimly lit hallway toward the stairway at the far end.

I stopped at the bottom for a moment, listening, my breath rasping like a faulty engine. But the silence was absolute, and I went up the stairs two and three at a time, ignoring my ankle's cries of protest.

I heaved myself around the post at the top, moving back toward the front of the house, then stopped, my eyes searching the hallway.

Six doors, all closed, only one showing a small slice of light at the bottom.

I hit it with the heel of my other foot, feeling the hard solid contact, hearing a satisfying crack as the latch gave way.

The door slammed inward, and I went in behind it, the grip of the .38 rough and reassuring in my hand, my heart lurching into my throat.

My eyes found her immediately, lying in the king-size bed, the pink satin headboard dappled with red, her slim body almost lost in all that vastness.

A small obscene hole glistened at her temple, ringed with a speckled band of black.

I stumbled forward numbly, stood looking down at her composed face, fixed and pale with death, a thin ribbon of blood trailing down into her ear and out again to form a growing puddle below her neck. Her bare right arm dangled over the edge of the bed.

A small smothered sound came from behind me; I whirled in a crouch, the snout of my gun weaving like the head of a nervous snake.

He sat in a high-backed velvet chair, wearing white pajamas, his hair neatly combed. His wrists dangled limply over the arms of the velvet chair, the gun in his right hand black, shining, and evil.

"You son of a bitch!" I yelled. "You didn't have to kill her! She wasn't your sister!"

"My sister," he said tonelessly. "She was my sister all the time." His lowered head moved from side to side. "I didn't have the courage to finish it."

"Drop the gun!" I took a step forward and thumbed back the hammer of the .38, the sound loud and clear in the large room. "Drop it, you bastard!"

His head wagged slowly, limply; finally he raised it, stared at me with glazed eyes, dark dirty holes in the taut white parchment of his face.

"My sister. You saw her shame! And she brought it to me. She brought sin into this house. She brought shame to our name."

"To hell with your goddamned name!" I shouted. "She loved you, you miserable bastard! She was better than ten of you! She was honest, loyal and . . . and she loved you, you hypocritical son of a bitch!"

"No! No! You don't understand. . . . My mother—"

"Oh, I understand," I raged. "I understand only too well."

He appeared to shrink, and his face was as white as his dead wife's. "No! Please! You don't understand. . . . I loved her. . . . Please . . . we couldn't continue . . . not . . . please, you must understand. . . . My mother, she wouldn't—it would kill her! She'd never accept—"

"We can't hurt her anymore, Arganian. She's dead. But you . . . you bastard! They'll have you in a courtroom in front of hundreds of people . . . and they'll hear it all from me. Every last sordid detail of her life."

"No!" It was a harsh flat sound, and he caught me flat-footed.

The gun came up. I saw the flash at the end of the barrel and felt a tug somewhere in my clothing at the same instant. There was a crash of glass behind me.

238

I twisted sideways and fired instinctively.

His thin body slammed backward in the chair; the gun bounced on the carpet. I watched dispassionately as he clapped a hand to the wound, his mouth moving, opening and closing in a soundless litany of despair.

I crossed to the gun, picked it up by the barrel and dropped it into my pocket.

He rocked back and forth, shoulders hunched, tears leaking around tightly closed lids.

I looked around for a telephone and found it on a small nightstand near the head of her bed. My shaky insides told me I wouldn't be able to handle that, so I went out of the room and down the stairs to the one at the bottom.

For once, Homer Sellers was at his desk.

"I'm at the Arganians'," I told him. "He's killed her, and I had to put one in his shoulder. It's not too bad, Homer, but I'd tell them not to dawdle."

I hung up on his questions and leaned against the wall. I was bone-tired and soul-weary, and all I wanted right then was to go home to try to apologize to Susie for what anger and fear had made me do.

But first I had to handle things here, and I reached wearily for a cigarette—and froze—a sound at the top of the stairs bringing me upright, my hand reaching for the gun.

He was there on the top step, braced against the railing, and he had found another gun somewhere.

He held it in both hands, the black bore yawning at me, the face behind it a white gruesome mask of effort.

He fired, and once again I felt the brush of death through my clothing, a light tug at my jacket near my waist, a paralyzing vise of fear around my heart.

I dropped to my knees, dove sideways, rolled, and came to my feet firing. He jerked, buckled limply at the middle, and tumbled headlong down the stairs, end over end.

He came to rest at the bottom, sitting drunkenly on the floor, his back against the staircase wall—and incredibly, he raised the gun again, face twisted in pain and determination, frothy bubbles of blood bursting at his mouth.

I shot him a third time, taking no more chances.

He slid slowly sideways, downward, and settled with his bloody skull resting gently on the first step of the stairway.

I took an automatic step toward him, then wheeled as my stomach went into a spasm, and I raced outside through the fractured door, squatted near the edge of the porch, and vomited into a row of soggy flowers, retching and heaving until there was nothing left inside me.

I glanced back toward the doorway, half expecting to see him come stumbling through.

A hell of a hard man to stop, I thought shakily.

I reached trembling hands for a cigarette, lit it, and sucked smoke deep into my lungs. I leaned against a tree and listened to the wail of sirens in the distance, blinking my burning eyes and trying to swallow a dry hard knot in my throat.

A damned hard man to kill, I thought again. A lousy shot. He had me cold twice and missed both—

I stiffened, cold fingers tickling my spine, a ghostly voice whispered in my ear: *"Phillip is into guns, handguns. He won the Texas State Championship. . . ."*

The cold fingers seeped inside me, closed like a fist around my vitals. Another voice: *"I didn't have the courage to finish it."*

Images, sharp and vivid, flickered unbidden across my mind: the pale serene face, the small dark hole still slowly oozing blood, ringed with black—gunpowder residue.

My mind churned. I felt loose, disjointed, fragmented, enlightenment coming like the flare of a match in pitch darkness.

With a reluctant hand I fished Phillip Arganian's gun out of my jacket pocket, flipped open the cylinder and stared at the shiny heads of the cartridges.

One cartridge fired.

Only one cartridge fired!

I tried to fit my mind around that fact, what it meant, refusing to believe, yet at once believing, accepting. . . .

Phillip Arganian had not killed his wife!

Loretta Arganian had taken her own life. That was where he found the second gun, on the floor beside her bed, lying where it had dropped from her lifeless fingers.

I stumbled back to the porch and sat down in the block of light spilling from the door.

A suicide pact.

Of course. The reflexive and inevitable solution to dishonor, misplaced pride.

But to be sane and take one's own life requires a special depth of courage. Courage had been the mainstay of Loretta's life, had carried her through to the end.

In all probability, Phillip's had never been tested, and so he had failed this ultimate test. He had said as much.

But it also takes a special kind of courage to march into the barrel of a blazing gun, to deliberately miss and draw fire.

He had done that, and I admired him for it.

He had also forced me into killing him, made me his executioner, the instrument of his self-destruction.

And for that, I hated him.

/ *41* /

Mrs. Arganian showed up on my doorstep two days after the double funeral, looking haggard and frail.

She was wearing a simple green dress. No adornment. No makeup on the ravaged face. It looked as withered and brittle as a frozen willow twig, and the blind eyes were dull and watery at the corners. Her steps were unsteady and halting as Sylvester silently led her into the den to the brown chair. He straightened abruptly and left without prompting, leaving her to settle her fragile bones into the firm contours of the chair.

I crossed to the seat I had used on her first visit, making small noises so she could follow my progress. I sat down and lit a cigarette, then cleared my throat and discovered I didn't have anything to say.

It didn't seem to matter. She looked across the room at me, staring into her private world. The strength had gone out of her face, the magnetism out of her spirit.

"I must know the truth, Mr. Roman." Her voice was dry and rustling, just above a whisper.

"You know the truth, Mrs. Arganian. They made a suicide pact. Your son couldn't bring himself to do it, so he made me do it for him." If there was bitterness in my voice, I couldn't detect it. I had buried my rancor along with the body of Phillip Arganian.

"Why?"

The word reverberated around the room, low and passionate and commanding, and for one startled, unguarded moment I almost told her. Not out of some misguided inner compulsion for truth, although my Baptist upbringing ranked truth right up there next to tithing. Instead, for one dizzying second I felt a sweep of dark perversity, a need to shatter and demolish for Nancy Taylor's sake. But I remained silent, and once again, it didn't seem to matter.

"Was she my daughter, Mr. Roman?" Her voice was as soft as a sigh, more statement than question, the dead eyes fixed on me as if she could read my face through her eternal darkness.

"Yes," I said, feeling an intolerable weight lift from my shoulders. The time for lies was past. If she knew enough to ask, she knew enough to find out for herself. "Yes. She was Loretta. How did you know?"

She sighed audibly and seemed to shrink inside her clothing, the thin neck settling deep between pointed bony shoulders.

"A man named John Sackett. He called me yesterday. He sounded drunk, or irrational . . . or perhaps even a little insane. He told me he loved her, had always loved her." She

242

stopped the flow of empty words, and her face turned toward the sunlight from the patio door. "I didn't believe him, of course. Not right then. Not until I heard on the news last evening that a man named John Sackett had taken his own life."

"Yes," I said. "I heard." And somehow I had not been surprised.

"It was then that I remembered the name. From Loretta's teenage years. He was a grown man, and my other daughter, Alice, was extremely upset because he wouldn't leave Loretta alone. He drank heavily and . . . and Alice said he treated her . . . shabbily."

"He beat her," I said bluntly, feeling a rustle of anger at her calm, matter-of-fact tone. "You all must have known that, and yet nobody did anything."

She faced forward again, a tight structured grimace on her lips. "Alice had her own problems during that time. She lacked . . . credibility. Phillip was living in Houston, assimilating our oil holdings into the corporation, and—" She stopped abruptly, her face emotionless again.

"And you?" I said, more harshly than I intended. "What were you doing? Why couldn't you have helped her? Did you try?"

Her lead lifted. "No. There was nothing I could do."

"Why the hell not? You were the strong one in the family. You told me that yourself. With your money you could have smeared John Sackett like a caterpillar on a doorstep. Why didn't you? She was your daughter. Didn't you care what was happen—"

"No!" The word sprang from her lips like a malediction, heavy with anger or pain; I couldn't tell which and didn't much care.

"I—I couldn't. I—I—" She made a noise that sounded like a muffled sob, then took a deep shuddering breath. She shook her sleek head. "I couldn't. I still hated her then, you see."

I stared at her, stunned, struggling with my expression,

then remembering that she couldn't see and letting the contempt run rampant across my face.

"That must take some doing," I said, my tone as flat and noncommittal as a cough.

She nodded silently, wearily, then brought one shaking hand up to touch a ruined cheek. "I can hear it in your voice, Mr. Roman, feel it all around me here in this room. Your anger and contempt. And that is all right. It is no more than I deserve, but before you judge me too harshly you must know the rest of it."

I remained silent, lighting another cigarette, snapping the top on the lighter so she would know I was still there. What rest of it? Nancy Taylor was dead and buried, and that was finally the end of it. No amount of soul baring was going to change that one iota.

"Loretta killed my husband, Mr. Roman. Her father." She said it without tonal embellishment, straightforwardly and simply, and it caught me completely unaware, rendering me speechless for the second time in five minutes.

"Jesus Christ," I said hollowly, more a prayer than a curse. "For Pete's sake, why? She loved him."

"We all loved him," she said, smiling for the first time, a cold smile, without humor. "And that was our undoing. All of us. We couldn't bear the thought of losing him. So . . . so, we put up with him through the bad times because it was so lovely during the good ones."

"He was a drunk," I said, feeling a flash of empathy, remembering my own youth, my own father, my unending compromises just to keep from hating him.

Her lips thinned, tightened, then segued into a wry smile. "Yes, he was a drunk. I prefer *alcoholic*. It sounds less . . ." Her voice dwindled, faded.

"Seamy," I said.

"Yes. Exactly."

"Why did Loretta kill him, Mrs. Arganian?"

She crossed her arms at her chest and hugged herself. She breathed air deeply and let it out in a rush of words: "We

244

never knew for certain. We—Phillip and I—thought he had tried to . . . to abuse her. We—we even thought that . . . that maybe he had . . . done something even before that night."

"Your daughter was only eleven years old, Mrs. Arganian."

"Yes," she said sharply. "I know that. Almost twelve, and well developed. Very pretty and very precocious. And the way they acted together—" She broke off and took another deep breath, the rush of air a dry sibilant sound through tightly clenched teeth. When she continued, her voice had turned suddenly thick and ugly.

"From the time she was nine, they never acted like father and daughter. It was easy to see that he loved her more than all of the rest of us put together—but it wasn't only that. When he was drinking, she was the only one who could handle him, the only one he never struck—" She stopped again, rocking slowly in the chair, the round sleek head lowered. "He never hit her. When he was drunk, he kicked and beat the rest of us like dogs, but he never hit her. Never! He never touched her."

"Then why would she kill him?"

"I'm not certain. I only know that she did. I only know that I heard the shot and found her standing beside his half-naked body, the gun still in her hand, her pajamas . . . her pajama bottoms on the floor near his trousers. Her legs were bloody. . . ." She shook her head and let her hands fall limply into her lap. "Phillip came in. Cyrus was dead. Loretta was still standing there in a trance. She couldn't, or wouldn't, talk to us. I—we decided what we had to do. We dressed Cyrus and Loretta, and Phillip carried her up to her bed. I pressed the gun into Cyrus's hand. Then we called the police. Phillip called our doctor." She fell silent, her head bowed over clenched hands.

I got up and walked to the sliding glass doors leading onto the patio. I lit a cigarette and searched the leaf-strewn lawn for the squirrels. The trees swayed gently with the breeze; nothing else stirred. Too early, or too late. They generally bedded down during the middle of the day.

From behind me Mrs. Arganian's voice came again, dry and husky with self-loathing.

"For a long time I hated her. I didn't want to, but I couldn't help it. No more than I could help loving him—even when he was treating me like some stray cur. I can't begin to explain love like that. Somehow I think debasement was a part of it. I sometimes found myself deliberately provoking him when he was drunk . . . just to . . . to get . . . something." She paused, her voice dropping. "It shames me, even now.

"It was a terribly trying time for me. I lost my husband and my daughter in one tragic evening. You can't imagine how devastated I was." A hint of a whine had crept into her voice, a thread of pleading. It bothered me. Maybe more than it should have.

"Perhaps I should have handled things differently." She paused. "But I don't see how." She had come full circle: from self-denigration to self-justification.

"You'll have to make that judgment call yourself." I said, thinking of two ways she could have done things differently—standing behind her daughter and telling her son the facts of his birthright.

"Yes, you're right. Well . . ." She made movements suggesting that she was pulling herself together. "If you would be so kind as to call Sylvester, I'll get out of your life." She coughed. "I am deeply indebted to you, sir. If—"

"Why?" My voice was almost a shout, a snarling raging sound erupting out of the guilt that spewed like corrosive acid. "Why, for Christ's sake? I pried and poked into her life, hounded her, cornered her, and . . . and got her killed—"

"You didn't kill her, Mr. Roman—"

"The hell I didn't! I killed her! You killed her! Phillip killed her! We all had our dirty little part in it. Phillip could have ended it, saved her, but he was too goddamned overwhelmed by his stupid pride and so-called honor—" I broke off and stared at her unforgiving image, frozen stiff and erect in the chair. I made a hawking sound of disgust in my throat, wheeled, and crossed the room to the doorway.

Sylvester leaned against a post on my front porch, immaculate and regally indifferent.

Minutes later I stood in the doorway and watched their halting progress down the walk to the waiting Rolls, feeling my righteousness ebbing away, feeling, illogically, a tiny rill of pity.

What did I know? Who was I to judge anyone? I had glimpsed fleetingly the moldy fabric of the Arganians' lives, mother, daughter, and stepson, and only partially understood what I had learned about them—and about myself.

I only knew that I was sick of other people's problems, tired of looking down the back side of other people's lives, at their sorry mistakes and deliberate manipulations, their scams and their hustles, their self-deceits.

I had my own problems to handle now. Susie was gone when I returned from the Arganians', and I had not seen her since.

Many people were wounded that night.

I could only hope that some of those wounds would heal.